OUR BONES IN YOUR THROAT

OUR BONES
IN YOUR THROAT

Megha Rao

**SIMON &
SCHUSTER**

London · New York · Sydney · Toronto · New Delhi

First published in India by Simon & Schuster India 2024

Copyright © Megha Rao, 2024

No reproduction without permission.

The right of Megha Rao to be identified as author of this work has been
asserted by her in accordance with Section 57 of the Copyright Act 1957.

1 3 5 7 9 10 8 6 4 2

Simon & Schuster India
818, Indraprakash Building,
21, Barakhamba Road,
New Delhi 110001.

www.simonandschuster.co.in

Simon & Schuster: Celebrating 100 Years of Publishing in 2024

Hardback ISBN: 978-81-974895-9-4
eBook ISBN: 978-81-974895-7-0

Typeset in India by SÜRYA, New Delhi
Printed and bound in India by Replika Press Pvt. Ltd.

FSC
www.fsc.org
MIX
Paper | Supporting
responsible forestry
FSC® C016779

For Dhanya,
who is little and wise.

PROLOGUE

R oman poets often wrote about half-bird, half-woman things that lured sailors to the altar of their deaths. Things that sang till the skulls on their island looked like precious ivory art. Dangerous, irresistible huntresses, dressed to kill. To me, it was the rumour that came closest to imitating a siren's song in real life. To be seduced by a rumour was to listen to this very song on loop.

You could tempt the world with a sensual secret. With the soft, feral striptease of a scandal. All it took was Henry's calculated lies to behead Anne Boleyn. Word of mouth that turned teenage girls into Salem witches. A single grapevine that led to the boiling of Jahanara's lover. I thought about her hiding her beloved until her father, Shah Jahan, heard of their affair. I thought about her waiting in her palace seconds before, soaked in perfume, ready to kiss ghazals out of the man's throat. I wondered if any of it was real, or simply good storytelling; an illicit romance built from thin air to ruin a princess's reputation in a time when reputations could be so easily ruined.

But it was in the forest that I first discovered a rumour in heat, rubbing against hungry ears. It was here, within the stone walls of St. Margaret's campus, that I learned to walk on fire. Here that I found myself caught in the sacred museum of bones in the closet. Here that I heard the myth of a woman who drowned in a lake, and became smitten by her in the very strain of Prince Salim.

The first time I dreamed about her, I thought she was bewitching. Her thick, charcoal-skinned hair bore the ancient sorcery of inebriating anyone who as much as looked at it. How did I feel when I saw her? Like there was no returning to my own name. And so, fearlessly, I walked towards her, as if I were moving towards the gates of the afterlife. She was singing into a riot with the entirety of her lungs, her spirit a boom box. I had no grace, no shame, no decency. I kept staring, following, even crying for her, enmeshed in the marrow-deep turbulence of her grief, grieving along, knowing I was eternally damned. When I woke up in the morning, I was left with a song in my chest, and I hummed it all the way to class, senses raging, heart illuminated.

I told nobody about my dreams. About the woman dipping in and out of the water until it turned into ambrosia. Not even the man I loved. I still remembered the nights kissing through cable-stayed bridges as the taxi drove on, when I almost told him. When we put our heads out the window and suddenly, the golden lights flashed above us, and in that moment, I felt like I was born for love. Only love. It had been another time. Another life.

Years down the line, the city of Bombay had grown to look like her. A dark fairy-tale. The trees were paler, the buildings felt older, the skies looked like smoke, and the weight of dreams and desperation was heavier, still. It was a difficult city to live in, a city that had a lot to tell. The Portuguese writer-historian, Gaspar Correia, had referred to it in his 'Lendas da India' as *Bombaim*, which meant 'good bay.' With the advent of the

British rule, it became 'Bombay.' And then, of course, there was Mumbai, another name, derived from the local deity, Mumba Devi. Mumba Devi was the patron goddess of the first people of the city, who'd mostly been fishermen and salt collectors, back when it had just been an archipelago of islands. Here, Rudyard Kipling was born. Here, the first ever bus service in the country began. Here, romantics came in search of their big dream of becoming a superstar, with nothing but a few train tickets and coins jingling in their pockets.

I remembered the last time I was in Bombay. I remembered the water ghoul, the sensitive boy from Kolkata, the frosty leader, and her political games. And then there was my first friend, Scheherazade. Scheher, who had always been a force to reckon with, a mystical sphinx. Scheher, with the silk robes and crystal bracelet and husky, suggestive laughter. Scheher, who had once sat next to me in the bus, anxiously biting her metallic nails after a lover's spat with her boyfriend. The first thing I'd noticed about her wasn't the hair painted the colour of warm autumn or the paper earrings swinging in the breeze. It was how fiercely vulnerable she looked. I'd never seen anyone wear fragility with such reckless power.

Her house had been gorgeous, a gift from her father. Photographs of Banksy's art and a large mood board lay framed on her wall. She'd been a hoarder. Books. Bus passes. Feathers. Sea shells. Newspaper clippings. Fancy containers. Collectible rare editions of classic novels. Anything, everything. Once she'd met a man selling potions at a carnival and had bought spell jars and vials with insomnia cure and witchcraft kits. And then, of course, there had been that ugly bamboo puppet at the antique store in Kala Ghoda. She'd kept it next to the infamous yellow table lamp with all the sticky notes on it.

And at Scheher's, a slice of rose scent always hung in the air. The smell of old wood and books clung to the turquoise tiles. Big windows, embroidered lavender curtains, and house plants added grace to the room. Incense sticks and ash trays left it rooted and truthful. A lone hand painted teapot with a Rumi quote decorated the otherwise simple kitchen. It had been our sanctuary.

We used to lie on her carpet and share a Marlboro and vada pav, Bombay's famous bread bun stuffed with potato fritters. We used to spacewalk on the possibilities of life as we stared at the cityscape outside. She would braid my big, carnivorous curls for me, and I would paint her nails. Sometimes, if we were in the mood, we would take turns riding her bike to the beach, and there, we would play jazz music. The night would break into complete darkness, except for the deck of constellations it wore like a bride. And then we would head back after gorging on desi Chinese food, just in time for some gin and unripe mango juice. We'd fall asleep gently under glow-in-the-dark stickers, and in the morning, I'd walk back to my apartment. That year had been lovely, and only the incidents that followed after had caused its beauty to age.

Had time suspended that year? Again and again, it felt that way. Because every time I was in the city, I could still see everyone's faces. Hadn't I returned during the spring festival only to be preyed upon by more memories of us tying each other's sarees and laughing when they came loose? When I sat making sugar crystal garlands with my new friends, didn't my mind still wander off to that time I'd done the same with Scheher, who'd ended up eating the whole garland because she'd been hungry? Hadn't it been so prosperous, three years ago, when we'd worn matching bracelets and danced in the terrace and made rasam together with sour tamarind and crushed tomatoes? How could I dream of getting it back now?

I stopped by a café to grab an espresso before heading to the Comedy and Music club we used to always be at. The

picture of Scheher in a denim jumpsuit, colourful beads in her
hair, still stood on the brick wall. It was vandalised on one
side, but everything else remained perfectly unaltered. Sucking
in my breath, I turned to the man standing behind me with
his mouth open.

'You're that girl who used to come for Scheher's shows,
right?' He looked older, much older, and if not for his smile, I
wouldn't have recognized him. I nodded curtly.

'Any idea where she is now?'

'I don't know. I came here to ask you.'

'Oh no, she stopped coming in years ago. Took her money
and left after her own people turned against her.' He looked
sad. 'I told her it would die down. Nobody stays cancelled
forever these days, right?'

'Right.'

'But she didn't listen. Straight up disappeared.'

'I know.' I had hoped to find something here. I had hoped
someone had seen her. This had been her favourite place. Hope
had been flirting with me for the past few years and leading
me on. It had given me nothing, but I'd gorged on it anyhow.

'What do you do? Where are you these days? Esai, right?'
he asked me.

'That's right,' I said. I wanted to leave. 'I'm in Kodaikanal.
I run a homestay with my family.'

We'd chosen Kodaikanal for its tranquil Southern woods.
For how easy it was to drift through the enchanting thickets
at twilight, to bask in the abundance of the blue, monsoon-
kissed Kurinji flower blossoms. For how easy it was to forget
everything that had happened. For how far it was from Bombay,
and how close it was to our roots. And some would call it
running away, but I saw it for what it was. The radical act of
choosing my own peace above everything else.

I'd grown into my own routine in Kodaikanal. I visited the

pines first, and then returned to the homestay for a light cup of rose tea before dinner. Dinner was a family affair. My uncle Pipi and my aunt Jolly would cook a variety of meals together, and I would set up the table with their daughter, Tendral. From seven-thirty onwards, the guests would begin to come down, scarves wrapped around their torsos. There would be music and dancing, under the faint golden glow of electric lamps. And on the weekends, there would be wine, the shade of liquid dawn.

'Kodaikanal sounds really lovely,' he said, reading into my thoughts. And then, when he realized I had nothing to add to that, he said sheepishly, 'She was our big star, that Scheher. She brought in the crowd. We could all feel it back then. She was destined for greatness. Anyway, if you find her number or address, could you pass it on to me? I'd love to catch up with her someday.'

I couldn't bring myself to tell him that he'd asked for the impossible. So I agreed and, feeling restless, I found a rickshaw parked right outside the building, the kind with flashy purple-green disco lights and Bhojpuri music. The film poster at the back glared at me. Its heroine's red lips glowed like the edge of a cigarette in the night.

Fifteen minutes into the ride, I told the driver to stop for flowers.

Half an hour later, I was standing in front of a barren plot of land. A crash site, an almost graveyard. The back gates were still there, but the main entrance was unrecognizable. I swallowed in the crisp air, the aquamarine sky. It used to be a degree less here, but now there weren't as many trees. Instead, I noticed beehives, mushrooms, beer bottles. I got out gingerly and folded my arms. So long ago, wild with the glories and tragedies of youth, we'd shown up here. I could still see it, Bagchi waking me up on Sunday to homemade Bengali breakfast, his fingerprints trickling down my thigh. Ira giving her election speech, cold and intoxicated by potential, like an invincible Arctic wolf, elegant like a dove. Nanda sir's messy silver hair, his dainty silver stubble. Joshua's broad cheekbones and electric eyes that Scheher had been fascinated with. The principal's room, the Banyan trees, the forbidden lake. The paper boats that had lingered over the delicate waves like haloes. All gone now.

Replaced with a ghost town. Broken toys, plastic, and other junk boring into its soil. I could still feel the cool water of the lake drawing goose bumps on my flesh, still taste the salt and panic in the air. Still see the look of joy on the Lake Woman's face when it all shot straight down to hell.

I knelt down and laid the flowers on the ground.

In memory of when *here* had been beautiful.

ONE

The first time I stepped into St. Margaret's, I was hit with a wave of euphoria and turmoil, faster than liquor hitting the gut. Here I stood, at the mouth of three hundred and fifty acres of one of the best liberal arts and sciences colleges in the country. Among nine thousand students in their late teens and early twenties. In front of stone towers, well-cut grass fields and mongoose gatherings. Like a new lover, I explored its body—loitering around the campus, infatuated with the pure, blue skies. I could smell vermillion, mint leaves, and enthusiasm wherever I went. A day café and an evening canteen stood facing each other, with nothing but plastic red-and-white chairs separating them. A screening room sat in the far corner, for the visual communication students. There was a water tower, an elevated structure that supported a water tank at its top. Students gathered underneath its shade. And when it got too crowded, they hit the *Dunes*, a series of stone benches near the fence. Within the fence was a big ground which was usually left empty until the annual college event took place. And then there was the library—time-worn and serene and absolutely glorious, where I found myself spending all my free hours. When I'd amble out, feeling slightly wistful, there would be at least five books in my bag, and one in my hand, for in-transit reading.

A week later, I found out why this wasn't a good idea.

Nose in the strange, yet compelling world of Girish Karnad, I didn't notice the much feared six-foot-one figure walking towards me, and ended up running into the college's most notorious senior student, Joshua D'Silva, and his gang of troublemakers. They were in the third and final year of their undergraduate courses, and they were looking for newcomers to intimidate. I'd seen them earlier, and I knew they'd been patrolling the first years' corridors.

Joshua was the heir of Joy D'Silva, a business tycoon with a belt of restaurants to his name. Their hotels were all over the city like billboards, and they had begun opening chains in the South as well. Joy had started from scratch and worked his way to the top, and his employees loved him. But his son?

He was a brat. A man child. He was one of those I knew I could never be friends with because of what they stood for. Fascism, hate speech, blaspheming minority religions. Joshua sought controversy and he got away with it because he was socially advantaged.

'I've never seen you around,' he said to me, narrowing his eyes. 'First year?'

'Yes,' I said. I'd heard so much about him, and none of it had been nice. He'd asked a nineteen-year-old Botany student to lick his shoes. At first he'd refused, but then he'd hit him. Threatened to use a metal rod on him and eventually gotten him to do it. Joshua had also asked two girls to recreate an explicit scene from a popular Hindi movie. Thankfully, they'd been saved by a professor's interference. I also had first-hand information from a reliable source that he'd asked a student to do the entire research for his dissertation.

I tried not to look at my legs or notice how they were

trembling like they were on a butcher's table. Instinctively, I began walking past him, but he kept blocking my way. 'What are you doing?' I asked, trying to remain unruffled. Was he attempting to get a rise out of me? Because if he was, then it was working.

'Do you have class right now?' he asked.

'Yes! Can I go?'

'Not yet. Is that your last class for the day?'

'Maybe.'

'What do you mean *maybe*? You don't know?' he asked, and then turned to his friends. 'The girls around here are so *dumb*. Look, she doesn't even know when her classes are.'

'I do, but I don't want to tell *you*.'

Around me, I could sense that other students on campus were stopping to watch the scene. They were mostly older, because the first years wouldn't risk themselves being caught looking. Joshua clenched his fist, and I was now angry and afraid. It wasn't a good combination. Once, after watching a man drive a burning truck into an abandoned field on the news, Tendral had made up a name for my kind of courage—fool's courage, she'd called it, every time I did something outrageous, at the cost of my own safety. I was moved to believe this was one of those instances. And so I stood facing him, holding onto the last flake of my fool's courage.

'Do you know what happens to juniors who talk back to their seniors?' he snarled.

No, I thought to myself. And I didn't want to know either. But before I could respond, he grabbed the book I'd borrowed from the library and flipped it around. Instantly, my hand reached out for it, and he swerved.

'A library book? If I tore this up, you'd be in trouble, you know that? You'd have to pay a fine, or worse, you'd be banned from the library. I could make sure of that,' he said. 'I could

make sure of anything. Even expulsion.' I gritted my teeth.
'Should I tear it?' he taunted.

'No.'

'Say no, *please.*'

I could have said it. It was just a word. But I didn't want
to say it, because one word would make all the difference. I
wasn't an idiot. Saying *please* meant surrender. I thought about
the classic look-behind-you trick, of yanking the book back into
my orbit and then running off. I also thought of buying a new
book for the library, an olive branch replacement. I was ready
to pay any price, but I swore to God I wasn't going to beg.

That's when I heard a low, silky voice behind me. A voice
with mischief's paws on it. I turned around swiftly, my hair
almost slapping one of Joshua's boys' faces, but there was no
time to react.

'Joshua, my brother! Just the man I was looking for!' he
announced.

And then I was met with hooded, mid-laugh eyes. A jaw
that reminded me of sharp paper cuts. For a split second, his
gaze lingered on me, and then it fell back on Joshua. Phosphenes
erupted in my vision.

As he spoke, I watched him in that unabashed way people
who were in love with strangers did. In the language of those
who carried a nameless, shapeless yet infinite desire. I was
suddenly, painfully aware of my own lithe self and whatever
space I took up, aware of the tangible mess of skin I occupied
like an ancestral house and the thicket of hair that curled around
my cheekbones like whirling Sufis in the breeze. I smoothed
the crease on my lilac shirt, subtly detangled entwined strands
with my fingers and tried my best not to be too self-conscious.
Hoping my oversized, hyper-expressive eyes did not betray
me and give away what I was feeling. Everything was a blur.
Everything.

I could see that those who'd stayed back for some drama were now walking past me again, a fleet of silhouettes, and things began shifting back into normalcy. But for me, nothing would ever be the same again.

The stranger had beautiful hands.

And I would never get over them.

'Aren't you supposed to be at the chairwoman's meeting?' the stranger asked, feigning politeness.

'I'm on sick leave,' Joshua muttered.

'You don't look so sick to me.' He patted him on the back happily, pulled the book out of his grip effortlessly, and then turned to me. 'Junior? Lost your way?' I immediately fell in love with the kindness in his voice.

'I've a class in the Arts Block, and I don't know where it is,' I lied.

'Follow me,' he said, grinning, and that was it. Joshua couldn't do a thing. As we sauntered away, I strongly resisted the urge to look back. But if I had, I was sure I'd have witnessed Joshua's version of *The Scream*. It didn't matter.

Meanwhile, in the short time we shared walking together towards the Arts Block, I noticed the smaller, more intimate details about my new friend. Like the key-shaped birthmark on the underbelly of his collarbone, and the thin cut over his eyebrow. Had the eyebrow slit been done on purpose, or was it a palpable memory of a knife fight? I couldn't get over the marvel of his shoulders. Or the landscape of his broad chest. Or the sweet susceptibility of his neck. Or the hollow altar of his throat.

'What're you staring at?' he chuckled.

'You. You've got very interesting features.'

'A very bold statement for a junior to make.'

I frowned. 'So what if I'm a junior? Am I supposed to behave a certain way because I'm new here? Can't I, for once, be honest, without anyone bringing up the fact that I'm a first year student?'

He seemed overjoyed by my outburst. 'Aha! A troublemaker.'

'I'm not a troublemaker, *Joshua* is.'

That seemed to make him very happy too. *Is he ever not smiling?* I wondered.

'Okay, agreed,' he said. 'A nonconformist, then. Just for the record, it's tough to pull through these woods if you don't comply around here.'

'Comply? With goons like him?' I retorted.

He shrugged, as if his diplomacy was a gift. 'Unfortunately, such *goons* also occupy powerful places. He's the Literary and Debating secretary of this college.'

I found that unbelievable. 'How did he even get there?' I asked. 'Who voted for him?'

'He bribed thousands of students with free daaru and dum biryani.'

So that's how it works, I thought. Of course, who could have said no to alcohol? And who could have dared say no to the aromatic, slow-cooked biryani rice with its rich, flavourful layers of meat? My mouth was already watering at the thought of it. 'Wealth can get you anywhere,' I mumbled, wondering how much it would have cost to buy all of that. But then again, didn't his father own all those restaurants?

I found it quite unbelievable that there was so much politics on such a micro level. That this was where it all started, where people learned to play dirty. I knew enough about what it was like in the country. I knew of sham political parties that existed just to dodge tax and I knew of journalists like Gauri Lankesh being shot dead outside her own home because freedom of speech came with a price. Every year, we entered into a new era of extremist violence. And before we were even given time to recover from it, we were bludgeoned with more dreadful news.

'So what does Joshua do as the Literary and Debating secretary? Apart from tearing books?' I asked.

He smiled. 'Oh, now, don't be too hard on him. He says a lot of things he'd never really do. Like his manifesto, for one. You see, he was a last minute candidate. The person who was actually, unanimously supposed to become the Literary and Debating secretary didn't have enough attendance, so he wasn't allowed to contest.'

'You need to have enough attendance to contest for a position in the student Cabinet?'

'Seventy-five per cent. That's the basic criteria.'

'And he didn't have it?'

'No.'

'Who was he?'

'Me,' he said, a faint dimple firing up on his chin. 'And if you make me angry, I assure you, I'm deadlier than Joshua.'

'Why, what would you do?'

He pointed at the book in his hand. 'I would give you spoilers.'

'No!'

'Did you get to the part where the snake drinks the milk?'

'Stop!' I cried, looking horrified. His laugh drizzled onto his cheeks. I stood no chance, I was going to think about it for weeks.

'I guess not. Look, we've arrived,' he said, returning my copy of Karnad's *Nagamandala*. I stared at it awkwardly, and then looked up and flashed him a generous smile. 'Thank you,' I said. His eyes glimmered with hunger for a moment, and then, as if it had been a trick of the light, it was gone.

'Catch you later,' he said gruffly, and disappeared into the hallway.

TWO

I was in the woods after class ended.
Ferns, freckled with green and gold, lined the path into the deeper sites of St. Margaret's. Initiation day was nearing, and I'd taken it up as a challenge to discover all the little, unexplored territories of the campus. For example, the spread of Gothic pillars that stood like guardians in place of some trees. I'd been informed that long ago, an old teak tree had fallen over another in that area, knocking a couple more to the ground. Instead of planting new ones, they'd chosen to install these obelisks and paint them a gingerbread brown. I'd also been lucky enough to spot migratory storks, stopping to quench their thirst in rain puddles. The more time I spent roaming around, the more I discovered new histories. I found the remains of a tiny snake temple that had once been a part of this land before the college authorities had bought it. They'd been told not to disturb it by the locals, but they'd still decided to tear it down. The colour of the soil changed in certain parts of the campus, and the temperature shifted every now and then with the density of the trees. There was so much to see, and so much beauty. I followed the squirrels, sparrows and animal tracks. The fruit bats

sleeping upside down on power lines. The apples bitten into, now decomposing on the grass. The colony of ants squeezing around the straw of a juice packet. Savouring the sweetness of whatever persisted. Everything about the place was wonderful, except for what was about to come next.

Initiation day.

It baffled me that the seniors had a ceremony where they made newcomers stand on chairs in formal wear and answer questions about the college. It was nothing but an opportunity for them to perpetuate abusive behaviour in the name of a long-standing campus *tradition*.

I could refuse to be a part of it, but I knew what happened to those who didn't go through with it. They were cornered, targeted and turned into social rejects. There was no counterculture, just misfits. And I wasn't ready to be one. So I resumed my rigorous training unwillingly, telling myself that it would be over in no time.

Just a few more days, and I'd be free. Just a few more days, and I would finally be accepted as a St. Margaretian.

But for all its worth, was it ever going to stop seniors like Joshua from being sadistic? And when something like this became a normalised ritual, wasn't it also sending a very obvious social signal that persecution was okay?

Besides, what was I going to do with all this useless information? What did I stand to gain from knowing that the college only had fifty students when it first began or that it was initially funded by donations and grants? Why did it matter that the Creative Writing course was only introduced last year or that it was the most sought after education department in the city?

Who's the founder of the college? Dr. Raja Dalvi, grandfather of current principal, Dr. Laxman Dalvi.

How old is the college? Ninety-two years.

I quietly meandered into a narrow street and took a quick left. Made a mental note of everything I had learned so far. *Who is the current chairperson? Ms Ira Saanvi.*

What is the hierarchy of the Student Union? The president, who is the principal. The vice president, a professor on campus. The chairperson, and then the convenors in the following order: literary and debating, academic, amenities, cultural and sports.

How many steps are there in the Arts Block? How many in the Science Block? Who started the library? When did they start it? In which year did the college function without a VP? How many lights are there in the exam hall?

I took note of everything. I made sure I knew St. Margaret's inside out, just in case they surprised me with difficult questions. I wandered ahead, took another deviation, and memorized five more answers.

I turned around, wary of the fact that I was all alone, but I kept going through the woods. The sound of the other students chatting about coursework and gossip died out.

What is the annual college fest called? Solstice.

Who is the evening canteen named after? This is ridiculous.

How tall is the Science Block Tower? Who cares?

How many blocks does the college have? Go to hell.

All of it played in my head, a monochrome film, rewinding and fast forwarding of its own free will. From the first brick to what it was today. I imagined what it looked like when it had just begun, a sequence of memories, almost as if it was my own: the inaugural function and the almost-drizzle that had worried the new professors. The founder, Dr. Dalvi, hoisting the flag while the first batch of students sang the national anthem. Dragonflies hovering over their heads and skipping queues, soaked in the enthusiasm of the crowd. The first prayer, the mic that stopped working midway. The scented candles in the old mess. The residences for faculty built on ground. The rapid expansion over the years into a flourishing academic institution. The grandeur and fervour of its transcendental existence. The pride of its forefathers. All of it played in my head—including the lake.

The lake, tucked away, like a skeleton.

It was the first thing every junior was told on day one—the mysterious lake that the management had banned anyone from visiting. There were all kinds of stories about it, but they were hazy. 'Just don't go there, all right?' was what a senior had told me the last time I'd tried to probe.

But I knew that places were forbidden for only two reasons: they were either full of blood, or jewels. Like the deadly Snake Island in Brazil, or the Coca-Cola vault in Atlanta, which held the secret recipe of the famous soft drink. Like Bhangarh Fort, once a splendid kingdom, now merely cursed ruins. And like every fool, my mind was drawn to the inaccessible.

Ever since I'd heard about it, I had wanted to see the lake.

I moved through the weeds, surprised by how well I knew my geography, when seconds earlier, I'd felt so lost. As I drew close, my skin tingled.

Somebody was singing.

I gravitated towards the music of the ripples. The glazed madness of its depths. The memories of its lifetime.

Just as I was about to take another step forward, I heard another sound. I stopped in my tracks. No, it wasn't a song. It was just a low, feminine growl.

I decided to follow it instead.

The first thing I noticed was the water. I had been led right to it, I realised. Glistening from all the rays that melted into it, it stared back at me. Koi fish lined its inner skin. The shadow of a banyan tree stretched on its bosom, an unconventional mattress. Breath-taking blue orbs levitated above the water. I rubbed my eyes, stunned.

It was the most astonishing lake I'd ever seen. It looked like an aquatic cave, and yet, light poured in from everywhere. The singing sharpened, and it echoed everywhere. It was suddenly pounding my head, pressing for entry.

I'm the one who's singing, I realised. The music was coming from inside of me. It was all I could hear.

And then, all at once, it stopped. I heard leaves rustle and then crack from the weight of someone's shoes. A woman appeared out of nowhere, looking flushed. Tendrils of hair had escaped her tight bun, and beads of sweat dotted her temple. She had a peculiar face. It took a mango-like structure, and tapered into an incredibly powerful, distracting chin. Her mouth was wide, her teeth perfect, as if she had worn braces all her life. But what was most distinctive about her was her height. She was taller than anyone I'd ever met, including Joshua. Including the boy with the beautiful hands.

Buttoning her blouse, flustered and livid, she asked, 'What are you doing here?'

And then, right behind her, I saw a familiar face, pulling a shirt over it.

'You!' I cried, aghast. His beautiful hands disappeared into his pocket.

He smiled, a little chagrined. 'Don't tell me. Are you lost again?'

'No. Yes. I mean, yes.' I had a feeling he was about to get rid of me.

'Good answer. We'll show you the way out.' He held me by the elbow and dragged me forward. I turned to look at the dishevelled young woman who was still putting her clothes back on. 'Is this the forbidden lake?' I asked. *Stupid question. You know it is.*

'Yes.' He sounded impatient. 'Now come along.'

I pushed him away. 'I've never been here.'

'For god's sake, girl, it's going to be dark in fifteen minutes!' he said, exasperated, and also a little embarrassed. A mild blush began to spread across his cheeks. 'Knock some sense into her, please,' he told the woman.

She leaned against the bark of a tree, bored eyes scanning me. 'I don't know. Maybe we should leave her here. After all, she's looking for an adventure.'

'Don't be silly. There are dogs here. And snakes. And we don't know what else.'

The woman burst out laughing, and pulled out a cigarette. Imported. She took a drag and blew out a perfect, bell-like puff of smoke. Her displeasure over how I had interrupted her rendezvous was glaringly evident. But it was him she chose to attack with her scorn.

'Don't tell me you believe that absurd folktale?' she jeered.

'There's a reason why this place is closed to us.'

'Because it's a legendary kissing spot!'

'It turned into that later,' he argued. 'For cheap thrills, *because* it was disallowed. And because it's highly unlikely to get caught here.'

'What happened here?' I piped in, intrigued.

'You mean you don't *know*?' the woman said theatrically. I couldn't tell if it was a serious question, or if she was merely ridiculing me.

'Stop it. We're not talking about it here, of all places,' he said, folding his hands.

'Listen.' He turned to me, his tone a little more compassionate now. 'I'm sorry, but none of us are supposed to be here. Not right now, not ever. So please, let's go?'

I looked at the lake once more, and nodded, albeit grudgingly. As we headed out and the excitement abated abruptly, I felt an unbearable grief pull me down. I knew of its origin, but didn't want to address it. I tried not to gawk at the couple, but I couldn't help it. They were oddly mismatched, and yet seemed to complement each other. Like a duet turning out wonderful despite being recorded separately. Occasionally, the two of them stared at me too, but with a detached sort of interest. Sooner or later, they always fell back into the solitude of their own thoughts.

When we finally reached the main gate, I stole one last glance at the strong-chinned, mango-faced woman. A third wheel, that's what I'd been all this while.

I held out my hand, nonetheless. It was the only thing I could do to dispel the awkwardness.

He looked at it, and it felt like deja vu. It put us in a little bubble, just the two of us, until she broke it again.

'Bagchi, where's your bike?' she asked him, fixing her bun.

Bagchi. I took note of his name. It surprised me that throughout the walk to my class, I hadn't asked him for it. But then again, he hadn't asked me for mine either.

'Over there.' He shook my hand perfunctorily and then pulled out his key. 'Don't forget to send me the budget draft for college auditions tomorrow, okay?' she told him.

'Yes, *ma'am*,' he said, in mock salute.

I followed him out of the gate and towards his bike. 'Can I drop you somewhere?' he asked. I shook my head, forcing myself out of the bubble again. 'I'll walk, *Bagchi*.'

He beamed. 'It's actually Shakti. Shakti Bagchi.'

Had *Bagchi* been an endearment reserved only for *her*? But why did I care anyway? 'Whatever,' I said.

'And you're Esai.' There it was again. That dimple.

'Oh? And how did you know that?' I asked him.

'I know all my juniors' names. Have you reached that part where the snake falls in love with the heroine?'

Irritated, I started walking away. He ran after me. 'You're easy to provoke.' As an afterthought, he added. 'You didn't thank me for helping you out of the forest.'

'Thank you,' I said tightly. I looked at him seriously. 'So
what's her name?'

He burst out laughing. 'Wait, you mean you don't know
her?'

'Am I supposed to?'

'Initiation day is in a week! They'll destroy you.'

'For your information, I'm fully prepared for initiation day.'

'Right,' he said, sarcastic. 'Well, that was *her*. The Iron Lady
of St. Margaret's.'

'Who?'

'Ira Saanvi. *Your chairwoman.*'

THREE

*W*ANT TO KNOW WHY ST. MARGARET'S LAKE IS
FORBIDDEN? YOUR SENIORS TOO GUTLESS TO TELL
YOU? ATTEND MY SECRET SHOW AT 6 PM IN THE BOMBAY
PERFORMING ARTS LOUNGE. I'M SPILLING TEA. AND SOME
KICKASS POETRY.
  YOURS TRULY,
  SCHEHERAZADE.

Scheherazade, I thought. *Why have I heard of this name before?*
I looked once more at the handmade flyer on the door of the
women's washroom.

I decided to go. It did seem a bit like a gimmick, but I was
willing to give it a shot. I needed to know.

A few hours later, I was at the heart of Bandra, the queen
of suburbs, and a place that held a very distinct memory for
me. My little cousin, Tendral, and I would come here for our
birthdays at midnight and cut our cakes in front of Mannat, the
gorgeous, sea-facing house of Shah Rukh Khan, the Baadshah of
Bollywood. Art murals of Madhubala, Amitabh Bachchan, Dev
Anand and Dadasaheb Phalke were entombed in old walls and
buildings, but my favourite would always remain the painting

of Anarkali and her lover on Chapel Road. Anarkali was a courtesan who fell in love with Akbar's son. The lost love of a crown prince who was destined to replace one of the greatest emperors of the Mughal dynasty. There were many versions of this story told through oral tradition as well as film, but I had a soft spot for *Mughal-e-Azam* starring Dilip Kumar, because of how many liberties it took with the truth. It twisted many facts, and above all, it left Anarkali alive, unlike all other retellings.

It was only when I thought about Anarkali that I realised why the name *Scheherazade* had sounded so familiar.

As I walked past the boutique shops and pubs, I saw more flyers for Scheherazade's show. I'd never been to the Bombay Performing Arts Lounge, but I'd seen it from the outside. It was a timeless Portuguese style building in a colourful artsy hamlet. There were a lot of scooters parked outside of it, and a single, pink door at its centre.

Inside, the Arts Lounge was a small, dark studio with large red curtains and a vintage face. Painted wine bottles lined the rows of wooden shelves, and caricatures of iconic songwriters from the seventies dominated the walls. A bar sat at the corner, illuminated by hanging bulbs and Venetian masks. Against the pale glimmer of the candelabra, as a group of teenagers spilled shiraz on the floor of the neon-signed inn, I looked for a seat.

I was surprised by the crowd. There were at least fifty people, most of them juniors. From the excited whispers, I realized they were all here because they were as clueless and curious as me.

It was the lake that brought us here. The thought made me uncomfortable. Had they heard the singing too? Or had it just been me?

A voice began to slither into the room. A voice that reminded me of strawberries in chocolate. It was so pure and crystal clear, so haunting and ethereal, I thought I was floating.

'When the Persian King, Shahryar, came to know that his beloved was unfaithful to him, he vowed to marry a new woman every day and then behead her the following morning before she could dare humiliate him.'

Everyone looked around, trying to make sense of where the sound was coming from.

'When his trusted chief vizier could no longer find anyone else, he gave up his own daughter as the sultan's bride, as per her request. The wise, well-read threat, Scheherazade. Scheherazade outwitted the sultan by telling a story every night, but leaving it unfinished with a dazzling cliff-hanger so he would have to wait the next day to hear it. He was so charmed by her tale that he would allow her to live an extra night to complete it. And from there, she would begin another one, and this went on until he fell in love with her. And so, the ingenious Scheherazade saved her life with her brilliant storytelling.'

The studio was suddenly lit with yellow and maroon. The woman who glided into the room was, by no means, beautiful. But in the stage light, wearing her tailored suit, beaded hair jewellery and classic cat eye, she could be almost stunning.

Her shoulders were broad. There was no symmetry to her mouth. It cascaded everywhere, teased too close to her ears, seeped into the strong curve of her chin. Her brows were irregular, and her lids could have done with longer lashes, for they looked empty. She was unusual-looking, almost alien-like at first glance, and then suddenly hypnotizing. Suddenly hard to look away from. In a swift movement, she rested her blazer on the piano stool. Between her lips was a fancy pipe, which she pulled out slowly as she fit the microphone onto the stand. The muscles on her arms tensed as she did, and I heard the momentary clang of her metal cuff wrist bands as they came close to the mic.

She was tall and lean; her body, a tower. The black

turtleneck was so sheer and snug that it looked like her shadow had been superimposed onto her. A leather belt clung to her torso, and the statement dragon earrings stood out more prominently because of the wet, slicked back hair.

'And then there was Minaxi, who lost her life to it. Our very own local legendary character. Also known as,' she paused dramatically. 'The Lake Woman.'

So that was what Bagchi and Ira had been talking about yesterday. The nerves, the disillusion. Perhaps Bagchi knew something that Ira didn't? Or was it the other way round? Had she been privy to information he had no access to, information that assured her she had nothing to be jittery about? Well, in the end, they certainly hadn't thought too much about it if they'd chosen that spot to have their tongues in each other's mouths.

Scheherazade continued. 'They said she was a freak,' she whispered, and the man next to her began playing the trumpet. 'She was demonic, always hysterical.' The piano joined in, and melancholy shrouded the room.

'She was a landslide
don't get on her bad side
they said she preyed on children
and cooked them in her cauldron...'

It was awful. Some people began sniggering. I moved towards the bar to get myself a drink, annoyed. I had to admit though, it was great marketing strategy. Baiting people with the lake to make them hear your poetry. Nonetheless, there was something likeable about Scheherazade's theatrics. All that spirited hand flinging and pointless rhyme was over the top for me, but for some reason, it felt genuine. Like she truly believed what she was saying. Unfortunately, I wasn't sure if that was a good thing.

'The forbidden lake is haunted,' Scheherazade said, moving closer to the mic. 'Oooooooo,' the chorus behind her sang. A Greek tragedy of sorts.

'Why?' Scheherazade looked around at us one by one, thriving from the anticipation of the pause. 'A woman drowned there, that's why. A woman called Minaxi.'

'Aaaaaaaaaaah,' the chorus continued. The double bass let out a deep, musical wail.

A death in St. Margaret's, I thought, as I looked around at everyone else, observing their reactions. 'Is she high on something?' a girl behind me asked, giggling. 'I've never heard anything sillier.'

'No, my roommate told me about the woman in the lake, even though he didn't say much. Some girl did die,' the boy standing next to her said.

'Really?'

They were interrupted by Scheherazade on the mic.

'Minaxi was a student in our college, our St. Margaret's,' she went on. 'They took her in because her grades were outstanding, because on her good days, she was amazing. But on her bad days, she was a monster! They saw her collapse on the ground in public, screaming into the sky madly, pulling her hair, half-moon marks on her face from her nails. She threw plastic chairs at the Student Union back then when they tried to calm her down. She became the problem child of St. Margaret's, and all the professors wanted her removed. And those who came in direct contact with her? Oh, absurd things happened to them. They had fevers that went above a hundred and two. They failed exams. Someone's phone went missing, and they were so sure it was her. Because they'd seen her do crazy things. Like wandering around campus after dark, calling to the hounds. Someone even saw her drink blood.'

I listened on in disbelief. The room felt unbearably small.

'And then one day, she showed up to class, dark circles under her eyes, wounds on her arms, sporting a new pixie cut. It looked choppy, as if she'd done it to herself. And then she disappeared. For a long time, she was on medical leave, and they knew she'd gone to the asylum or prison. But a few months later, she showed up again, in the middle of the night, only to do something terrible. She'd kidnapped someone's child, and rumour had it that she'd stolen him for a human sacrifice. And rumour had it that she was trying to hide him in St. Margaret's, can you believe that? That's why she came back. So the management sent some members from the Student Union to look for her, and they set out into the deep woods at that odd hour, only to find her in the lake. She had drowned, and the baby was nowhere to be found. They say they were too late, that he was sacrificed and buried somewhere she alone knew. And they say Minaxi turned into a sea spirit, or a sea witch. That she's still...*here.*'

She threw her bangle onto the floor and screamed. 'This is the story of the Lake Woman, Minaxi. Or is it?' Her eyes were huge and glassy as she looked back at us. 'I am sure there is more to it. I don't trust history, no.'

'I heard someone saw her when they got lost in the deep woods!' a boy shouted from the audience.

Scheherazade burst into laughter. I had never heard anyone laugh like that. From their belly. Fully into joy. Baring all teeth. Mouthy and so explosive that it almost felt violent. 'But did *you* see her, my friend? That is the question.' She put a hand to her chest and looked at the ceiling. 'For all we know, it could just be a beautiful myth.' Nobody said a word. They wanted to hear more.

But Scheherazade had come to the end of her soliloquy. Or at least, as far as the lake was concerned, she was done. 'You know what isn't a myth?' She looked around. 'Do you?'

Everyone waited for her answer in bated breath.

'Power. Rigid systems. Corruption.' The students looked around, struggling to comprehend the sudden shift in topic.

A lot of them hadn't even realized that the story of the Lake Woman had ended. 'Just look at what's happening to us,' Scheher said. There was an angry lilt to her voice. 'How can we think about some Lake Woman who doesn't even exist when we've got other things to worry about? Like learning college facts and getting on a dumb stool? What is this initiation anyway, huh?' Silence. 'It makes me sad. Traditions like this are exactly how the capitalist class controls the proletariat in a bourgeois society. These things are tools for exploitation, they're part of the superstructure. Laws created to legitimize the power of the dominant class. And there's nothing we can do about it, is there?'

She nodded at the chorus to begin again. This time, it was the saxophone that took centre stage. 'When I feel helpless these days, the only thing that keeps me going is love. Yes, love.' People looked at one another again, this time, a little jaded. As if they'd jumped from one train of thought to another, and now all they wanted to do was go home. 'I want to write poems for my queer family, for the people who are part of the big fight for freedom. All kinds of freedom.' She cleared her throat. 'This is a piece I wrote about a girl I was crushing on. I never got to find out if she was into me.'

So finally, the true intention of the gathering was exposed. This had been nothing but a rallying call to sell snake oil, to listen to her incomprehensible performance poetry. Nonetheless, some people clapped and hooted, while others continued to look dubious. But that didn't stop Scheherazade. She had a few more poems about the girl she loved, and then one about police brutality, and then another about her cats.

By the time the show wrapped up, it was nine. I still couldn't make up my mind about whether I liked the flamboyant Scheherazade or not, but I had to give it to her, she was definitely interesting. As people began filing out the door, I made my way towards her.

'Grab dinner with me,' I said.

She gave me a once over. 'Why?' she asked haughtily.

I quickly came up with an elevator pitch. 'Well,' I began. 'I had some questions about the Lake Woman. And…I'll buy you dinner?' I didn't know if that was enough, but then she said, 'Ah, why not? I'm free anyway. And I'm assuming you go to St. Margaret's like me. Right?'

'Yes. Yes, I do.' And that was it.

Dinner was at Candies. It made me feel nostalgic, even though I'd never been there before. Across me sat Scheherazade, who was downing food as if she'd gone hungry for days. 'God, I'm famished,' she said. 'Performing live does that to you. I can't believe the organizers told me not to come back.'

I could. 'So Scheherazade is your real name?'

'It's Firoza Wadia, actually.' she said, between bites. 'Scheherazade is my stage name. But you can call me Scheher. It means the city. And I like that, I like this city. It's a fine vibe.' I couldn't help but agree with her. Bombay's charm certainly was stimulating. People loved and hated it at the same time. It had an overpowering presence, a signature of its own. Life was enthralling when the arts festivals and cultural events came by, when actors put together Eve Ensler's *The Vagina Monologues* or improvised plays based on Ismat Chughtai's stories. It also became unsightly when it ushered in the monsoon season, and dead rats and sewage water blocked the roads. Everyone turned cranky, and bridges collapsed from the brute force of perpetual rain storms.

'What are you doing in St. Margaret's?' I asked Scheher.

'Journalism,' she quipped.

I leaned forward. 'And how did you know the story about the…Lake Woman?'

'Just a lot of asking around, really. A lot of these seniors start talking if you buy them a beer or two.'

'Noted. And if I wanted to go see her for myself...'

She shook her head. 'No. Don't do it. People say all kinds of things about that place, you know.' She pulled out a deck of cards from her bag and began shuffling. I realized they were tarot cards and leaned back.

'I don't believe in any of that,' I said. She smiled, and continued to spread them on the table.

'So tell me, what exactly do people say?' I asked.

'Well, they say if you dip your foot in the lake, it turns into a mermaid's tail.'

'That sounds ridiculous.'

'I don't know. I don't know what to believe anymore.'

She stared at the cards for a few seconds. And then tapped on the one at the far right, and flipped it around.

The Devil.

'Every time,' she said.

'So the devil lives there?' I asked, cynical.

She shook her head again. 'The Devil card means temptation, addiction, bondage. *You* need to stop being so obsessed.'

'I'm not obsessed.' *Liar.*

'Why do you want to go to the lake anyway?'

I didn't tell her about the dream. Or the humming. Or that I was there for a fleeting second, and the spectral orbs spoke to me. 'I'm just curious. And it sounds like a fun...outing.'

She dusted the crumbs off her pants, and got up. 'My boyfriend is coming to pick me up. Do you want a ride home?'

'He won't mind?' There was a moment's hesitation, and then she smiled. 'No, no. Just come.'

'Drop me off at Aram Nagar, if that's okay?'

'Done.'

For the next few minutes, we had nothing much to say. I was preoccupied with the lake, and Scheher had delved into her own world. An hour passed, and then one more, and there

was no sign of her boyfriend. 'He'll be here soon,' she kept
reassuring me, and soon, the reassurance turned into apologies.

By the time he finally arrived, she was in tears. She pulled
open the door of the car, and signalled at me to slide in. She
climbed into the passenger seat and leaned back, resting her
head on the soft cushion. I thought she was going to pick a
fight, but she wiped her eyes quickly, and said, 'The show went
really well, Jo.'

'Sure.' I had an instinctive urge to jump out when I
recognized his voice. To rinse my skin, to unravel the familiar
knot in my stomach.

There, in the damned driver's seat, sat the one and only
Joshua D'Silva.

I need to leave right now, I thought, the hair on the back of
my arm straightening. But before I could listen to my intuition,
he started the engine. And although he didn't seem to pay any
attention to me, I was still stressed. I told myself it was a good
sign that he was more focused on Scheher, or rather, the version
of Scheher that was now in the car with him.

The Scheher on stage had been so different from the
Scheher in Joshua's car. On stage, she'd seemed unshaken,
volcanic, a tall, architectural wonder. Eccentric, perhaps, but
definitely confident. In the car, however, she'd shrunk out of
her wildling self and into a trance, listening mutely to Joshua
as he went on about how he thought she ought to stop writing
altogether.

'You need to set realistic standards for yourself, Firoza.
You're not cut out for it.' She had ignored his jibes throughout
the ride.

Only when we'd entered Versova did she say, in a small
voice, 'Jo, could we stop at Aram Nagar to drop Esai?'

I recoiled when I heard my own name, because that was
when he noticed who'd been sitting behind him all along.

Seething, he adjusted the mirror and let the tension build up, before saying, 'You think I'm your personal driver, Firoza? If that's what you need, why don't you ask your rich Baabaayi to hire one? Anyway he's bought you a house to get over the guilt of not taking care of a child he didn't want.'

'Do *not* talk about my Baabaayi.'

His eyes looked red. I wondered if he'd been drinking. 'I'll talk about him all I want.'

'I should've dated Lehar when I had the chance. Then I wouldn't have ended up with an idiot like you.'

'Ha! Firoza, you can't even please a man. You think you can please a woman?'

'What's that supposed to mean?'

'It means you don't know the ABCs of fucking.'

'If fucking means getting me stoned and then grinding against me when I'm passed out, Joshua, then let me tell you, you're the one who can't fuck. Actually, you know what? Stop the car. I want to get down.'

He stopped the car, turned to her, and glared. And then his hand reached out and coiled around her neck. She screamed, and so did I.

'How dare you insult me in front of your friends?' he spat at her as she coughed. He retreated, and then turned to me. I couldn't stop staring at the red trails on her throat. 'Get out,' he said to me.

Gladly, I thought, and jumped out of the car as fast as I could. 'Scheher,' I said, still shaking. I could taste the blood in my mouth. At some point, I'd probably bitten into my tongue. 'A-are you coming?' She looked at me, her eyes twin pools now, and slowly shook her head. My heart sank. And then, before I could say anything more, the two of them drove off. I stood there for a good five minutes before getting onto a rick and heading home, my body lapsing into shock the whole ride.

He'd choked her. In front of me. He could have killed her.

The scene ran in my head for hours. The screaming turned into a chorus as the night grew. I paced back and forth in my room, keeping my head down, struggling to breathe. It was as if a big boulder was pressing my chest down, digging deeper into my lungs and nestling into the abrasion. Morphing into an arrow, and then a barb, and then an inexhaustible vessel of shame, like the legendary copper bowl in Hindu mythology that never ran out of food. All night, I was the keeper of a very ugly truth. And the repercussion? Tremors for hands.

I resisted the impulse to call her and ask if she was all right. What if they were still in the car? What if seeing my name on her phone aggravated him further? What if...? I lay on my bed and took a few deep breaths. It bothered me that she'd passively refused to come with me. It bothered me even more that I hadn't done more, that I had no clue what to do about this, no power.

The night didn't wait for me. As I turned host to all my unwelcome thoughts, the moon washed away into a stroke of pale fuchsia. The street lights began to shut down, and the city stirred awake. I pulled my curtains close and admitted defeat.

By the time I finally fell asleep, the sun had already risen.

FOUR

I was nine again and sitting in front of my aunt, Jolly. She was massaging my head. We were in the balcony, and we were watching a pigeon hopping back and forth with twigs in its talons. The bottle of oil next to Jolly smelled of hibiscus petals, Indian gooseberries and some herbs she'd used to make it. To kill time, I asked her for a story, and she told me about the man in the puppetry show when she'd gone for the Isakki Amman festival in her hometown. The folk dance his puppets played out for her was a retelling of an old legend: a woman-turned-guardian spirit to Tamil districts such as Tirunelveli and Kanyakumari.

'She wasn't Isakki Amman at first,' Jolly told me.

'Then?'

'She was called Ambika.'

Ambika was a housewife who loved her husband, Somasharman, and her two sons. They were gearing up for a special ceremony that offered food items to the ancestors of the family, when a hungry sage arrived at her doorstep. Because her husband had gone to bathe in the river and Ambika did not know what to do, she offered the sage whatever she had prepared for the ritual. When her husband returned, he was furious that she'd interfered with the process of the rites, and so he drove her and her sons away from the house. Somasharman later repented his actions, and went looking for her. Ambika, in her fear of her own husband, took her life. She eventually regained her human form so that she could come back and take care of her sons, and this was the reason why her idol always had a child or two by her side. Ambika, now the goddess Isakki, was awarded a shrine by her worshippers, and was usually recognizable from her red dress and the cactus plant used to decorate her abode.

It was Isakki who came in my dream, running from her husband, her eyes full of terror. *Help*, she screeched. *He's trying to kill me!* And then she turned into Scheher, and she was running too, this time, from Joshua. She had a trident in her hand, and her hair was loose. She escaped into the forest in search of a place to rest, and I followed her.

In the forest, she was Minaxi. She was wailing, her arms bruised from the branches that had stood in her way, and she was crawling towards the lake.

'Minaxi,' I said, and she turned.

I took a step back and gasped. It wasn't Minaxi. It wasn't any of them.

It was *me*.

I woke up with a jolt, a car screeching to a halt. With watery eyes, I looked at the clock and cursed. *I should skip first period*, I told myself. It was Vikas sir's class and he hadn't taken any of his classes so far. Maybe he wouldn't show up this time too?

No, I couldn't afford to take the risk. I'd heard he was a tough one. Reluctantly, I dragged myself out of bed. On my way to class, I walked past Scheher, and noticed a bit of red and purple on her arms. I went rigid. I didn't know how to bring it up, and I didn't know if I was allowed to. She smiled at me edgily, and I smiled back.

'I'll catch you later, I'm late for Media and Cultural Studies,' she said, and I never saw her again that day.

I distracted myself with back-to-back classes and two hours at the library, but I was jittery. The incident in the car still had me shaken up.

In the evening, I looked for Scheher, but I was told she'd left early. And because I wasn't ready to return home just yet, I found myself walking towards the lake again. This time, it was deserted. This time, it was easy to find my way to it. The deeper I went, the denser the forest became. But there were also fragrant champaka trees leading the path to it like lighthouses. And just before entering the lake's grounds, I saw painted pebbles catching moss and bathing in the sun. Were they there before? Or had they been left there for me?

I thought about the things Scheher had said during the show. I thought about her tarot card, and the silly little poem she'd written about the Lake Woman and her insanity. I had so many questions. Was Minaxi's body still in there, or had they taken it out? If I were to reach the deep end, would I find bones, or absolutely nothing? Would I turn into a mermaid if I took a dip, or would I stay the same? I was delirious.

I bent down in front of it, assessing my image, hands on my lap. Whispered a prayer to the waves, played with the rocks guarding it like a small fortress. In my reflection, I saw a trace of fear.

The orbs held their breaths above the lake in harmony, waiting for me to react. I hitched my skirt and walked along the edge of the lake to its opposite side. It wasn't a very big lake. In fact, it was smaller than my classroom.

A woman had drowned here. A crazy woman, Scheher had said.

I closed my eyes and felt the cool wind settle on my skin. The earth was damp, and I created tiny circles on it with my

finger. It reminded me of a time not too long ago, when I'd
hiked my way up a mountain with Jolly. We'd spread ourselves
on the grass, depleted and flushed with the acceptance that the
universe was too big, too chaotic for us to understand. Devoted
to the philosophy that our existence was wonderful despite that.

When I opened my eyes, I saw another reflection. The
reflection of a woman ruined by absence. The emptiness of a
fallen economy reflected in her eyes. I moved closer, and looked
again. She was gone.

'My child, just what do you think you're doing here?'

Jumping, I turned around and came face to face with my
intruder. I'd been caught. 'Sir.'

It was Nanda sir, the head of the Physics department.
Short, old and weary, he was a major astronomy enthusiast.
All his students had outlandish anecdotes about him. I'd been
told about the one time he went to class with a half-shaved
moustache and two different kinds of shoes. About his obsession
with Galvanism and aliens and even the discovery of nuclear
weapons. About the jinxed telescope in his house. About him
getting so easily side-tracked with topics unrelated to what he
was teaching that he was far behind the other professors; but
none of the students cared, because they loved his antics. They
said there was nothing he didn't know. Except, perhaps, the
syllabus. For every time he'd begin the subject, he would have
something more fascinating to talk about. And then from there,
they would go on a space mission, and when they came back,
textbooks simply didn't matter. The *nutty professor*, that's what
they'd labelled him.

'I ought to take you to the principal straight away,' he
grumbled.

'How did you find me?' I was defiant, armed to the teeth
for a confrontation. Every alphabet tasted bitter on my tongue.

'I was tipped off by a young man that a very stubborn

junior might show up here. So I've been patrolling the place every now and then.'

Bagchi, I thought, offended.

'I wasn't doing anything illegal here,' I argued. 'Really.' It was true. It wasn't as if he'd caught me necking like Bagchi and Ira.

'*Being* here is illegal!' Looking a little resigned, he asked, 'What are you doing here?'

'I heard a story last night and I just wanted to come see. It was an enchanting story.'

He sat on one of the bigger rocks. 'I see.'

Trying to buy time, I continued, 'I was told a woman drowned here after trying to escape a mob. She'd kidnapped an infant and they believed it was for a ritual.' God, I sounded silly to my own ears.

'Really?' He raised an eyebrow.

I was the first to look away, faintly weighed down by liar's shame. I sat on the opposite rock, face in my palms. 'I'm sorry. It's mostly rubbish, isn't it? I don't know what came over me. I won't come here again.'

'Have you heard of Johannes Kepler?'

I looked up, disoriented. 'No, I haven't.'

He grinned, and then broke into a spontaneous lecture. 'Kepler was an important astronomer and mathematician at a time the Church was against all kinds of great thinkers.'

'Like Galileo?'

'Galileo came in much later. Yes, he was notorious for his theories and an ardent support of heliocentrism. But Kepler wasn't any less controversial, you know. He had his fair share of treacherous stances too. In 1596, he wrote his first public defence of the Copernican system. It was an era of opposing beliefs, a time when everyone was at risk of persecution if they argued that the sun was the centre of the universe. Do you follow what I'm saying?'

I nodded, wondering where this was heading.

'Kepler's three laws of planetary motion changed the world,' Nanda sir explained. 'In the world of Science, there is not a single person who doesn't know him. But what most people don't know is the odd, gruesome account of his mother.'

'What about his mother?' I asked, drawn.

'She was accused of witchcraft.'

'Oh.' I leaned forward. 'Was she? A witch, I mean.'

'Nobody,' Nanda sir stressed. 'In that time, or even now, could ever be a witch. It simply started with a rumour, a rumour that the devil gave certain people special powers in exchange for their allegiance. Children under pressure from magistrates blamed innocent women of being the devil's slave. It was a game of power and suppression, and of course, mass delusion. Some of the first women who were accused were a homeless beggar, a Caribbean slave, an old lady. They found targets everywhere, and they executed them for nothing. Not that Katharina Kepler was executed, she was actually released eventually, but she died a year later. After being put through so much suffering.'

'That's so sad,' I said bleakly.

'Anyway, it started with Ursula Reinbold, who went around crying that Katharina had given her a potion that made her sick. The truth was that Ursula had a personal issue with Katharina. And it didn't help that Katharina was raised by an aunt who'd been burned at the stake for witchcraft. And it didn't help at all that Katharina had anger issues. Soon, more rumours about her spread through the streets of Leonberg. Every bad fortune was pinned on Katharina. If someone became lame, or went hungry, it was all her fault.'

And those who came in direct contact of her? Oh, absurd things happened to them. They had fevers that went above a hundred and two. They failed exams.

'What are you trying to say?' I asked, mistrustful.

'That there are no witches. Simply casualties of hearsay.'

'I see.' So he knew about the myth, and he knew something that the others didn't.

'Shall we leave, my dear?'

Involuntarily, I stood up and lifted the bag which I had carelessly tossed onto the ground earlier. 'All right.'

As we walked back to the main area, I felt a familiar disappointment, the same vague feeling of regret. I thought about Minaxi running in a white gossamer gown, her dark mane flying around her, her nimble feet carrying her to safety, or perhaps to the devil.

Long ago, when Tendral and I had broken Jolly's favourite sugar jar, leaving Jolly in a puddle of tears, my uncle Pipi had told us about the Neeli pisasu, a Tamil ghost lore. He'd cooked up the first half of it, claiming this was a phantom that ate children if they behaved badly, but the second half of it had been borrowed from a well-known myth of a dead woman who sought to tear her husband, a merchant, to pieces for murdering her and taking another wife. Just as the merchant was passing through a forest in Tiruvalangadu for trade, the angry ghost showed up before him, impersonating his new wife and child. He sensed it wasn't them, and fled to the custodians of the village for protection. But the tear-laden Neeli told them that he was her husband and he'd forsaken her, and so they locked the couple up in a hut for a night, hopeful that it would make things right. But as dawn stopped by, his body was found in strips, and the spellbinding young woman was gone. Ever since, Tendral and I had tried to call Neeli using handmade Ouija boards, to Pipi's disdain. His trick to discipline us had rebounded, and we were back to square one again, breaking glass vases and causing trouble, praying this would provoke the aggrieved phantom and give us a glimpse of her.

It had been an easy myth to believe. There had been no loose ends whatsoever, nothing to question.

But Minaxi's tale was in slices, just like Neeli's husband. Parts of it just didn't make sense. Everyone who had opened up about it had a completely different version of it. My head buzzed as if knotted wires ran inside it.

As we crossed the canteen, I saw a couple of seniors, sitting at one of the tables and sharing a dirty joke. Some members from the Student Union Cabinet I didn't know, the chairwoman, the deceitful Bagchi, and of course, the one person I never wanted to see again, Joshua. Pulse speeding, I tried to conceal myself behind Nanda sir, but it was too late.

'Esai!' Joshua yelled from his chair, as if we were good, as if I hadn't witnessed his physical assault on Scheher the previous night. 'Come here!' I walked towards him warily. 'Where are you off to with Nanda sir?'

To my surprise, Nanda sir didn't say we were going to the principal's office. Instead, he remarked, 'She got lost. So I'm just showing her the way home.' Nice, I was off the hook. At least for now.

As Nanda sir turned to the other seniors and began asking them about their electives, Joshua nudged me. 'So, my little Madrasi, did you ever get your class timings sorted out?' I blanched at the regional slur. Madrasi was a blanket label used for anyone from South India, by those who couldn't bother to learn that Madras wasn't the only region in the South. For me, what was more galling than the word itself was the way Joshua had said it. I ignored him and fixed my gaze on Bagchi instead.

Bagchi blushed tellingly when he realised the spotlight was on him, and Ira's face was an indecipherable code. In that moment, I felt a surge of loathing towards the chairwoman, towards everything that she represented. Power. Apathy. Arrogance. Old money. And so much more.

But lord, Ira was very beautiful. Divinely beautiful. Porcelain skin, straight black hair pulled back into a harsh bun like a ballerina or congresswoman. A full, glossy mouth, almost always pouting and turned downwards in distaste. Fingers that looked like they could play the piano like a wet dream. The well-built body of a policewoman. Anyone would be envious, especially a first year nobody like me.

I suddenly became aware of how easily their doctrine had spilled into my nervous system. I had just trivialized myself for being a first year, even though it had been a subconscious thing. I vowed I'd never do it again. I tried to remember something Scheher had said during dinner the other day.

Being a first year meant we had a lot of brand new experiences in store for us, a life ahead that was packed with curiosity and originality and nobody could take that away. The way a fresher saw St. Margaret's was nothing like how a senior did. Freshers came in with priceless susceptibility and dreams, and if anything, those were the things to be envied. Hopes in the interim. The enthusiasm of new beginnings, the experimental friendships of the first months. The jubilation, the eagerness to please, the determination to be something great. Yes, I would wear all of them like a prefect badge.

'Shall we move on?' Nanda sir asked quietly, breaking into my thoughts.

'Do you find Joshua evil?' I asked him out of nowhere, the minute we reached the main road. 'Don't you think he treats people badly?'

The following silence was so long, I thought he wasn't going to answer at all. 'There's always at least one like that in every batch,' he finally responded, reproach lacing his voice. 'Always.'

I wondered if there had been someone like that in Minaxi's batch too. Someone who called her names, just like Joshua had called me *Madrasi*.

I also wondered if there were people who had just watched and done nothing at all while it all happened. People who were ready to devour any sickening news, even if it didn't sound right. *They'd find her wandering on campus after dark, calling to the hounds. Someone even once saw her drink blood.*

I eyed Nanda sir. Why had he reacted to the myth in such a personal way? Was he always this protective of the reputation of students, or was there more to it? I felt an immediate, deep-seated urge to investigate the timeline of these incidents. I visualised Minaxi moving past the trees, crying for help, her public panic attacks crawling up her spine again. Her toes were tingling; her face was numb. Frantic, terror-struck. Tears tumbling down her cheeks, begging for shelter. Left to erode, as everyone played jury at her trial. They vilified her, called her a sinner for her rage storm, for her lack of self-control. For crashing and falling to pieces in broad daylight. It wasn't normal, they said. *This behaviour.*

There were gaps to this. And I didn't know what to fill them with, so my imagination took over. I only knew that whatever the truth was, I would never be like Minaxi. To survive, I would have to be like Scheherazade, the original Scheherazade. A true queen of yarns, and not a victim of them.

At the gate, I thanked Nanda sir, finding it a little funny that I'd been caught in a repeat of that day near the lake; only now, it was a different person walking beside me. But then, just as I was about to split ways, Nanda sir said something I would never forget. Something that reinstated my trust in the unique timelessness of every new day, every new episode, every new conversation.

'I knew her, you know,' he said sadly. 'I knew Minaxi.'

FIVE

At last, it was initiation day.
Dousing myself with two rapid glasses of water, I jumped
out of bed.

Last night had been a montage of night terrors and too
much tossing and turning. Visions of the nightmare I'd had
replayed in my head, and known faces sprang up. Joshua and
his allies tying me to a chair—or had it been a stake?—and
brandishing their lit torches, as everyone else, including Bagchi,
called me a *daayan*, a witch.

The word cut into my mind like a sharp C-section incision.
They were going to turn me into a witch today. I could already
taste the fire on my tongue.

Hadn't we anticipated this day since we'd arrived in St.
Margaret's? Hadn't we studied harder than we'd studied for
our tests? And if I knew I had all the answers I needed, then
why did I still feel like something bad was about to happen?

Tendral entered my room, a plate of round, fluffy and
perfectly made gunpowder idlis in her hand. She was a great
cook, but she rarely entered the kitchen, so I was taken by
surprise. 'Yes, yes. I made them,' she said, taking one look at

my expression. 'So no skipping breakfast.'

'You made them for me?' I asked incredulously.

'Well, I made them because it's Raza's birthday, but trust me, you were in my thoughts.'

'Thanks anyway,' I said, sitting back on my bed and yawning loudly.

Tendral met Raza at her engineering coaching class. Tendral was trying for Computer Science, and Raza, for Electrical. They'd bonded over things that Bombay people usually bonded over. Rent and Bollywood. He'd helped her solve a sum in class, breaking the ice. And then they'd gone to Dheeraj sandwich shop after their lessons, debating over who was the best Khan in the industry, the archetypal dispute that decided whether two people could be friends.

They'd decided they would be lovers instead.

A shared latte and a kiss later, he'd asked her about her leg, and why they had to remove the part below her knee. She'd opened up about her life changing pneumonia and dry gangrene, and then proceeded to show him her prosthetic. He'd told her she looked like Iron Man, and it had made her laugh.

Ever since, they'd been inseparable. And ever since, Raza had visited the house so often that he turned into our permanent resident. 'I'll wish him when I go downstairs,' I said, stretching lazily. Picking up my toothbrush and paste, I sauntered into the washroom.

Five minutes later, I heard Tendral's impatient voice through the door. 'Are you going to eat these idlis or not?'

'Obviously. I'll eat anything at this point. I need to be standing on a stool today for God knows how long, looking straight into thin air.'

'Really? Why?' she asked as I opened the door, all dressed up.

'It's this ceremony where juniors have to prove themselves to their seniors,' I explained. 'You get to be a true St. Margaretian only if you pass a test. They ask you stupid, irrelevant questions.'

'Good luck,' Tendral said, smirking. 'It's going to be a long, long day then.'

'The longest. Longer than the summer solstice.'

As I was leaving, I quickly embraced Raza, ruffled his hair and promised him a birthday cake as soon as I got back from college. The walk to the bus stop, which was usually my moment of peace and solitude, was now punctured by self-doubt.

Daayan, daayan, daayan, my head screamed at me. Every street lamp looked like a stake. Every passer-by seemed as if they would point at me and split into a banshee cry. Everything appeared as a bad omen.

My bus dropped me a little behind the main gate. There, I ran into Scheher, and slipped into a brisk walk right next to her. We didn't say anything to each other, merely nodded in acknowledgement and carried on, all wound up in our devout recital of St. Margaret's facts. After that sermon at the Arts Lounge, I hadn't expected to see her here, all buttoned up and obedient. I assumed she'd gone against her own advice and chosen to give in to the seniors' demands.

We entered Richardson Hall, where all the big events happened, and took our seats, sincerely praying for everyone we knew. This was bigger than any exam. This was an exam of first impressions, an exam that proved our allegiance to the college. An exam that nobody dared fail, because if they did, it would mean being targeted for the rest of your college life. It would mean being cornered and mocked and shoved around until you began living each day in fear.

The Cabinet members sat at the front, with the exception of the president and vice president. Vikas sir, who taught us Speculative Fiction and Literature from the Margins, was the vice president of the Cabinet. As usual, he was absent. The principal was the president, and he'd given his approval for the ceremony, as long as it was kept within its limits, but I didn't know what exactly he meant by limits. On a scale of zero to problematic, what was a limit? Wasn't anything above zero already vile enough? Anyhow, he'd excused himself, saying he had more important things to do than partake in Fresher's Day.

This was not Fresher's Day. This was Seniors' Day. Everyone knew that.

'Welcome everyone, and please settle down fast. We will begin shortly,' Joshua announced, right after Ira whispered something in his ear.

Interesting, I thought. I hadn't noticed it before, the odd way Joshua and Ira behaved with each other. It seemed to me there was an impenetrable friendship between them that even Bagchi didn't understand. A friendship built on a shared secret. I didn't know if I was reading too much into it, but my instinct told me they had some kind of history. It could be that they were both from extraordinarily rich families, and so they understood each other's lives in a way those who'd been born middle class didn't. Or it could be that they were family friends and had known each other since they were babies. Literally chaddi buddies, literally *friends since their diaper days*. The more I watched them, the more it became plain to me that there was something. Definitely something more than what met the eye.

'Scheher,' I said. 'How long has Joshua known Ira?'

'Maybe three years? I mean, they met on their first day of college.' She didn't seem as interested as I was in them. 'Listen, I really want a treat after this. Let's go have banoffee pie later?'

'That's specific.'

'I'm craving it.'

'All right, all right,' I said, distracted.

I also noticed that for the first time, Bagchi was not by Ira's

side. He was sitting where all the other seniors were, at the
back. He smiled at me, and I smiled back.

Relax, he mouthed. I showed him a thumbs up from where
I sat.

They began to call names in alphabetical order. All seniors
were allowed to ask a question each, but it was the Cabinet
that asked the most. They were all well-versed in the facts,
and Joshua particularly, felt the urge to keep asking about the
names of the current Cabinet members, so that he could hear
his own. Eventually, Ira shot him a dirty look, and that stopped
him for good.

Everything was going well, as well as I could have imagined.
And then, right before me, a lean, long-haired boy shot up, and
got onto the stool. The seniors asked him to get back down
and tie his hair. Once he was done, he asked their permission
to get onto the stool. One of them said no again, pointing out
that he hadn't removed his shoes. By the time he was finally
on the stool, he was trembling.

His fear excited them. And because they were out to draw
blood, they started with the difficult questions. He knew some
of them, but when he admitted that he didn't know the others,
the seniors sulked and whispered among themselves. Scheher,
seated onto my right, whispered, 'I'm glad that's not me.'

'Same,' I said, staring at my open palms, unable to watch
the scene unfold.

'Do you know who built the library?' I heard Ira's voice
ring through the auditorium. He answered, but he'd begun
stammering.

'Which year?' Joshua asked. Scheher groaned, probably
sensing he wasn't going to let it go. 'And day, and month.'

'Can you tell us who the college is named after?'

'Who was the first chairperson of St. Margaret's?'

I could tell that he was about to break down. 'M-may I

get off the stool, p-please?' he whimpered. His hands started twitching, and someone behind me said, 'He's got a fear of speaking in public. He was telling us yesterday.'

Had they ever failed anyone before? And what happened when someone with a phobia of facing the crowd had to stand in front of one?

'P-please may I get down?'

'Not yet,' Ira said, and I gritted my teeth. Scheher shifted beside me, her nails biting into her palms.

Ira turned to the rest of the seniors. 'Does the floor have any questions for Mr. Darshit?'

I could see Bagchi vehemently shaking his head, but there were too many raised hands for anyone to notice him. Here was a boy, almost about to cry while standing on a stool, being turned into a fool, and yet glued to the same spot. It was painful to watch. If he wasn't initiated today, he would have to wait till the next year to be initiated with the new batch. One year of not being a St. Margaretian? Coming to campus every day and being heckled and driven insane? How could anyone bear something like that?

They pounced on him. 'What are the names of the two labs inside the Science Block?'

'Amarjith lab and...' He looked around. Nobody breathed a word. 'Amarjith lab...'

'And Dr. Francis lab.'

He nodded.

'Say it,' Ira said. 'Dr. Francis lab.'

'Dr. Francis lab,' he said quietly. The seniors at the front could hear him, but I had to read his lips to understand what he was saying.

'Louder.'

'Dr. Francis lab,' he said, and this time, his voice hit the back of the auditorium.

'How many acres is the campus?' A second year student asked. I had seen her before, under the water tower.

'Three hundred and...' The bloodlust on the seniors' faces, it was almost cannibalistic. He saw it too, and clammed up. Suddenly, he was very much aware of everyone in the room. He stared back vacantly.

'Darshit? Answer the question.'

It didn't look like Darshit could hear any of them. He bowed his head till his chin hit his chest, and the only thing I could hear now was him breathing heavily.

I didn't know what got into me at that moment, but I rose from my seat.

'Wait, what are you doing?' Scheher asked, but I was already sprinting past the chairs towards him.

When I was right in front of him, all eyes turned to me. It felt like the whole room was suddenly still, and I could hear nothing but heartbeats racing in suspense.

I tugged at his sleeve and told him, 'Darshit, just get down.'

'Absolutely not!' Joshua roared, springing from his seat. He looked livid.

'Really, just get down,' I said, mildly. 'You can do it.'

He raised his head a little and looked at me. I smiled encouragingly, and gave my other hand. He took both, and stepped down, keeping his eyes on the floor.

'You,' Anisha, the cultural convenor snarled, pointing at me. 'How dare you interrupt the sacred initiation ceremony? Are you going to get off the stage or not?'

Fool's courage kicked in. Nothing mattered. Not this initiation nonsense, not the Cabinet's disfavour, not anything at all. So I looked straight at her and replied, 'No. Not yet.'

Darshit went back to his seat, and Scheher immediately offered her water bottle to him. And then, before the seniors could even begin to complain, his friends began to crowd around him, asking him if he was all right.

'Silence, silence,' Ira said, and some of the juniors booed at her. 'Go outside and check on him. If he's not fine, then take him to the counsellor.'

The group moved out immediately, and I saw Bagchi follow them quietly.

'Esai,' Ira said. 'You're next.'

I'd walked into the noose; my impulsivity had consequences. I removed my slippers and hoped to God that I didn't appear skittish. They weren't going to let me off the hook so easily. They were going to have me for supper.

I took a deep breath and stepped onto the stool.

The first few questions were easy, but within a minute, the tough ones started sliding in. It slandered them to see me answer them well, and their questions assumed an injured tone, becoming more complex as each one was won over.

'How many shelves does the library have?'

'Sixty-seven.'

'How many tiles does the floor of the computer room in the Economics Department have?'

'A hundred and forty-three.'

The senior who asked the question turned to the Economics students. 'Is that correct?'

None of them knew.

Soon, they became indignant, and all hope fell on Joshua to cross the line, to do the dirty work, which he did. Rising from his seat, he asked me, 'What would you do if the principal asked you to strip?'

From the corner of my eye, I watched Bagchi enter the room, and then stop in his tracks.

'He's not going to ask me to do that,' I said.

'Answer the question.'

'I wouldn't do it,' I said stiffly.

'Good,' he replied. 'That's what I wanted to hear. After all, if you're going to be a true St. Margaretian, you shouldn't obey any of the teaching staff blindly.'

'Or the seniors,' I said sweetly.

There was a sudden hush-hush in the room again. 'Silence,' Ira repeated, annoyed.

'Would you sleep with your professors for higher grades?' Joshua continued. From where I was standing, I could see Scheher getting up from her seat and storming off. Another chair moved, and then another.

'Maybe tone it down a bit,' Ira told Joshua, looking at the thinning crowd.

'No, wait. Would you?' He glared at me.

'I'm not failing in my classes like you, Joshua,' I said slowly. One of the seniors at the back snorted, making it quite obvious that not all of them were his fans. 'I don't need to be doing any dirty deeds. So maybe you're the one who should be answering that question.'

Someone erupted into heavy laughter. 'Bloody hell!' they cried, wiping tears of mirth. A sense of triumph washed over me. It felt good to see Joshua squirm and scuttle around for a good comeback. He had none. I'd won this over purely by wit.

I looked straight at the seniors, burning with the newfound knowledge that most of them were on my side, even though they just didn't know it yet. 'May I get off the stool, please?' I asked firmly.

'Yes,' Bagchi was the first to speak.

The word sent a ripple of relief down my spine. And one by one, everyone reiterated after him, until there were hundreds of vibrant, emphatic yesses. It was astounding. Minutes ago, they'd tried to turn me into a target in a firing range. And now they were championing me, screaming my name like there was no end to it. I couldn't stomach how fickle they were. Were they really that gullible? That easily swayed? Was that all it took to change a person's perception of you? Guts, and a few smart words? Did every madman walk to the podium and speak into the mic before starting a mass homicide? Hadn't Mark Antony himself, in one quick-witted speech, turned an entire audience against Brutus?

My mind was reeling.

I stepped down gracefully, walked towards my seat and picked up my bag. Without looking back, I began walking out of the hall, and heard the resounding outbreak of applause behind me. And a very displeased, yet captivated Ira grumble, 'Well, well. A young Jhansi Rani and all, isn't she? Maybe we need to get her on my Cabinet.'

SIX

Outside, Joshua caught up with me, seething. I had just crossed the street to get to the main gate, when he circled my elbow with his fingers and turned me around.

I stared back at him coldly. This was a man made for wickedness, from wickedness. He hadn't just hurt me. He'd attacked my friend; he'd terrorized a junior just minutes ago. One look into his eyes and I knew I would never be able to get over the image of his hands closing around Scheher's throat. I was back in that car again, screaming my lungs to death, goose flesh all over me. My pulse had catapulted so high it had taken hours to return to normalcy. I couldn't bring myself to tolerate him. I couldn't forgive him for who he was.

In my eyes, he just couldn't be redeemed.

'Why are you overreacting to everything?' he sneered.

I could see the faint red marks his unyielding grasp was making at the base of my upper arm. 'Stop that.'

'Next time you open your mouth and cause a scene, it's acid for you,' he spat, fuming. It was evident. The entitlement in his voice, the menacing promise.

I wrenched my hand out of his grip. But before I could turn on my heels and run, he stalked off first.

Next time you open your mouth and cause a scene, it's acid for you.

It burned a hole through my gut. I took three deep breaths, and then some more. Told myself it had just been an empty threat, that there was nothing to worry about. But every time I thought about it I felt unsettled. My elbow throbbed from the tightness of his clutch. His words parked themselves everywhere. I caught myself jumping every time I heard a sound. I told myself I was getting paranoid; he wasn't going to spring out of the bushes with a vial of acid around his neck. Where would he buy it from anyway?

No, he wouldn't have to buy it from anywhere.

He'd have enough people to buy it for him. In fact, he would even have enough people to do the deed for him. Realizing that only made me feel worse.

It was late evening now, and all the campus shops were closing, but I still went ahead and seated myself in the canteen, at one of the empty tables. One of the waiters offered me a tissue, and I thanked him profusely. The silence was interrupted only by the wild crickets, and the sound of plates being dropped into the sink.

When the chair across me creaked, my head snapped up. Nanda sir plopped himself on it, and gave me a small, timid wave.

'I don't like seeing my students cry.'

'I'm not crying.'

'Of course you're not.'

I wiped my tears angrily. 'Was she treated this way too?'

'Who? What way?'

'Minaxi,' I said, heaving. 'Did the others give her a hard time too?'

'Oh. Yes,' he admitted. 'In fact, back then, it was worse than what you saw with Darshit.'

I realised he didn't know I was referring to what had happened with Joshua just now. He didn't have to know either. For some reason, a part of me was ashamed to admit that it had frightened me. I wanted to laugh at it, feel more enticed to riot against it, but I knew I couldn't. Fear had managed to shut my voice, at least for the day. I knew I would bounce back, but at the moment, I held my silence like a shield.

'Were you there at Richardson Hall today?' I asked Nanda sir.

'No, but I heard what happened.'

'Of course, you did,' I said, sniffing.

'You know they destroyed Minaxi's project? I remember for weeks she'd stayed up late in the lab, constructing this model of a water purifier that did not remove essential minerals. And then, because she hadn't been initiated...'

'She hadn't been initiated?'

'She refused to go through it,' he said, smiling. 'She was the first person who said no to it. She was a bit of a rebel, actually.'

'Wow. How come I didn't know about this?'

'People only want to talk about the nasty things, my child. Not the glorious feats you achieve.'

'Especially if you're a woman,' I said. The tongue was a scorpion's tail, after all.

He nodded. 'If Joan of Arc can be spoken ill of, then anyone can be.'

'Right. What happened when Minaxi rejected initiation?'

'The Cabinet at that time struck back. They vandalised her project and told her she didn't belong here in St. Margaret's. That she wasn't a true St. Margaretian. That was the day...' His voice trailed off.

'The day?'

'That she threw the chairs at the seniors. That story was twisted as it was being told. They'd ambushed her in Richardson

Hall and told her they were giving her one last chance, but through and through, she refused to be initiated. Now people only talk about the whole affair as a matter of her losing her mind, but the truth is, they'd pushed her too far. They'd made her hit her breaking point, and then they'd behaved like victims.'

'Why didn't you do anything about it?'

'I did. But it was my word against everyone else's,' he said woefully. 'They just didn't like her. She was spontaneous and valiant and so full of life. And they were threatened by that. They didn't want anyone else to like her.'

'I'd have liked her. She seemed like a very interesting person. Complicated, but interesting.'

'She was,' he said poignantly. 'She was the brightest young woman I'd ever met.'

We fell into silence, guilty of two parallel narratives. To him, she had been a favourite student. All I had, though, was what I'd heard during Scheher's performance. All I knew was the Lake Woman, the water spirit, the girl who'd drowned.

'Esai?'

Both Nanda sir and I turned around. Even in the narrow, dim entrance of the canteen, against all that golden hour light, I could recognize his silhouette instantly.

Bagchi.

He stood there, haggard, as if he'd been looking for me everywhere. He hurried in, greeting Nanda sir as he grabbed a chair from the opposite table and sat next to me. Ordering three cups of coffee, he patted me on the back. 'What a day, right?'

I didn't know why, but I was rattled, and at the same time, pleased to see him. Moving my chair away from him, I said scathingly, 'Aren't you going for your Cabinet's victory party? Oh wait, you're not part of the Cabinet.'

'That's right, I'm not,' he said, unperturbed, looking around as if he wanted to order food too. My stomach chose that very moment to growl, and Nanda sir jumped in, 'Don't eat anything here, Shakti, my boy. My wife is making dinner. I've already told her to make extra.'

'Oh, excellent!' Bagchi smacked his lips. 'Have you ever tried Shilpa aunty's food, Esai? Absolutely delicious.'

He was trying a little too hard to get me to warm up to him. I decided I would give him a tough time. 'When were *you* there?'

'Oh, I went once or twice when I was sad. But...'

'*All the time*,' Nanda sir said. I smiled. It was no surprise that Nanda sir had taken Bagchi home. Had it been someone like Vikas sir, he would have completely ignored him and left him to spiral. But Nanda sir took his role as a professor on campus very seriously. He knew that there was a reason some professors had been given houses on college grounds, and it wasn't just to make sure the students were on their best behaviour. It was also to be a local guardian, if they ever needed one. And some professors did have a problem with Nanda sir's friendliness with the students, but he didn't care.

'All the time? Now that's an exaggeration,' Bagchi said, and I was brought back to the conversation.

'All the time,' Nanda sir replied. 'What a nuisance of a boy, really. At one point, we had to kick him out.'

'The first time I went there was actually right after the college elections,' Bagchi continued, a cursory smile skimming along his face. 'I was walking alone on campus, grieving over my lost Literary and Debating Secretary post, when he found me. Nanda sir has a knack for taking the downtrodden home.'

'Like I told you,' Nanda sir said, proudly. 'I don't like seeing students cry.'

'I wasn't crying!' Bagchi said indignantly.

'Lies! You were,' I retorted.

'How do you know? You weren't even *there*.'

It didn't take long for them to shut down the canteen. We bickered all the way to the professor's house, a small cabin next to all the other staff houses on campus. It was a narrow lane, entirely isolated from the main blocks and canteens. A tamer part of the forest, where the grass was neatly trimmed and the earth was replaced with smooth tar. Vehicles and bicycles were parked near the gates, and mailboxes with house names queued up like trees in a row.

'Is this lane where the principal lives too?' I asked.

'Right at the end, the very last one.' Nanda sir pointed at the stone-walled building. 'Looks like a cathedral of sorts, doesn't it? They were all built by Raja Dalvi. Of course, it was Raja's father, Gagandeep, who'd owned the land and started off the initial construction of the Arts and Science blocks. But he never lived to see his dream of starting a college. Raja Dalvi picked up from there, and under his supervision, the project was complete.'

'Sounds like a family project,' I said, searching for signs of agreement. If Bagchi felt the same way, he didn't say anything.

Nanda sir had a different take on it. 'That always happens,' he said, distracted by his own thoughts. 'Legacies are always passed on to children, and there's not a lot you can do about that. As long as the college runs well, there's nothing to complain about either, is there?'

I wasn't too sure about that. Personally, I had a lot to complain about.

From the corner of my eye, I watched Bagchi cancel a call from Ira on his phone. I wondered if, after the whole initiation fiasco, they weren't on speaking terms. I hated that I hoped so.

'Here we are,' Nanda sir said, knocking. 'Shilpa?'

A short, amiable woman opened the door and welcomed us in. She had the loveliest pair of wide set eyes, hooded with long, thick lashes. She was in a beige nightgown, her hair braided into a fish tail, and she looked like she'd been about to turn in for the day. 'I hope we're not imposing,' I said hastily, as we entered the house.

Shilpa laughed. 'Of course not. Nanda brings home students all the time, especially this one,' she said, looking at Bagchi. 'Sit down, please. Would you like some biscuits?' She rummaged through a big plastic container. 'Cream? Salted? Eggless?'

'All of it,' Bagchi said, digging in.

They had a lovely place. It was decorated with colourful lamps and a minimalist wooden desk, where Nanda sir had set up his computer. They had no TV, just a radio in the kitchen, and I could hear old Lata Mangeshkar songs playing on it, one after the other. The curtains were the shade of Scotch mist; the walls, water chestnut. I immediately took a liking to its cosiness, and the distinct warmth it emanated, just like the house I shared with Pipi, Jolly and Tendral.

'Who plays?' I asked, pointing at the tabla in the corner.

'Me,' Shilpa said. Instantly, Nanda sir glowed with pride. 'She does a concert every now and then with her troupe.' He ran towards the twin hand drums and tapped on them, shaking his head vigorously to the beat.

'Oh, Nanda! Stop,' Shilpa cried, giggling. 'He's always being such a clown around the house.'

'Esai, come on,' Nanda sir said, nudging me towards the biscuits. 'No formalities. Look at Shakti.'

'I'm hungry,' he said. 'I didn't have breakfast or lunch.'

'A growing boy shouldn't skip breakfast,' Shilpa warned.

'He was stressed about initiation. I could tell.' Nanda sir ruffled his hair.

'How did that go?' Shilpa asked.

I was the first to speak up. 'It was dumb. I'm never doing that to my juniors when I become a senior.'

'You'll be surprised to see how many of your own batchmates want to do it to their juniors next year,' Bagchi said. 'It's in their blood. Ask around. Now that everyone's initiated, they're probably already waiting for the new batch to come in.'

I couldn't dispute that, so I didn't say anything. The landline rang, and Nanda sir rushed to pick it up. When he put it back down after a brief conversation, he told us, 'All right. So I have an electrician coming in to fix our tube light in a couple of minutes. I hope you don't mind.'

Bagchi and I shook our heads. The whistle chose that moment to blow.

'Why did you call him now, when we're just about to eat?' Shilpa asked, as she ran into the kitchen. 'This was the time *he* gave me,' Nanda sir complained, and then went in to assist her. I got up too, to help set up the dining table. Bagchi joined me, arranging the spoons parallel to the plates.

'Stop copying me,' I said to him, irritated.

I didn't want him standing so close. I could smell baby powder, a faint whiff of smoke and pepper. Rosemary and cumin, the subtle dampness of his skin, the sun-kissed freshness of his hair. The scar on his eyebrow now appeared as a sickle, half the Marxist party symbol, a mole right above it that could easily pass off as a little star. Why did some men roll their sleeves like that? Sure, it was summer, it was sweltering, but why wear full sleeves then? Why did he tuck one tail of the shirt in, and leave the other hanging loose over his cotton pants, as if he was always in a hurry? And what were those hands, anyway? *Just what were those hands?* As they spread the table mats smoothly, working their way towards assembling the cutlery, I assessed them. Poised. Slender. Strong. But above all, promising. Of what, I didn't want to know. Or maybe I did. Maybe I was dying to know, and I just wasn't willing to admit.

'What do you mean? I do this all the time with my mother,' he said.

'Don't lie.'

'I'm not lying! Stop being so distrustful of me all the time.' Our eyes met for a second, and a missile darted across my chest. 'I'm distrustful of everyone. Don't take it personally.'

'What you did today, that was really daring.' His voice fell into a whisper, barely audible. 'And kind.'

'It wasn't kind, Bagchi,' I said. 'What everyone else did was evil. What I did was normal. I'd expect any decent human being to do it. But the way Darshit was after that, God, he was so thankful. There was nothing to thank, he deserved to not be...*bullied*. *Harassed*. It's his basic right, to not be treated badly. He should know that. Everyone who steps into this place should know that.'

After a long pause, which I liked to believe was him agreeing to all that I'd said, he asked me, 'What did Joshua say to you? I saw him. Confronting you and then walking away. I saw your face. I know he said something dreadful.'

'Nothing.'

'Look who's lying now.'

'He threatened me with an acid attack.'

There was a pause. 'He doesn't do half the things he says he will.'

'So there's still a fifty per cent chance of him mutilating my face?' I said. In an instant, Bagchi was at my side, and his fingers slipped through the spaces between mine. The gesture confounded me. 'It won't happen. I'll make sure it won't happen,' he said.

'*I'll* make sure it won't happen.'

I knew I had his word, but it was his touch that calmed me down. It had my head spinning, the sweet shop of his hands. The soft curve at the tip of his fingers, a lot like jamuns dipped in jaggery. I was suddenly hungry for serving after serving, skin on skin. A need to run through the sugarcane fields of his tall body, limb on limb, a whole summer of sugar rush. It reminded me of a particular afternoon a few years ago, when Tendral had read me news about the butchery replacing the confectionery, the whole street stinking of dead meat, when once, it was halwa-scented. What was it about beautiful things that made me so uncomfortable? Oh yes, their endings. The way they spoiled like rice pudding under the sun, the saffron old and the cardamoms flavourless, the milk decaying and making me sick. Time could rot anything good, even love.

I had no business getting involved. It was a shame, because this boy was beautiful inside out, but I would rather starve than have my pessimistic heart eaten at. To trust anything at all was to betray myself.

I disengaged, and he stumbled back.

Thankfully, the doorbell rang, as if on cue. A saving grace. Nanda sir came out of the kitchen to answer, and ushered a young man with a low ponytail inside.

'The electrician is here,' he announced, looking at us expectantly. We stared back, blank and unbothered. He shook his head and moved into the hall.

For the next couple of minutes, Nanda sir watched the electrician like a hawk while he worked on the light. It was funny how he kept picking up all the tools from his box and observing them with child-like curiosity.

'Nanda, let him work in peace,' Shilpa said, exasperated. 'Come eat, it's already eight. And the food is hot.'

'You start; I just *have* to look at this.' His eagerness seemed to make the electrician uncomfortable, who was looking over at the rest of us, hoping we would take him away.

'Nanda sir,' I spoke. 'In my house, it's a tradition to eat together. We call it commensality; you must have heard of it. Anthropologists say it's one of the most important things for social community-building, relationships, health and well-being. The family meal. So we can't eat until you join us.'

Nanda sir looked alarmed. And then he beamed, impressed. 'Oh, child. If you put it that way...' He got up and sat next to me. Patting me on the head, he began helping himself to some rice and dal.

'The time has come when your own students are outsmarting you, Nanda,' Shilpa remarked impishly.

'What can I say? Except that it makes me very happy.'

At half past eight, as we huddled in the kitchen, doing the dishes and drying them, Nanda sir's tube light began to flicker, plunging into a beautiful yellow. 'Look at that!' Shilpa said, clapping.

'It does look lovely,' I said.

'I've been telling Nanda to get it fixed since forever.'

I smiled. 'Glad it's finally done.' I checked my watch quickly. 'Listen, Shilpa aunty, it's getting late, and I need to be home. Thank you so much for the dinner.'

'Of course, of course! Please come again, dear. Any time.'

'I will.'

'I'll drop you,' Bagchi said, joining me. 'Thank you, Shilpa aunty. Thank you, Nanda sir.'

As we said our goodbyes and walked into the cool St. Margaret's woods, I caught a glimpse of the electrician, just as he was about to start his bike. He looked up at us, his helmet on. Bagchi didn't notice him, as he was busy telling me about all that had happened after I'd left the auditorium. Apparently the Cabinet had had a very long meeting just to slander me, but the other seniors thought I was supremely cool.

'That's all really great, but I don't want to be a part of your drama,' I said, pushing my hair to a side.

'Well, you're a St. Margaretian. There's always going to be drama.'

'I'll hide.'

'Where?'

'In the library.'

'There's drama in the library too.'

'What're you saying?'

'You didn't know? The other day, a girl hit her boyfriend on his head with a really big book. Tolstoy, I think...because he cheated on her.'

'With a junior?'

'You watch too many movies,' he teased.

'Life's literally a simulation of that, you know.'

'Right.' There was a pause. The trees appeared still, as if they'd been painted into the background. He looked at me, distracted. 'Do you guys know each other?' he asked, out of nowhere.

'Sorry?'

'You smiled at him. The electrician. Do you know each other?'

I shook my head. 'Didn't think you were the jealous type.'

'Ah, shut up.' He rolled his eyes. 'You wish.'

I stared at him pointedly.

'Come on. Don't look at me with those big eyes.'

'Why not?' I asked stubbornly.

'It's scary.'

'Scary?' I chuckled. 'Nobody has ever said that before.'

'I was joking. You've got really pretty eyes.'

'Thank you. Really.'

It hadn't been a great day. In fact, it had been appalling, and now I felt drained. But Bagchi's silly antics had lightened my mood somehow. Smiling up at him, I wound my arm around his, and on we went, as a trail of *what ifs* followed behind.

Satisfied with the crumbs of banter for now.

SEVEN

Something about the evening with Bagchi kept me up. The playful touching, the wisecracks, the deer eyes flashing like an ambulance in the night. I was feeling hot all over. I wanted to throw clothes and civilization to the wind. I wanted to fish gasps out of him, my body as bait and hooks for hands. I wanted to say prayer after prayer before each meal I made out of him. I wanted it all.

I didn't know how, but I was going to kiss him.

I lay there in my bed, brazenly thinking about him, attuned to the rhythmic drum beating within my chest. The new novel I had borrowed from the library lay untouched next to the pillow. It was too late to be in love with anyone at all, too late for anything but the nurturing routine of sleep. But I was wide awake under the starlight, utterly damned, as unholy thoughts about him wrapped around me like a shawl. I didn't know if I could endure this any longer. I rose to close the curtains, before catching one last glimpse of the horizon, ambushed by the moon's haze.

I was just about to switch off the lights when my phone rang.

'Esai?' The voice on the other end was in a frenzy.

'Yes? Who is this?'

'Esai! Oh my God. You don't know me, but I'm Priya, Scheher's flatmate...'

I rubbed my eyes. 'Hi Priya. Is everything okay?'

Priya broke into sobs. 'Scheher got into a fight with her boyfriend. I'm on my way to the hospital with her.' I sank into my bed abruptly, and ended up sitting on my reading glasses. I heard the frame crack, and quickly pushed it away from me. I felt numb.

Just a few days ago, Scheher and I had gone to a café to have her favourite banoffee pie. We'd ended up sitting there for hours, talking about initiation and the catastrophe that followed it, and eventually about our own lives. Scheher had told me about her broken family, and I'd told her about mine, and how I'd grown up with my uncle, aunt and their only daughter. About how I had never once felt like a third party in their home, and how Scheher had always felt like a liability. I learned things about her, and the more I did, the more I came to see that she was not as artificial as I'd assumed her to be. In fact, she was funny and selfless and nice to talk to. And for the life of me, I couldn't imagine why she had chosen to be with someone like Joshua.

'The *hospital*?' I said. Suddenly, my throat felt extremely dry. My mind conjured up a million different possibilities. Had Joshua strangled her again? Had she hurt herself after he'd left? What had happened? Whatever it was, it must have been ghastly if she'd had to go to the hospital for it.

'Which one?' I choked out.

'The one right behind Heller Hall's gate. Outside the campus.'

'Okay. I'm coming.'

I slipped a shirt over my body, grabbed my wallet, and ran.

I called Priya again on my way there, and listened in horror as she told me about all the letters to friends and family in Scheher's room. Letters she wanted discovered if ever Joshua killed her in one of his fits of rage.

'I had no idea it was this violent,' I said.

'It keeps getting worse,' she said, grimly.

'Has anyone ever tried to interfere? Her parents, maybe?'

'Scheher doesn't really talk much to either of them. And they don't seem to be bothered with her life either.'

'What about friends?' I asked.

'I did tell her he was bad news. But I stopped after a point, because she kept running back to him.'

I had guessed that was the case. Especially after that night, when I'd gotten out of the car and asked her to join me. She'd still stood with him. 'I'll be there in five minutes.'

At the reception of St. John's Memorial Hospital was a girl my age, full of tears. Her hair was still wet from a recent shower, and she was wearing bathroom slippers. Her eyes were round and disoriented, and her lips bore the marks of being chewed on. When she saw me enter, she heaved a sigh of relief. 'She told me to call you.'

'Where is she?'

'In the ICU.' My stomach dropped. A wave of anxiety crept over me, and I was afraid to see her in her battered state. I had never seen such violence up close until now. What did she look like? I tried to imagine a busted lip or a blackened eye, but I couldn't think beyond that.

'What exactly happened? Were you there?' I asked.

Joshua had come over for dinner, and then decided to stay back. Priya and Scheher had had a pact right from the start: boyfriends wouldn't sleep over unless it was some kind of an emergency. So Scheher had tried to make him leave, but he had been difficult. Priya had sensed it was going to get bad, so she'd told them it was all right. He could stay, just this once. It had been a mistake.

In the middle of the night, they had started arguing again. Over what? She had no idea. But vaguely, she remembered them talking about him disappearing on her again. Most fights had been about him devaluing her and then discarding her anyway. Scheher had told Priya about how he'd punish her with the silent treatment when he wanted to avoid confrontation. 'He's got the emotional intelligence of a five-year-old,' Priya said to me bitterly.

'What happened when they began fighting?' I asked.

'It escalated.' Priya had tried to open the door, but they'd locked it from inside. There had been wailing, there had been yelling. And then he'd barged out, and Priya had jumped in, and there Scheher had lain. She'd spat her own blood all over her face.

'Is Joshua here?'

'He's in the parking.'

I froze. 'The *parking*?' My voice sounded shrill.

'I think he's gathered some friends with him, and they're all playing card games inside his car with the air conditioner on.'

It was getting to me now. Scheher and I had never spoken about Joshua that day in the café after initiation, but once in between, she had brought up love. I'd seen the look in her eyes, I'd seen hope and warmth and sacrifice. I'd realized that she was passionate about the people in her life, no matter how they treated her. She was the kind of person that would take a bullet for someone else, even if that someone else was the bullet.

I rubbed my chest subconsciously. It did not help. I could feel the pounding growing harsher. 'Did he say anything at all?'

'He got mad at the nurse.'

'For trying to save Scheher?'

She shook her head. 'He didn't think she needed to be put

in the ICU. He said they were just doing it to get money out of us.'

'I hate him.'

'Me too.'

I was tempted to storm into the parking and cause a scene, but right now, I knew it would be sabotaging Scheher's situation. Knowing how Joshua would react and who would face the brunt of it if I fought with him, I continued to walk on tenterhooks.

Compassion fatigue swept over me. I sat there on one of the empty chairs, massaging my temple. 'Be honest. How bad is it?'

'It was bad,' Priya admitted. 'But I don't think they'll keep her here for too long.' She shuffled her feet. 'What do I do, Esai? I have a test tomorrow.'

'Go home, it's okay. I'm here anyway.'

She stood there, unable to make up her mind, her cheeks flushing with guilt. 'Are you sure? You'll be alone.'

'I've got these nurses,' I said, pointing at the ones walking around brusquely. 'Really. Go sleep, go study in the morning, do your exam well. I'll keep you posted on this.'

A few minutes after she left, the hospital had new visitors. Bagchi and Ira streamed into the hallway, and I realized Joshua had probably called them and told them.

I knew why they were here. To cover up.

'That idiot boy,' Ira said angrily. 'He's going to be the death of us.'

'Will you stop thinking about the Cabinet for a minute? A girl has been assaulted.' Bagchi stared at his shoes, fidgeted with his shirt tail. I could tell it was killing him to take a side.

'Do you think she's going to file a complaint?' she asked him.

He shrugged. She turned to me. 'Oh, Esai. Have you seen Joshua?'

'He's playing cards in his car.'

'What?' She pulled out her phone from her bag and called him. 'Where the fuck are you?' I couldn't hear what he was saying on the other end, but her face was growing redder by the minute. 'Quit tooling around and come upstairs if you don't want to be suspended.' It wasn't a request, it wasn't an order, it was a warning.

I didn't think I could even look at the man. Especially because the last time we'd had a conversation, it had essentially been a confrontation. The image of his hands clawing at Scheher's throat had given way to new mental images of him walking around campus with a vial of acid around his neck. I had believed it would take time for me to get that picture out of my head, but after today, my imagination procured new visuals. Now all I saw was him and Scheher arguing in her room and then the thrashing.

My hands shook with indignation. He was on his way here, and there was nothing I could do. I didn't want to treat the hospital like a bar, brawling like I was drunk, only to be thrown out. If Scheher needed me around at any point, I'd have to be here. So when Joshua finally waltzed in, I clenched my fists by my side and suppressed the burning in my knuckles.

'My brother, what're you doing here?' Joshua asked, looking at Bagchi. 'You like my girlfriend, don't you?'

'You're so *disgusting*.'

'Shut up, you two,' Ira snapped. She turned to me. 'I'm so sorry that your friend is going through this. I'll personally see to it that the management pays her hospital bills.' I wondered if her apology was genuine or simply to save face. After watching her domineering behaviour during initiation, I wasn't sure if I could trust her to be sympathetic towards anyone.

And then I realized what her statement meant. She was trying to buy my silence. She was trying to buy Scheher's silence.

We don't need your money, I thought. But could I actually tell her that? What if Scheher did want financial support? At this point, I was still unsure how much money she received from her parents, keeping aside the big apartment she owned.

I felt helpless. I decided to stay silent until Scheher woke up and had a say in this matter.

'Joshua,' Ira said. 'Brief me on the situation.'

Brief? Was this a Cabinet meeting, for her to be speaking like this?

'Well, she really got on my nerves, so I had to-'

Ira put one hand up to silence him. 'I don't want to hear the gory details. I'm asking about the situation now. What did the doctors say? Is she going to be all right? What can we expect when she wakes up?'

'She's already recovering. She just needs some bed rest,' he admitted.

'And when Firoza wakes up, she won't turn against you?' she asked. I wondered why their relationship was so important to her.

'No. Absolutely not. Firoza loves me.'

'Sure,' Ira said, folding her hands against her chest. 'I just need to know the police aren't going to get involved in this. We don't need any cases of domestic violence blackening the name of St. Margaret's.'

No wonder. For a moment, I had hoped that she had spoken out of kindness. I had hoped I could offer her the benefit of doubt. But it was evident to me now that it wasn't Scheher's health she was concerned about. She was protecting the college; she was making sure nothing would happen to her ancestral property. In that moment, I felt nothing but spite towards her.

Joshua patted her arm, and she wrenched it away from him in revulsion. He looked disgruntled. 'Relax, Madam Chairwoman. It won't happen. I know Firoza. She pretends to be fierce and all, but she's actually a softie. She'll forgive me in no time. I can bet on it.'

We both knew this was the pattern. The abuse and then the love bombing. The sudden show of emotion and repentance if she even dared to get help for herself. Bagchi and Ira stepped to a side, still discussing the issue at hand, and Joshua leaned against the wall, looking bored. His gaze zeroed in on me, and then he walked towards me.

'So Scheher's got a new friend, eh?'

I didn't say anything. I didn't want to talk to him.

'What you saw in the car that day,' he said, contempt dripping from his voice. 'Was really nothing. *Nothing.* You should see the cigarette burns on her chest.'

I turned away from him, horrified. Before he could say anything more to me, I quickly walked towards the pantry. I placed a hand on the pillar and clutched the front of my shirt. Breathing in and out slowly, I regained the peace he had swindled from me. Why had he said that to me? Of course, it was a show of power. He was sending me a clear sign: *There's nothing you can do about this but watch.*

I looked at him once more, and he grinned. *Don't start a fight,* I told myself. *Not now, not here.* I walked ahead, trying to get as far as I could, so that I didn't have to see his face. I spent the rest of the night in the hospital lobby, watching patients clamouring for medicines in the store opposite to where I was sitting. Meditating to the sound of babies wailing and needles clicking. Feeling spent to the bone.

In the morning, when the nurse said Scheher had been shifted to a room where visitors were allowed, Joshua was already there by her side, holding her hand, doodling on her arm.

How ironic. He was writing on her cast; over the very bones he'd broken.

I hovered by the door, waiting for Scheher to invite me in. Her room was small and white. It had a vase of fresh flowers on a plastic peach table, and one tiny window without a view. It faced the next hospital building, and it was a drab, blank wall. The sound of ambulances was more prominent in this room, and the metal bed didn't look one bit comfortable. Neither did I. But then again, who enjoyed hospital visits anyway? The last time I was in one was during Tendral's routine check-ups. But it hadn't taken too long, and it hadn't been a crisis.

Scheher had been chatting enthusiastically with Joshua when she noticed me. Her eyes widened, and she looked both touched and scared. 'Esai! Oh my god, you're still here? Oh no, did you stay the whole night?' I hadn't meant to. She had asked for me, and I had responded with my heart. I didn't know her well enough to feel so protective, but I couldn't help it. To me, she was this abandoned little thing, left on the road to fend for herself, alone all her life. I should have known better than to pick her up, but I did. I still had time to leave, to back out of all this toxicity. But she was a girl without a family. From what she'd told me during our conversation over banoffee pie, I was her only real friend. I had to stay.

'Yes,' I admitted.

'No, you shouldn't have! Go home, get some rest, this is nothing. Really, I promise.' Her eyes kept darting towards Joshua, and then at me. Suddenly, I felt stupid for staying back.

'Are you sure?' I asked. Why was she being so dismissive?

She'd always been excited to see me. But today she was acting as if my presence was an embarrassment to her.

'Of course, go! I'm okay now. Everything's fine.'

I was feeling hot all over. If everything was fine, then why was she on a hospital bed?

I wanted to hold her by the shoulders and shake her hard, I wanted to tell her she was hurting me by choosing Joshua's abuse over my friendship. I wanted to plaster her with logic, point out that she needed to leave him right away. That this was not *normal*. 'Did he make you say that?' I asked.

Scheher looked at Joshua, and then she turned frantic. 'No! Jo is innocent,' she said, and I stared at her incredulously. 'Esai,' she said, and my name sounded like blasphemy to my own ears. 'Listen to me. He's innocent. He didn't do anything wrong. I'm the one, I did this to myself. I wanted to get back at him.'

'You know that's not the truth.'

'What do you know about the truth?' she snapped.

I turned on my feet and started walking out. *This is what happens when you help people who don't want your help*, I thought scathingly. *They bite you.*

'Esai! It wasn't him! Don't go around spreading lies, okay? It wasn't him!'

Outside, Bagchi and Ira were sharing a cigarette, laughing over some private joke. Thunder reverberated around us, and dawn light weaved itself into the roads and buildings. The world was stirring awake and everything was golden, but I wanted to cry. I was mad at myself for being there, and madder at Scheher for pushing me away. I nodded at Ira and Bagchi, and before they could come talk to me, I climbed into a rick, and sped away.

Throughout the ride, I was sleepy. My eyes kept watering, and I blamed it on the hot wind. Once I was home, though, I felt my weight all over. I managed to drag my feet up the stairs, and I hit the bed like a hammer. Had it only been last night that I'd lain on the same bed, dreaming about Bagchi? I'd seen him at the hospital, and I'd felt nothing. I'd been ransacked by worry, and left completely disarranged. I pressed my face onto the pillow and screamed into it. There was nothing new about this feeling. The heart was in hell, but it would heal. It would have to.

EIGHT

At the start of August, Scheher returned to class. She'd only stayed in the hospital for two days. 'It started getting really boring in there,' she'd told Priya. She'd shown up the day Article 370 was scrapped, ending the special status of Jammu and Kashmir. Internet and mobile services were suspended, and a classmate of ours who had family in Bandipore stopped hearing from them—he'd been so distraught the whole time. And then Vikas sir had said something terrible about the revocation to him, and he'd never come to class after that.

Vikas sir. Three months into term beginning was when he'd finally decided to show his face to us. He'd breezed in casually, one-fourth of a chalk in his right hand, and a stack of papers in the other. He'd erased the beautiful quote someone had written at the top of the blackboard. He'd confiscated phones. He'd asked a student to tuck in his shirt. He'd turned the room gloomy.

'I thought he was going to bail on us for the whole year,' Scheher said, opening her bag and pulling out a notebook. She was particularly chirpy, and I could see cakes of concealer on her scars, in a weak attempt to hide them. A handmade bookmark fell out of the bag, and she looked embarrassed. 'Jo made that for me.'

It was in the shape of a peepal leaf, and a strip of pink ribbon snaked through the punched hole at the top. On it was a painting in white and mauve, of the doomed lovers, Heer and Ranjha. A short little note was scribbled at the bottom, and I ignored it deliberately.

'Nice,' I said, irate. He'd been hoovering her the whole week, buying gifts and pulling her back into his toxic radar. I couldn't believe that she was reciprocating to something so obviously pretentious, and I was still nettled by the things she'd said to me at the hospital. But she was adamant about talking to me, and was trying her best to win my friendship back.

So she kept talking. 'I'm glad I took Literature from the Margins as my elective. I get to sit next to you once every week.' She looked around at the fifteen odd students in the room, and nodded in acknowledgement at the boy behind her. 'Besides, who can sit through Vikas sir without company? You'd die, I'd die.'

'Shouldn't be a big deal for you,' I quipped sarcastically. 'You almost did.' The moment I said it, I wished I hadn't. Scheher turned pale, and immediately looked away.

I was about to apologize, but then Vikas sir interrupted, and suddenly, his pompous accent filled the classroom. Something about him was almost reptilian, so very foul. And to top it all, his mood matched his face. The minute everyone saw him, I could tell that they regretted taking this elective.

Up until now, I'd only seen Vikas sir in photos pasted on the Cabinet bulletin. In his own way, he was handsome, but he had a steely, conniving gaze that bothered me. In the photos, it hadn't been so palpable. But in person, there was no breaking free of it. It followed you everywhere, and it lingered. If you caught someone staring, didn't they usually look away? Why did he continue to stare in such an unabashed manner?

'I've marked your papers, and I'll say this. I'm not too happy,' he announced. Everyone exchanged worried glances. I could tell the students weren't too happy either; of course everyone had hoped for good scores because the substitute faculty had been lenient. And now here he was, telling us that he'd been the one to look at our assignments. Indeed, such bad luck.

'But before I hand out your answer sheets, I have something to say.'

'Where is he getting that fake accent from?' I asked Scheher. His D's sounded like T's, and he was sputtering out so many big, archaic words. I could barely understand a thing he was saying.

She shrugged. 'He's always asking people to listen to the BBC. But it doesn't sound British, does it? And it doesn't sound American either. It sounds like something he made up on his own, I suppose?'

'It's all *bakwas*,' I said. *Nonsense*.

'He's definitely forcing it,' she said, holding back a smile. 'Wannabe.'

'Lately, many of you have been going to the porn site,' he began, and a boy behind us sniggered.

'Now how did he find that out?' he said slyly, and Scheher and I burst into giggles. The professor shot us a look.

'The porn site is *dangerous*. If you get lost, there is no coming back.'

'Oh, definitely,' the boy said.

'Saif, shut up!' But Scheher's rebuke made no mark on him. His comments continued on the side like subtitles, and left us in splits. A temporary reprieve from what was to come.

'The other day,' Vikas sir said. 'The principal caught two students doing ungodly things in the porn site. Oh, God!' A tremor ran through him, and his face contorted in distaste.

'Oh, God!' Saif moaned, and we bowled over laughing.

'Saif!' Scheher hissed again, clutching her stomach.

'They were punished, although not severely,' Vikas sir went on, absolutely immune to us. 'But be warned. The next time, if we catch you going to the porn site, you will be suspended.'

'Where is all this even coming from?' I asked, shaking my head.

'Ungodly things in the porn site,' Saif repeated in Vikas sir's artificial accent. I covered my mouth with my palm. 'He sounds like a bishop.'

'Oh no, guys.' Scheher's eyes were bulging. 'I just realised something.'

'What?'

'*Pond side.*'

'What?' Saif looked like something had hit him between the eyes. He scowled. 'What're you talking about?'

'He's saying *pond side*! Not porn site! He's talking about the lake!'

'Don't be ridiculous!' Saif said. 'A lake is not the same as a pond.'

'I think he doesn't know that.'

'We love a nice, misinformed professor.'

Scheher raised her hand. 'Sir, did a girl drown in the... porn site?'

'No, no,' Vikas sir said, grimacing. 'That's just a cooked up story.'

'There you go,' she whispered to us. 'He was saying pond side all along.'

From then on, we refused to look at one another, because we knew we wouldn't be able to control ourselves. I stared at the crack on the desk intensely, as if my life depended on it. Scheher played with her pen loudly, and the girl next to her put her head down every now and then. I was sure she was covering up her giggles like a crime. Saif ran out of the class with the flimsy excuse that he had to use the washroom. He never returned.

Towards the end of his lecture, Vikas sir began distributing our papers.

'He's so good looking,' the girl next to Scheher muttered under her breath, ultimately recovering from her hysterics. 'But no good when it comes to marks.'

When the department head dropped my answer sheet on my lap, I noticed a big, red forty-nine out of a hundred. At first, I was filled with shame. I'd failed. I'd let myself down. I had done so well in every other class, and this was now going to bring down my grade point average. St. Margaret's English department didn't have a reputed Masters course. I'd hoped to get into another university after my three years here as an undergraduate student. But a score like this would definitely affect my chances. It also meant that I would have to resit this paper next term, and I just didn't want to do that. I quickly went over my answers and realised there had been a misunderstanding.

'A fifty-six,' Scheher groaned. 'Not fair. I'm over seventy for everything else. And this is an elective, for godsakes.'

I stared at my paper again. 'He failed me. By one mark.' It felt intentional.

'What?'

'He *failed* me.'

She grabbed my paper and studied it intently. 'This is terrible.'

'Really?' I asked, surprised.

'No, as in, it's brilliant. The fact that he's failed you for this is terrible. Your answers are...I mean, I wish I could write like this. You should ask the other professors to read it.'

'Or I'll ask Vikas sir to read it *again*.' Just as I rose, she yanked me back down. 'No, don't.'

'Why not?'

'You don't know him. He's not going to like it if you question his integrity.'

'He has *no* integrity. He barely shows up to class.'

'I know. But he'll torture you the rest of the year if you start a fight. Trust me on this. I heard it from the seniors.'

Ignoring her, I made my way towards the professor. He looked up at me from his desk, and furrowed his eyebrows. 'Yes, Esai.' *He knows me*, I thought. *He's been keeping an eye on me.*

'I think there's been a mistake,' I said. 'You haven't graded my thirty-mark long answer question.'

He took the sheet from me and glossed over it. 'Professor Prajnesh never taught you this novel, so why have you written about it?'

'It's in the syllabus. I read it, liked it and wrote about it.'

'The next time, answer a question we've taught you. Don't get over-smart.'

The nerve! I narrowed my eyes at him. 'I see. Is that why you've failed me? Because I wrote about a book you didn't talk about in class? Why didn't you? You were supposed to cover it in our first term.'

He shrugged, indifferent. 'Some books don't get covered. End of discussion. Now get back to your seat.'

I didn't move. 'You were never going to teach this book to us, were you?' I asked angrily. 'No, I don't think so.'

'What's that supposed to mean, girl?' A lone vein throbbed in his forehead. His eyes turned into slits. I was tempted to take a step back, but I stood my ground.

'My answer is *perfect.*'

'The question required you to write an essay on the folktales of Meghalaya.'

'And what about the *alternative* question? The one about the theme of homosexuality in *Funny Boy* by Shyam Selvadurai?'

'It's invalid if we haven't taught it to you.' He shot me a revolted look. 'And honestly, I don't know why you'd bother. It's such an ugly book.'

Ugly? I'd loved *Funny Boy*. I'd loved how gently I'd grown up alongside the gay protagonist in Sri Lanka, amidst the Tamil-Sinhalese war; its innocence despite such a tumultuous setting; everything about it. And I knew then in my very bones exactly why Vikas sir hadn't, and never would.

'There you go.' I turned around and faced my classmates. 'You guys heard that, right? Sir thinks *Funny Boy* is an ugly book.' It didn't look like they cared. I realised they probably hadn't even read it because it hadn't been taught. I turned to him again. 'What's so ugly about it?'

Vikas sir leapt from his seat, both palms on the desk. He leaned towards me and hissed, 'Get out of my class. I know girls like you.'

'What do you know?' I taunted.

He pointed one finger at me. 'I've heard enough about you from the other professors and your seniors. You're nothing but a meddler.'

I bristled. I couldn't stomach his arrogance. Or how coolly he'd just admitted that the staff gossiped about the students. Or that he'd already formed a bias about me without even knowing me. So that was how he had graded my paper? By already deciding I would fail? 'And you're changing the topic. You hate that I wrote about *Funny Boy*. You hate the book, and you hate that I see right through you. Tell me why you think *Funny Boy* is ugly. Tell me.'

'You're overreacting now.'

Gaslighting, I thought. I had every right to feel the way I did, and he had no right to tell me it was too much. If he wanted to see overreacting, then I would show him overreacting. 'Tell me!' I slammed the sheet on his table. The whole class looked bewildered.

'Get out.'

'Because the main character is gay? You're homophobic, aren't you?' I wasn't asking. I was confirming.

'Enough! That's enough. Get out of my class.' His finger now pointed towards the door. 'If you don't, I'm sending you to the principal.'

To hell with you, I thought, as I collected my things and put them inside my bag.

'And stand outside for the entire period. Stand where I can see you.' *In your dreams.*

I was met with the petrified expressions of the other students and the sudden stillness of the room. As I grabbed my bag and stalked out, I heard Vikas sir announce, 'Anyone else not happy with their marks?' I didn't have to look around to know they were all shaking their heads. I hovered near the door for a few seconds, and then began walking away, far enough so that he couldn't see me.

Within a few minutes, Scheher caught up with me, panting.

'What're you doing?' I asked. I hadn't meant for it to, but it came out like a little bark. Moderating my tone, soothing it out of its temper, I said, 'I mean, why are you here?'

She pursed her lips and said, 'I wanted to go check on Saif. He's been in the washroom for so long, I've a feeling he's got diarrhoea.'

A smile teased its way out of me. I gave in. 'You know he never went to the washroom, right?'

'I know, I know. I'm just joking.' She chuckled. 'It was such a boring class, I thought I'd bunk. Do you want to go around campus sticking posters for my next show?'

I knew she hadn't left for the posters. She'd left for me. Her loyalty was touching. I nodded, not trusting myself to talk. For a while, we stood that way, overcome with emotion. And then she saw my eyes welling up and said to me, 'Hey now, don't be sad about this. It's not worth it.'

I looked down at my feet, unable to collect myself. 'Just...
why? Why'd he do that to me?'

'Don't take it personally! He's a terrible man. You don't
know what all I've heard about him.'

'What?' I asked.

'Hardcore illegal things, like money laundering. I'll tell you
later. But you know, right, that most of the professors here
are alumni?'

'Vikas sir too?' I asked, dazed.

'Yes. He graduated from the English department, applied
for work here, and immediately got in.'

He'd probably loved the power he'd wielded as a senior,
and now he loved his power as a professor. He'd definitely seen
initiation too. And he glorified that culture because he grew up
in it. It all made sense to me now.

'He also comes from a very specific school of thought fed
by religion. Respecting our elders. Besides, Indian patriarchy
can't stand women having opinions. You know that,' Scheher
said, resuming the conversation.

'Speaking of Indian men and the patriarchy...' I let my voice
fade away. Suddenly, the air was thick with tension. We both
knew what I was going to say. The question was, how. I wasn't
sure if we were good enough friends for me to interfere. Or
even if we were, why would she open up to me? She knew I
did not support her relationship. She knew I hated Joshua. In
her eyes, I had vilified him, and she didn't trust me enough to
talk about him to me. But I couldn't help wanting to know. I
couldn't help inserting myself in their malicious game. It wasn't
curiosity. I wanted to help her. One look at her face, and I
knew I would feel terrible if I let this slide. The concealer had
washed away from the sweltering heat, and the blue on her skin
had now turned to black. I recalled the night in the hospital
and the horrors that trod on its heels. It had been a while since
then, but it continued to make me uneasy.

'Are you doing all right? How's your arm?'

'It's fine. I'm fine.'

I took a deep breath. Here came the question I dreaded asking, but had to. 'Why do you stay?'

She picked at a scab and took her time answering, almost as if she were looking for the right words to explain her situation. 'I guess I don't feel this way with anyone else. With him, I'm always on a high.'

'But he's not good for you. Scheher,' I whispered pleadingly. 'He hits you.'

Her eyes gleamed with tears. 'I know. But I can't be the first one to leave. I just can't. I don't know how to do that, I've never left anyone before. And besides, I've just given up too much to leave,' she said ruefully. 'Too much.'

I didn't know how to respond to something like that, so I simply asked, 'Have you been together for a long time?'

'Yes. He went to my school. He was the one who asked me to apply to St. Margaret's.'

'So that's why you're here.'

'That, and the fact that St. Margaret's has one of the best Journalism departments in the whole city. And there's never so much coursework that I can't do the other thing I love doing.'

'Like writing and performing poetry,' I noted. 'But he doesn't like that you're doing gigs, does he?'

'He hates it.'

'But you do it anyway.'

'What can I say? I love it,' she said, her face brightening. Suddenly, she looked like the Scheher on stage again. 'No, I'm *in love* with it. I couldn't sacrifice it for the world. You know what I mean?'

I nodded. I could tell it took a lot in her to bypass him. That standing here, pasting posters everywhere wasn't easy for her. It made my heart swell with pride. 'Come on, we've got work to do.' I snatched one half of the posters from her hand and walked ahead.

'Come for the show, okay?' she said. 'It's this Friday night. And since you're my friend, you can bring a plus one.'

'Isn't it a free event?'

'Okay, yes. But you know what I'm trying to say. Bring everyone you know. I need that.'

'Got it.'

We ambled around the campus, sticking colourful papers onto trees and pillars and walls outside classrooms, making as much noise as possible till it pissed the professors off. When we reached the second floor of the Arts Block where the third year students were, I caught a glimpse of rolled sleeves and deep dimples. Before I knew it, Bagchi was walking towards us.

'Speak of the devil,' he said.

'Who, you?' I retorted.

'Good one.' He folded his arms. 'What're you kids doing here?'

Scheher and I looked at each other. 'Kids?'

And then Scheher said, 'Help us paste these everywhere?'

He picked up one of the posters from the stack in my hands. Tried too hard to disguise his laugh as a cough and then said, 'Who in God's name calls themselves Scheherazade?'

Scheher looked offended. 'Me.'

'Oh! Firoza.' The tell-tale blush was adorable. 'My heartfelt apologies. I had no idea you were a poet.' He looked around. 'All right. Where exactly do you want these pasted?'

'All the happening places on campus,' I said. 'And you'll be my plus one for the show?' I asked, blinking innocently.

'It's Friday night,' Scheher explained. 'And it's a costume party. Esai is dressing up as the Lake Woman.'

'Absolutely not! I've already decided, I'm going to be Neeli pisasu.'

'I don't even want to know what that is,' Bagchi said, grimacing.

Scheher's phone chose to beep that moment, and she jumped. She looked torn. 'Oh no, I forgot.'

'What?' I asked.

'I have to meet Jia ma'am about my Broadcast Journalism assignments. She's out of campus tomorrow onwards.'

Bagchi removed the stack of posters from her hands. 'We'll take care of this. Go.'

'Really?'

'Yes.'

She grinned. 'You're the best, *kid*.' I nodded approvingly at the cheekiness of her remark, and watched her jog off towards her department. The ruthless warmth of the summer descended on us, and I was alone with Bagchi.

We were surrounded by ghosts again, trapped in bubbles. I wondered if he could feel it too, the tension; the thorny, ticklish sensation all over. I looked at him, and he looked away. 'Let's hand these out, then. Unless you've got something else to do.'

I shook my head. There was nowhere else I'd be, now that I was here with him. But it wasn't enough. I wanted more. The thought of this moment coming to an end when we were done pasting the posters made me panic. 'So are you coming for Scheher's show or not?' I asked him, hoping I didn't sound too eager. 'She really needs people there,' I added. *Good*, I thought. Now I'd made it sound like I was asking for a friend, and not for myself.

'Let's make a deal,' he said. 'If you come for Ira's pre-Solstice house party this Wednesday, I'll come for the show.'

Ira. Of course, Ira. It was always about Ira and her mini campus government.

'Pre-Solstice?' I asked, trying to bury my disappointment. 'Like a prep night for the college fest?'

'More like a celebration after the budget approval meeting. Ira wants to get to know you more. I think you'll be good for her.'

Was he asking me to be her friend? Be a good influence on her? She needed more than me to become a better person. I couldn't teach her how to put people before things. To treat Scheher and Darshit and everyone else around her the same way she treated the grounds of St. Margaret's. These were things she had to learn on her own.

'Good? How?' I asked.

'Well…' He toyed with his hair as he rummaged for answers. 'You're brave and kind. She needs that on her team. She knows how to be brave, but she needs someone who can teach her to be kind. It's the only way she can get on the side of the students. There are a lot of seniors who hate her guts, and of course, the juniors barely know her or are intimidated by her. Think of it as…'

I knew where he was going. I felt thoroughly let down. 'Rebranding?'

'Exactly.'

'What would I have to do?'

'Be a sort of advisor. Since you're a fresher, you can't be on the Cabinet anyway.'

'As if I wanted to be, in the first place.'

'Just hear me out. We want you to act as a spokesperson among your batch. Since they love you already, it shouldn't be too difficult.'

'You make it sound so *appealing.*' Our gaze met when I said that. Just for a fraction of a second. It could have even been a trick of the eye. And I would have assumed it was, if not for how his hands emerged out of his pockets for a moment, almost as if he wanted to touch me, and then slipped back in again. I looked at him, and he looked away again.

'Tell your batchmates we're good people too. That we want to help them.'

'Basically be your mascot,' I said, still thinking about his hands.

He looked peeved. 'No, absolutely not! Listen. Maybe I'm not explaining it right,' he said, fidgeting with his watch. I noticed that he did that a lot when he was nervous. Had I made him nervous? 'Maybe we should wait till Ira explains it. Just don't jump to any conclusions. Come for the party, and then you can decide, okay?'

I nodded, tearing my attention away from the way his fingers were circling his watch. 'Can I bring Scheher as my plus one?'

He agreed, but seemed a little unenthusiastic about it. 'Just don't tell anyone else. It's...'

'Elite. Got it.'

'Smart girl. You're learning fast. So you'll be there?'

'Yes.' *You're asking, how could I say no?*

He was about to say something else, but then his eyes widened and fixated on a spot behind me. I turned around, and saw Joshua leaning against the wall, chatting with a girl from the first year. They were deep in conversation, and they were standing a little too close.

'Am I reading too much into that?' Bagchi muttered, a little uneasy.

The girl grabbed a fistful of Joshua's hair. He shoved her hand jokingly and moved in. She pushed him away, and then they started walking away. 'I think we should follow them,' I said.

'I think you're prying.'

'Follow me.'

I grabbed Bagchi's hand and ran after them. They headed out of the gate, dived into a rickshaw, and so did we. The dusty wind belted my face as I looked out impatiently, praying we didn't lose them. Bagchi kept fidgeting, and that drove me further to the edge. 'Will you stop that?'

'I can't help it. I don't want to know what he's up to.'

'Because you know it's no good.'

'And you do too. So why bother finding out?'

'It's like Schrodinger's cat. Until we open the box, do we really know?' I challenged.

'Esai, I'm going to say something very clichéd right now...'

'Don't say it.'

'Ever heard, curiosity kills the cat?'

I groaned. 'And you're like a cat that closes its eyes while drinking milk. You think if you don't watch when someone does something wrong, it disappears.'

'Isn't that a South Indian proverb or something?'

'You know what I mean.'

We got down at the beach. I was glad it wasn't a café, they might have spotted us then. 'We'll watch them from here,' I said, hiding behind a tree. 'Classic,' Bagchi drawled, amused. 'Come here, fool,' he said, placing his hands on my waist and pulling me closer to the bark. 'Your big hair is noticeable from anywhere.'

'Oh my God, Bagchi. Look!'

Joshua and the girl were holding hands. She stood on tiptoe and planted a tiny kiss on his cheek.

'Maybe they're just being friendly. Maybe Firoza knows,' Bagchi suggested, his voice laced with uncertainty. 'I mean, some girls know and they still stay, right?'

'Will you just shut up.'

'What?'

'They're together *exclusively*, they're high school sweethearts. She definitely doesn't know.'

'Then maybe he's polyamorous or something.'

'If he is and he didn't tell her, that's very unfair,' I shot back.

'Okay, okay! Stop glaring at me like I did something wrong,' he said. 'Are you going to tell her?'

'I don't know.' Joshua placed his palm on the girl's back, and slowly began lowering it. 'He's squeezing her ass in public. What a guy.'

'You've seen what you wanted to. We should go now,' Bagchi said. 'I don't think you should tell her. It'll wreck her. And she won't really believe you. She might even get mad at you for it.'

I didn't respond. I knew I wasn't going to tell her, because I'd seen how she'd behaved that day in the hospital. She'd stood up for her abuser. She'd bought into his lies. So why would she take my word against his? But I didn't want to give Bagchi the satisfaction that I agreed with him.

All the way back to college, we sat in silence. The driver tried to make conversation with us, but gave up after a point. Once we were back on campus, Bagchi waved at me awkwardly, and walked away.

After that, it didn't take long for the whole college to find out that Joshua was cheating on Scheher with a junior girl called Simrat. Political Science department, part-time model, second runner-up for Miss Ludhiana or something of that sort. After all, it was St. Margaret's. And we weren't the only ones who had seen them.

By night, it was confirmed that Joshua wasn't just cheating, he had broken up with Scheher for the new girl. There was no going back even if she wanted to. I tried ringing her up, but she'd switched off her phone.

For the next few days, Scheherazade was nowhere to be found.

NINE

In her grief, Scheher was rabid.

After I'd finally caught hold of her the other day, I'd taken her to B. Merwan & Co. for mawa cake. It was her favourite Parsi diner in Grant Road. We'd been there before twice after class, and had had some of the best conversations about art and philosophy and food and men in the presence of their masala chai and broon maska. We'd wandered into shops, trying out perfumes that smelled like honeysuckle and balsa wood. We'd gone up to strangers with two different scents on our wrists and asked them to smell and tell us which was better. We'd bought drinks for random girls in clubs, we'd told a boy who'd been shamelessly flirting with Scheher that she was married and had two children. But this time we'd gone, she'd looked like a ghost. She'd said nothing, eaten nothing, simply stared at the walls. She hadn't even bothered to change out of her t-shirt and track pants.

Today, she'd turned around completely.

Right before we left home, I'd asked her, 'Are you sure?'

She'd been uncompromising. She'd been in denial, and then she'd descended into retaliation. She'd wanted to show Joshua what he had left behind. She'd wanted to call up an old flame and have him on her arm at the party. I'd flat out rejected the idea. And then she'd suggested dressing to kill. 'All right,' I'd said, and then shopped with her for a whole hour, helping her pick the perfect revenge dress. 'Like Diana,' she'd said. 'Diana, the same night Charles had confessed he was having an affair with Camilla. I want to be the showstopper at this party.'

She'd scrubbed tear stains with wet tissues. She'd sprayed rose water on her face until she shone. She'd come out of the dressing room looking unforgettable. And then she'd sobbed relentlessly for the next thirty minutes. I'd sat next to her and stroked her back as she refused to look at me. 'I think you should stay home. I can also stay with you,' I'd said.

'No, we're going.'

Now, at half past seven, she stumbled into the front yard like nobody's business, in a long, V-neck maxi. Curtain bangs helmeted her forehead like a rash, daredevil decision. Her hair was now the length of a pocket knife. On her, it didn't look like a haircut gone wrong. It only made her appear younger, emphasized her cheekbones more prominently. Her silver sequin heels were more moonlight than moonlight itself. And throughout the night, I couldn't recollect a single moment the marble cigar pipe wasn't in her mouth. I'd told her multiple times she didn't have to come along, but she was stubborn, she was manic.

'Are parties allowed to be hosted at the principal's house?' I asked, staring at the archaic Viking structure that stood in front of me.

'Yes, yes, don't worry. Ira does this the minute the principal and his wife are out of town.'

'Perks of being the principal's daughter?'

'She's loaded with privilege, that one.' Scheher took another puff. There were dark circles under her eyes. The bruises on her face looked like they'd begun to heal, but they hadn't yet disappeared. 'And she flaunts her privilege, but at the same time, never accepts it.' Streaks of wet mascara had begun to collect around her cheeks like turbulent black rivers. 'Do I look fine?'

'Yes,' I lied. 'You look beautiful.' *But not fine*, I thought. Of course, there was no need to tell her that.

'That's not enough. Do I look better than the girl he's with now?'

Frankly, I didn't even remember what Joshua's new girlfriend looked like. There were so many students in college, and I hadn't seen her until that day when I was sticking posters with Bagchi. I tried to conjure up her face, but all that came to my mind was the groping and the giggling. I shook my head. This wasn't going anywhere. 'You've always looked perfect to me, Scheher. I don't really know any other way to answer that.'

'Then why isn't he picking up my call anymore?' she asked miserably.

I winced. 'Why are you calling?'

'I need to know if I did something wrong.'

I was tired of reminding her it wasn't her fault. But at the same time, I felt bad for her. 'You *didn't*.'

'Then why isn't he talking to me?' I could tell where this was going. Her wounds were still raw. She was still in *that* phase. She would be for a while. Someone didn't want her. And somehow, that seemed to define her entire personhood.

'He's never going to talk to me, is he?' she asked, and I didn't know how to tell her the truth without hurting her.

'Scheher,' I said in disapproval. I knew there was no point making her feel responsible for herself, especially when she was already in such a dysfunctional place. I knew that wasn't what she wanted to hear. She wanted me to tell her he still loved her. She wanted her delusion to be validated. She wanted to hold on to denial for as long as she could.

For Scheher, the truth was the real monster. Not Joshua.

We'd spoken before coming to the party. I had told her to put herself first, but all she had wanted was to look stunning in front of him. She had wanted to parade herself and make him want her again. She had arrived with a master plan to cajole him back into her life, and now, at the entrance of Ira's house, it had finally hit her that it had been a foolish decision.

'If he's never going to talk to me again, then I don't want to talk to him either.'

'He manipulated you. He played sick mind games on you. Of course, you shouldn't want to talk to him,' I said.

She nodded, but I wasn't sure she heard me. She was still staring at the door, looking determined. What if she went in there and tried to seduce him? Or worse, begged him to take her back and cried in front of him? I knew everyone would laugh at her. And I would be disappointed that she'd done that. But then again, how could I expect her to get over this so easily? So soon? I couldn't judge her like that. She had showed up into the relationship dedicatedly. He'd cheated, he'd hurt her. Yes, she'd repeatedly gone back to him, and some would say it was a choice, but they wouldn't understand that it was a manipulated choice.

It was easy for people to say it was her fault that she stayed in it. From what she'd told me, I knew that at the start, Joshua had been incredibly charismatic. I'd understood that abusers never revealed themselves as abusers when they met a potential victim. The mask only fell off over time. Scheher was made to believe he was capable of love, made to second guess herself all the time. He broke her self-esteem. He broke the faith she had in her to do right by herself. He'd made her feel stupid and selfish and crazy for leaving him when he hurt her. He'd fed her the wrong narrative, and she'd made her decisions based on that wrong narrative. She never had the truth. Never. That was how he took her power away.

'Scheher,' I said. 'We've been standing here for a while.'

'I know.'

'Let's go in?'

We looked at each other, long and hard. Two women, burning sacredly, outside the principal's house. 'Yes,' she finally said, her lower lip trembling. 'But just tell me one thing before we go inside.'

'Yes?'

'Why...me?'

Why her? It was so evident to me. The empath and the sociopath. The fated, treacherous combination. He had chosen her deliberately because she was full of love to give. 'Because you're good and forgiving and some people use that as a weapon against you, when it's your weapon in the first place. Always is, always will be,' I said.

She seemed oddly at peace with my statement. 'Let's just go inside, okay?' I said to her, letting her process it. 'We'll get you something to eat, and you'll feel better.'

We stepped into the large house and I instantly regretted it. I had a feeling we looked terribly out of place. We were complete strangers to the area and the people occupying it.

The interior of the place was elegant, with its slanting roof and polished bronze mirrors. The curtains were lace, and the walls were filled with portraits of old men and women, probably the Dalvi ancestors. I recognized Raja Dalvi from one of the photos I'd found of him at the library. Here, he looked younger, less mousy. Something about the entire family, though, made me feel a bit antsy. Like they were hiding something, something vicious.

In the dining area, I found Bagchi holding a glass of wine in his hand, chatting with Ira. 'Esai!' he called out, and waved at me. Was he really that happy to see me, or was he just drunk?

I made my way towards them.

Bagchi was in a tux. Ira was wearing a collared shirt with pearl buttons and a long black skirt to go with it. Her hair was in a massive side braid with rhinestones on it. Her gaze moved in on me, but I couldn't read her. I wore my poker face like a veil and stared back.

'Why is your name Ira Saanvi and not Dalvi?' I asked.

Ira was caught off-guard, but then she answered, all composed, 'Saanvi is my mother's name. I don't get along that well with my father. When I was fifteen, we had this big fight, and then I legally changed my last name to my mother's. Better, isn't it?'

'Sure. Patrilineal surname conventions are super outdated at this point anyway.'

Bagchi chuckled. 'Ira, she talks like you.'

'I had a feeling she would.' Her eyes bore into me. 'And what about you? You're Esai *what*, exactly?'

'I'm from the Tamil community. A lot of us gave up our surnames because it contained our caste. It was right after Periyar started the self-respect movement in the state.'

'Ah. I see.' I didn't think she did, though. 'You were really great during initiation. I mean, Anisha and some of the other Cabinet members were pissed. But I thought you had spunk.'

'Thank you.' I didn't know what this was leading to.

'Do you know what today's party is about?'

'A pre-Solstice get-together?'

'We passed the budget for Solstice, so we're celebrating. That's why you'll see mostly Cabinet members and their friends here. And, of course, the newly chosen core committee for the annual fest.'

'Right.'

'And now that we've passed the budget, we want the fest to be a success.'

Bagchi intervened at this point. 'What Ira means is that we

want everyone out there saying they loved it. How do we do that? We have the money, and we have all the manpower and resources, but how do we get people to like us?' He smiled sincerely, hoping I wouldn't misunderstand him again like the last time. 'Also, can I get you a drink?'

'Red wine, please.' I faced Ira. 'What exactly happens at Solstice?'

'Everyone gets sloshed and passes out eventually.' A tiny smile crossed her face, but it was brief. 'Let's see. Outsiders who have no connection with St. Margaret's, people from big political parties mostly, enter the campus and try to get votes. Sometimes, they even recruit new members. There are banners everywhere and teenagers having unprotected sex. Missing wallets, lucky draws, fancy dress stuff. But overall it's fun. It's a fest. So there'll be a lot of bands playing.'

'What kind of bands?'

'Metal, death metal. Folk, alternative rock. We haven't decided yet, but now that the budget has been passed, we'll begin discussing internally.'

I let that sink in. 'Internally, as in among Cabinet members.'

'Yes.'

Bagchi was back with a glass of wine for me, and a beer for himself. He inserted his presence into our little conference without any disruption. But I felt all of it.

'Don't discuss it internally,' I said, and quickly looked at him. He leaned forward.

Ira blinked at me, confused. 'Okay?'

'Make it a democratic process,' I said. I had Bagchi's full attention now, and it excited me. 'Find out what bands the students want to invite. Not you, not Anisha, not Joshua, not the VP. Know what everyone else wants, including the freshers, and then get those bands to come. That'll make them feel heard, and that'll also get them saying nice things about you and this year's Solstice. Know what I mean?'

'Interesting,' Ira said, rubbing her arms. Bagchi immediately offered her his sweater and went into the hall to look for the AC remote. A pang of jealousy swept through me, and I tried my best to suppress it. 'That's actually a really good idea,' Ira said. 'Maybe I can—'

Just then, someone bumped into me, hitting my shoulder as they stormed past. I turned around to see who it was, and realized it was Scheher. She ran out of the door and into the night, her dress billowing behind her.

What had that been about? 'Listen, I'll be right back,' I said to Ira.

I stepped out in search of Scheher. She was under the porch light, hugging herself tightly. The golden light cascaded all over her like a shower, and the satin of her dress gleamed in the dark. 'Scheher?' I said, taking cautious steps towards her.

She whipped her head around. 'Who do they think they are? I know them, I know what they've done. I know the kind of politics they play. I'm going to expose them. I swear I'm going to expose them!'

'What happened?'

'Look at this!' She handed a crumpled letter to me.

I peered into it, not sure what to expect. It was a stick drawing of her in the ICU. 'Anisha made this, which means he probably told her about that day in the hospital.'

'What was the point of making this cartoon?' I asked angrily.

'They're just trying to ruin my night. Give me a hard time.' She clutched the sides of her head tightly. 'Those two, when they get together, can be really mean. I've seen them.'

'Anisha and Joshua?'

'Yes.' She rubbed her mascara stain with her index finger. 'I try to forget it, and nobody lets me.'

'We shouldn't be here. You shouldn't be exposed to these people.'

'It's who they are. They enjoy seeing others in pain.' She played with her bracelet, absentminded. There was a moment's silence before she asked, 'When I was in there, I saw her. Do you think she's pretty?'

'Anisha?'

'No, Joshua's new girlfriend.'

'Scheher, just drop it.'

'Why should I?' She was tearing up again. 'Oh, Esai.' She covered her face with her hands and began sobbing into it.

'I am so sorry, Scheher. I truly am.' I kneeled down with her and held both her hands tightly.

'Why are you sorry?'

Someone has to be. 'Can I take you home?' I asked.

She rocked back and forth, foetal position slowly setting in. 'People don't just leave, you know. They leave in a way that makes you feel abandoned.' She flinched at the drawing in my hands, and then shrunk away. 'They're all going to talk about this now. They're going to paint me like some use and throw, like some hysterical idiot. I'll only be remembered for this, for being dumped and replaced.'

'Stop that!' I said in dismay. 'You're Scheherazade. Female rebel, teller of stories. You're a poet, a badass tarot reader. You're the books you read, the things you believe in. Your passion, your big heart, and so much more. And those are your identities. Not some dumb loser.'

She smiled a wan, teary smile. 'I guess you're right.'

'Talk about it,' I said earnestly. 'Through your art, I mean. You don't need to be telling Minaxi's story or some old Persian queen's story. It's your story the world needs to hear. Don't let him get away with this. And don't let them mock you for it. Turn it around, reclaim your narrative, reclaim your power. You aren't who they think you are. You are who you know you are.'

She nodded, a little harder this time, and let go of my hand. 'Thank you.'

Violet rings hung under her eyes from sleep deprivation. I didn't tell her, but I found it staggering that someone could go from looking so invincible to utterly powerless in such a short span of time. It was like she had completely retired into herself. She continued to look lost, and something just had to be done.

'I'll be back, okay? Stay here, we'll be leaving in a minute or two.'

'Where are you going?'

'Some unfinished business.'

I ran back in, and looked around for Joshua. He was standing next to Anisha and some other girls, and they were all engaged in some bawdy joke.

Wine in my hand, I marched right into Joshua, and threw the rest of its contents onto his face.

'What the hell!' he roared.

'Esai!'

Bagchi grabbed me by the shoulder and tried to move me away. 'Let go, Bagchi!' I screamed, pushing him away. 'Stop. Being. Such. A. Pushover.'

Ira stepped between us and put a palm on a frothing Joshua's chest. 'It's okay, it's okay. I'll talk to her. Here, take this towel, go change in my mother's room. You know where it is.' It took a couple of other seniors to reign Joshua in and drag him upstairs. He glared at me, and I returned the glare. On his way up, he said to me, 'I'll hit her if I want to, and I'll dump her if I want to. I want to see you try and stop me.'

Bagchi carried me into a room on the opposite side of the kitchen, and locked us in. It was a tiny room, with pastel pink walls and medieval wardrobes that could easily belong in a museum. Paintings of fruits and landscapes hung everywhere. Had I not been so riled up by what had happened, I would have been thrilled at the opportunity to be alone with him.

Covering the door with his lanky frame, he looked me in the eye, and said, 'This time, you've really pushed it, Esai.'

'You don't even know what happened!'

'Try me.'

'He taunted Scheher! As if breaking her heart wasn't enough, he taunted her! And he...' I couldn't tell him about the other stuff I'd heard, like how he'd forced himself on her after getting her high. Or the attack in the car after her show. I couldn't tell anyone. It wasn't mine to tell.

'He what?'

'Nothing.'

'He hits her, right?' he said, and I grimaced. Of course, he knew. He'd been there at the hospital too that day. 'I mean, who wouldn't notice the black eyes and blemishes she keeps sporting to campus anyway? We'd be blind not to.'

'You notice it and look the other way, right?' I said condescendingly.

'No,' he said, gritting his teeth. 'I've tried talking to her about it.'

I squinted at him, trying to understand whether he was telling the truth or simply virtue signalling. Had he really gone against Joshua and told her to leave him? Had he, then, been troubled by what he saw? It felt strange to even ask that question, when what was happening to Scheher was so obviously triggering. Anyone would have been affected by it. But then, hadn't there been instances where passers-by took photos or videos while victims bled to death in the streets, post hit-and-run accidents? Instead of getting them medical help, hadn't people simply walked by, as if it was none of their business? Didn't the world do nothing but stare and watch in that voyeuristic way when someone was dying? What did they owe us, and what did we owe them? Hadn't that been our motto throughout history?

I continued to watch him. He didn't look away. I took that as a sign that he wasn't hiding anything. But the more the eye

contact persisted, the more I felt the room revolve around me.
I'd never been claustrophobic before. So why now?

'Esai,' Bagchi said to me. 'You need to stop doubting me
all the time.'

I nodded. I knew Bagchi was probably being truthful in
this case, but I still couldn't bring myself to take his word for
it. Nonetheless, I asked him, 'How did Scheher react to that?'

'She defended him,' he said. His words had slowed down,
become deeper after that prolonged eye contact. The energy in
the room had changed, and we both knew why. 'She begged
me not to confront him. When I did, he denied it. And she
denied it too.'

'I hate him.'

'Esai, you need to stop reacting to him. It'll only make him
more aggressive.'

'So what's your point? I should shut up and turn the other
cheek?'

His features were sharp and cold now. 'No, I'm just saying,
save yourself for bigger battles. You're better than this, picking
fights with some immature overgrown child. Acting like an
immature overgrown child yourself.'

'Oh, so standing up for a friend is suddenly immature and
childish.'

'I'm just *requesting* you to cool your blood down a bit. It
isn't helping anyone. It isn't helping Scheher. For all we know,
Joshua might get nastier towards her because of the trick you
pulled today, now that he knows it provokes you. And didn't
he just threaten you with an acid attack a while ago? Or did
you forget that?'

I didn't, I wanted to say. But it killed my ego to admit that
he had a point.

'You never,' I said, wiping angry tears. 'Never take anyone's
side.'

'Esai, I'm literally on your side,' he said, galled. 'The fact that I'm in this room with you and not him, means that I am on your side.'

The silence that followed was invigorating. We'd muted the sound outside with our breathing. There it was again, that look in his eyes. And then I saw my reflection in them. Lips parted, hair a big cloud around my head. 'Really?' I asked, tilting my head to a side. 'Is that why you're in this room with me?'

His hands sought his pockets for shelter. I knew what that was code for. I knew him well. 'What do you mean by that, Esai?'

'You know exactly what I mean.'

I took a step closer, and so did he. And then another, and then another. Standing a little too close. Palms brushing. Breaths syncing.

I could feel the room begin to shrink.

'You have nice hands, Bagchi,' I said. I picked up his limp arm and folded it towards me. I ran my thumb along his knuckles, along the veins, along the wrist bone. 'And nice fingers too.' I looked up.

All my senses were heightened. In a wink, we were in a magnetic field, and the room was a kettle. Did he feel it too? The tingling neck. The slow fever building up the spine. The back arching from a simple stroke of the breeze. Simmering, boiling. Slow dancing with danger and liking it. I wanted hungry canines to the flesh like a red, hot fever dream. I wanted the fire to hit my belly, I wanted my body to break into a broiling summer.

Just then, a bottle crashed outside, pulling us out of our trance. More gasps, and then a gin-soaked male voice asking for tissues drifted into the room. A few people giggled.

And then the party went on.

For a second, we looked at each other, confused. And then I pushed him away and ran down the stairs.

How was it that I was mad at him just a few minutes ago and now…now I wanted to be under him? For Scheher's sake, I was upset with myself.

'Esai, wait,' he called out. He charged after me, but I lost him. Someone chose that moment to block him and start talking to him.

As I exited the building, I found Scheher standing exactly where I'd left her.

'Let's go,' I said gruffly.

She grinned at me. 'While you were in there slaying those dragons, I was up to some funny business too.' She opened her bag and showed me the bottles lying inside. 'It's ten and we're still on campus, may as well make the best of it. Want to get drunk near the lake? Turn into mermaids for the night?'

Of course I said yes.

TEN

The blaze of the stars was in our bloodstream as we giggled our way into the forest. Two bottles down, we were already tipsy. At this hour, St. Margaret's forbidden lands seemed different—carnal, alive, on the prowl. From far, the trees looked like giants in dark cloaks, foaming at the mouth with their leaves. There was something animalistic about the woods, as if any moment now, anything could swallow us whole.

My phone hadn't stopped ringing since we'd left, but I had no intention of picking up and listening to Bagchi convince me that he was with me on this one, when clearly he was playing safe again. I pressed the *reject call* button once more.

Near the lake, the orbs were resting. There was a sourness in the air. I had a vision of hands rising out of the water, twisting, turning, and beckoning. Clean, feminine hands, the kind you would want to rest your cheek on. Suddenly, my head felt heavy, and my throat, parched. 'Scheher,' I called out. 'Scheher, where are you?' The hands immediately dropped back down like lotuses closing at the end of day. 'Scheher?'

'I'm right behind you.'

'Do you see the hands?'

'What hands?'

There was white mist everywhere, and I squinted my eyes. There was a figure at the end of the fog, but I couldn't see much of her. 'Where's all this fog coming from?' I called out.

'What fog?' Scheher asked. Whatever else she said to me, I could barely figure. She'd become all muffled tone and incomprehensible words. Hadn't she been walking close? Why did she feel so far away now?

There was a woman standing in the middle of the lake, but she wasn't drenched. The closer I got, the clearer her face became. 'Scheher? Is that you?'

No, it wasn't. And I knew it, so why was I asking? I'd seen this woman before, in my dreams. I'd heard that song before, and I couldn't help but join in.

'Stop humming, Esai!' Scheher said, but her voice had begun to fade. 'You're scaring me.'

'Sorry, I'll stop. Do you see her?'

'Who?'

'The Lake Woman.'

'Now you're *really* scaring me.'

A sharp pain shot through my temple and I fell on both knees. I could hear Scheher's footsteps approach, but it wasn't the only thing I could hear. Somewhere, somewhere far away, there were people laughing. A professor screamed, 'Silence!' and it echoed all over my body.

I was sitting inside a classroom.

I looked at the window pane, and for a moment, was surprised to see someone else staring back at me. It was her, the Lake Woman. I touched my face delicately, and everything felt different.

It's just a dream, I told myself, trying to stay calm.

But then a monologue started to run in my head, and it wasn't in my voice.

I had always been a firm believer that Newton wouldn't have been able to escape the apple even if he had wanted to. That the moon, even after all these centuries, would stay put because of gravity, and there was absolutely nothing it could do about it. That love was also a long experiment of surface tension and eurekas and explosions in the laboratory, and its science was a puzzle as confusing as the existence of God. That no matter how light or heavy or tall or short or skinny or muscular I was, I would still be a test rat for Galileo's falling bodies. Falling, accelerating, crashing.

I was the only person in the room sitting alone, studying a current carrying coil and taking notes in my little graph book.

'Is this seat taken?' the boy standing near my table asked, clearing his throat. He had the face of a barn owl, serious and composed. I shook my head, vexed by the interruption. He eased into the chair and pulled out his notebook too. Truth be told, he looked like he had no clue what to do. Across us, Nanda sir was absorbed in his own parallel universe, playing with magnets, completely oblivious to the rest of us.

'Do you have an extra pen?' he asked me timidly.

Who came to class without a pen? I pushed a ball point towards him and continued to write down my observations.

He tried to indulge in small talk. I mumbled one word answers back to him, but he was ambitious. He took the conversation forward even when I ended it. Told me the class was unfairly quiet. Do you like quiet? He asked. Yes, I said. Or rather, I was comfortable with it. And him?

He said the last time he remembered being in such a dull place was during dinner, inside his spacious, oak framed house, built in the quaint architectural style of the Vikings. He'd sat at the dinner table, his mother watching her television drama on mute because his father hated it, and his father reading documents on the side as he crammed portions of rice into his

mouth. It had been a quarter past eight, and he'd taken his
bicycle out for a ride in the woods. In his mind, he'd heard
radio noise, voltages fluctuating. And then a young deer had
crossed his path, and he'd skidded, cutting his arm.

His head throbbed so bad he thought antlers were growing
out of it. And then all he remembered thinking was, how good
it felt to feel anything at all.

I thought he was a strange boy. But I liked strange things.
I usually didn't care about the lot, but this one made an
impression on me. Was it his pitiful emptiness? His self-
deprecating jokes? It was surprising, how much he had my
attention. My heart was sweating into my chest every time
he said something to get me to open up or did something
magically, remarkably normal. My jitters didn't make sense to
me, because he was rather plain-looking. And yet, there was
something in the way he held his pen, in how he was enlivened
every time he arrived at a solution and identified the problem
with his graph. I was pulled in by how he looked so laid back,
like life could be simple, if we wanted it to be.

'R? What's R?' he asked, five minutes later, gaping at the
questions in the book.

'Radius,' I said.

'Radius of what?'

I turned to him, grinning. 'Radius of the loop.'

'Ah, all right,' he said. He was suddenly self-conscious. 'I'm
sorry, I'm no good at this.'

I rose from where I was sitting, picked up my notebook,
and walked towards Nanda sir.

Nanda sir, who now looked over twenty years younger. I
had a vision of him with grey hair and thicker glasses. So very
unlike the Nanda sir in front of me, and yet so eerily similar.
My head suddenly hurt, as if the time warp was happening
inside it. The classroom flickered into the forest, and then back
again. In a flash, the pain was gone.

I positioned the book right in front of the young Nanda sir, and said, a little proudly, 'Done.'

He sifted through it, his small, grey eyes a little fatigued from lack of sleep. I had a feeling he'd been up all night evaluating those magnets, almost forgetting that he had a class so early in the morning. I'd heard so much about him, and it was all remarkable. Did he really have a telescope in his house? Did he use it often? And when he wasn't teaching, what was he reading? Did he have a personal laboratory and did he invent things there? Hadn't someone gone as far as to say he was secretly creating a human being just like Frankenstein had in that gothic Mary Shelley novel?

He was really such a character.

He grew smitten by my answers with every passing second, and then his mouth formed a small O when he saw my final deduction.

'That was fast! And it's accurate.' He checked his watch. 'There's still twenty minutes left to this class, but since you've finished, you can leave.'

I pointed at his magnets. 'Sir, are you testing chaos theory?'

He arched an eyebrow. 'What do you know about that?'

I tapped on the pendulum in front of him. 'Where this stops, is unpredictable.'

'Go on.'

'The magnetic forces it feels at five milliseconds after its release are highly dependent on the forces present at four milliseconds after its release. This is because of the many feedback loops among the variables.'

Nanda sir's eyes stretched open.

'Which makes it a system whose output is extremely influenced by very small, initial conditions that may, to the common eye, seem insignificant.' I wiggled my finger solemnly. 'But they're not.'

'Genius.'

For the next twenty minutes, the professor and I engaged in rapid, delightful conversation. Everyone had noticed, everyone had pretended not to. By the end of the class, as the bell rang, they all rushed out, relieved that they no longer needed to tune in to us.

The only person hanging around was the boy.

He came up to me, a little shy. 'Here's your pen,' he said. He hadn't used it at all.

I smiled. 'Thank you.'

'I'm new here,' he began.

'Oh, aren't we all?'

'Well, yes. But...I was wondering if you could show me the day café.' I noticed he stuttered a bit when he said that. I'd never once had a boy act nervous while talking to me. I'd never had a boy talk to me at all. Or maybe I'd been too in love with my books to ever pay heed.

'Of course!' I said, and wrapped up my discussion with Nanda sir. We promised we would pick up from where we left off during the next class.

'You'll have to finish your assignment early the next time too, then,' Nanda sir said, issuing a challenge jokingly.

'I will,' I said with confidence.

The boy and I took the long route to avoid some of the seniors, because I'd agitated them earlier with something irrelevant. One of them wanted me to call them ma'am and not by their name, and I'd refused. She'd complained about me to her friends, and they'd come after me.

Not relenting still had landed me in more misfortune. I was now their favourite castaway.

'And that's Bharati Sports Ground,' I said to my friend, as we crossed it. 'It was built by Dr. Dalvi's brother, who's now started a new political party and won one seat, I think, though I can't be too sure. And that,' I said, pointing at the library. 'Is a new addition, and it opened only last year, can you believe that?'

He shook his head. 'Wow.'

'But I've been inside it more times than even the people who constructed it, you know? They've got these huge shelves, made of pine, and they're painted white. The books are all new, but they've got some old, yellowing ones too on the top floor. Not all of them are academic, though, I found a lot of novels too, the fast, thriller type. And some erotica.' I wiggled my eyebrows. 'Who knew I'd find those there? Or maybe I was never supposed to discover them. Ah look, we've already arrived. The day café. There are two people who work shifts here. In the morning, from eight to one, it's Savitri didi, whose two girls go to school in Lower Parel, and post noon, it's Dharmesh uncle, who makes one of the best Bombay sandwiches in the world and saves a mango-flavoured milkshake for me because he knows I love it. In fact, back in my town, everyone loves anything related to mangoes. We make mango chutney, mango pickle, mango pudding. Our town is even known for the police stealing mangoes from roadside shops at midnight.'

'Seriously?'

'Seriously.'

A little later, he admitted that he'd lived on campus all his life, but he hadn't wanted me to know that. He'd wanted to talk to me, he said.

'So then that tour of the campus went to waste,' I said, sulking.

'I loved it,' he said. 'You're the best tour guide I've ever met.' And then he told me about how he'd grown up in silence. In the silence of his locked room, in the silence of gloom. It didn't take long for that silence to fossilize into discomfort. He'd been a by-product of his parents' marriage, nothing more, nothing less. An insignificant outgrowth, a derivative of two incompatible people. He'd never once considered living outside of the quiet.

And yet, here he was, all ears. Something about my outrageous chatter, he said, felt safe.

'Do you want to get some tea?' he asked, just as I was about to leave.

I thought about it a while, and then walked inside. He followed me towards the table I'd chosen, and we were hit by the aroma of pastries and savouries and spicy fried rice.

'You're a nerd in every sense. You know way too much about St. Margaret's,' he said. 'Even I didn't know about the sports ground. You're going to do really well in initiation.'

I laughed mirthlessly, and then leaned forward. 'No, I'm not.'

'Yes, you are. I already know it.'

'Maybe, if I give it a try. But I'm not doing it.'

'What?'

'I'm not doing initiation. I'm not getting on a stool and reciting answers like some puppet. Not for *them*.' I looked towards a bunch of seniors at the next table. 'Not for anyone.'

That remark left him highly strung. He told me nobody had ever disobeyed the codes of initiation. Of course, it was a taxing, pressurising task, but it was also duty. Didn't I want to be a true St. Margaretian? He asked. I already was, I said. How did initiation make me more of one?

After a while, he gave up trying to wheedle me into it. He didn't know anyone who had gone against it, he admitted. And although he'd had nightmares of fainting on the stool or going numb when they questioned him, he knew, deep down, that all this was a part of St. Margaret's culture. At least, that's what his father had told him. And nobody disrespected tradition.

'It isn't tradition, it's just another way of brainwashing people into being suppressed,' I said.

He looked dejected. 'But won't you get into trouble if you skip it?'

I shrugged. 'I'm here to learn, not monkey-dance.' I thanked the waiter as he placed two cups of tea on our table. One sip, and he made a face. 'Too sweet for you?'

'It's fine.' But I could tell he was lying, because he took an awfully long time to finish it. A part of me itched to peek into his cup, but I knew that would be crude. He waited for me meekly, and I liked that he had only been concerned for me when I told him my plans, unlike the others, who had been vengeful.

Once I was done, I pulled out a pill from my bag and swallowed it.

'What does that do?' he asked.

'It gives me magical powers,' I joked. 'Actually, it's for my mood swings.'

'What kind of mood swings?'

'What kind? Well...' I held my breath. This was going to be tough to explain. 'It's complicated,' I said lamely. 'I'll tell you one day, just not now.'

And so we talked about other things. I told him about the love letters I'd written to Marie Curie, my idol, and the first time I'd fallen for the wonder of electricity as a young girl. I told him how my little sister and I had made a life for ourselves after our parents died, and I told him about the relatives who had tried to take away our inheritance. We'd escaped their deceit, we'd studied hard, and we'd even picked up freelance jobs while in school. We'd made it somehow. Alive and happy.

Meanwhile, he amused me with his tales about childhood, about all the times he'd felt like he'd been born a grown-up. Instead of saying things, he acted them out, and I was enraptured by the high-spirited movements of his hands and the flurry of expressions on his face. Joy, rage, grief, and my favourite, which was unique to him alone, the dorky squirrelly look. The one he'd had on throughout class, when he'd first started talking to me.

I'd barely known him for a few hours, but I found him so endearing.

He looked at my empty cup, and then at the food around us. Before I could get up and leave, he said, 'Listen, I'm hungry, and I hate eating alone in silence. Do you want to grab some lunch with me?'

I beamed at him. 'I thought you'd never ask.'

'And since we're having lunch together anyway,' he said, holding out his hand. 'The least we should know is each other's name.'

'Minaxi.'

He looked grateful the tension was gone, and fell back into the novelty of our unfamiliar friendship. 'Laxman,' he said. 'Laxman Dalvi.'

Laxman Dalvi!

I blinked. The vision stayed. There we were, sitting next to each other, but I couldn't hear the conversation anymore. I flitted from the chair to an external world, as if there was a tear in the universe. I had just met eighteen-year-old Laxman Dalvi, and all I could think was, he looked young, really young. But it was him, all right. There was no thick neck pouring into his shoulders like a waterfall, no receding hairline. But he had the same watery eyes, the same papery face.

'Laxman Dalvi,' I whispered to myself. And the minute I said his name, he grew faint.

'Sir,' I said out loud, and he looked directly at me. It was as if he could see through me, and I felt exposed. I touched my face again, and felt the squared jaw and the fullness of my mouth. The whole place began to melt away. The cafeteria was now an open ground, and it was midnight.

'Esai?' Someone called from behind one of the trees. It sounded like a distant echo.

Esai, Esai, Esai.

'I'm here!' I cried out. The scene had completely dissolved by now, and there was nobody around me. The students had gone. Their laughter had chipped away. And all I could see was a light in the distance. It was a young woman, holding a kerosene lamp.

I did a double take when I saw who she was. 'Esai!' she said, walking towards me.

My first reaction was to run away from her. But as she quickened her pace, the sound of her feet somehow brought me comfort. As if it was trying to tell me there was nothing to be afraid of.

'Esai, stop. Please.'

I turned around. There she was, with the thick black hair and red dress, standing in front of me, waving. She was me. She was the version of me from the party. I looked down at myself to see what I was wearing.

The red dress.

I held on to the image before me, still stunned. Drops of water fell onto my face as I got closer. I pressed my palm against the figure, and the forest swayed.

Blood rushed to my head. I felt like I was inside a tunnel, and yet, I could see the trees swinging around me. I could see the black clouds, and the lightning that drew silver half moon shapes over them, and then suddenly, everything came to a dead stop.

In no time, I was lying on my back, drenched in sweat. The first thing I saw was the sky, painted with stars, circling towards me. And then Scheher's concerned face.

'You passed out,' she said, looking worried.

'Did you see that?'

'See what?'

'The woman. From the lake.'

'No.' She looked around. 'But maybe we should just head back. This place was a bad idea.'

ELEVEN

A slice of daylight crept into the room through the curtains. Scheher had taken me back to her place, instead of dropping me off at mine.

Her flatmate, Priya, had moved out after the grisly hospital incident, and Scheher was living alone again; it was her place, after all. It was the only tangible memory she had of her family.

When we reached her house, Scheher had done everything in her capacity to see to it that I was well-fed and well-rested. She had even left a packet of biscuits next to my bed, in case I woke up in the middle of the night, feeling hungry.

She had sacrificed her single bed to me, despite my protests. I didn't remember much of last night, just that I'd been groggy and she'd half carried me home. It had rained badly, and we'd been drenched. She'd helped me out of my clothes, and let me borrow her old Powerpuff Girls t-shirt and pyjamas.

Now that I was fully awake, I decided to take a tour of the studio. It was neat, sophisticated. A banner of Malcolm X rested on the pastel wall of her living room. A pair of large, rectangular mirrors hung on either side of the window. The house was marinated in sun. There was a small balcony where she'd kept her plants, mostly Japanese maple. The more I looked around, the more I realized the house was filled with Feng Shui things. A lucky bamboo, an evil eye wooden hanging. A crystal lotus, a dream catcher and lots and lots of origami. Had she made those? The paper crane, the boat on the kitchen slab, the levitating airplane perilously balanced on a single thread? A big tapestry of the High Priestess, a card I'd recognized from her tarot deck, was spread on the wide kitchen door. Lilac post-it notes with couplets she'd written were pasted on the drawers of a classy study desk. Next to it was an antique bookshelf that reminded me of traditional cabinets from a different time, the kind that belonged in the quarters of queens. She had a lot of books, and most of them were poetry collections. Forugh Farrokhzad. Anna Akhmatova. Arthur Rimbaud. Yehuda Amichai. Nikki Giovanni. Kamala Das. Tagore. Audre Lorde. Some from the Beat generation.

'You can borrow them whenever.'

I turned around. Scheher stood there in her slip and shorts, combing her hair with her fingers. 'It's all yours.'

'Good morning to you too,' I said, smiling.

'Hmm.' She moved around the house, dragging her feet as she went. I knew she was still thinking about last night at the party. I knew she was terrified of everyone in college talking about her. I knew she was afraid of how long it would take her to let it go. She'd begun to believe this was what life was all about. A layer of hurt over another, piling up like a stack of unread books. All this unfinished business with herself, lying in a pile of dust. She didn't see a point in cleaning up if more demons were anyway out there, waiting to have a piece of her.

Awful, bothersome thoughts kept her up these nights, and she didn't spare me from hearing about them. What was she going to do with all these memories lodging in her brain? She still remembered the two of them in his extravagant apartment, slow dancing in such alignment. And in the end, had it been such a tall order to ask for mercy? To not be dropped and replaced in such a dehumanizing way? Who was there for her now? Who would even care to love her again? And who the hell was she supposed to be if not a lover?

I had no answers. But I knew someone who might have. And so I told her. 'I'm going to get you a copy of Plath's *Ariel*.' It had saved me once, when I'd been fifteen and in a rut. 'I want you to give confessional poetry a try. I feel like it's just the thing for you. For your next show.'

She looked thoughtful. 'I'm writing new poems. Maybe you can look at it later, tell me if it sounds right.'

'I'd love that.'

I lounged around the living room, going through everything she owned. I loved the pale décor and the huge windows, and I loved the way she had colour co-ordinated everything. The only thing I didn't understand was the framed one-rupee coin on the coffee table. I looked at her, confused.

She chuckled. 'Joshua's photo used to be there. I needed to replace it with something.'

'So you put a one-rupee coin?' I couldn't hold myself back. 'Scheher!'

'That's his worth, isn't it?'

'It's less than that, of course,' I said. 'But look at you! Savage.'

'I know, I know.' As an afterthought, she said, 'So are you feeling fine now? How's your head?'

Last night, I thought it was going to burst. I could feel the blood in my nerves, I could hear everything tenfold. But come morning, it had vanished. I was back on my feet again, with just the memory of a dream.

'It's stopped hurting, thank you. What about you? Are you doing good?'

'When I went to sleep last night, I was okay. But then I woke up in the morning and I thought, God, not this life again, where I die and I die and I die and I die.'

'Oh no.'

'Sometimes it's pitch dark, you know.'

'I get it. Hold on to your dream, whatever it is. He can't take that away.'

Her tears sprang back again, and she couldn't restrain them. 'You know my dream. And you know how he always tried to mess it up.'

Indeed, I knew her dream. She wanted full auditoriums. She wanted to put her poetry in an album. She wanted bookshelves in her name. She wanted little girls to look at her and think they could achieve big things. It wasn't out of reach, not for her. I truly believed that.

'I made Scheher up when my Baabaayi left,' she explained. 'I think it was my way of dealing with the loss. And ever since, this idea of Scheherazade has kept me hopeful that I can be brave. It's like she's a philosophy, this superhero suit I can wear whenever it gets really tough. She's my ideal self, the best version of me, and a coping mechanism. Knowing I could be her on stage, when I wore her clothes and did my hair like she did... knowing I could be Scheherazade, the Scheherazade I created, saved me. It helped me survive Joshua's abuse. It will help me survive the breakup. Firoza is weak. Easy to hurt. Firoza chooses the wrong people. Scheher isn't like that. Scheher is all claws, Scheher is all fire. Scheher is this desperation to escape sorrow and eat the sun. And without all of that, I know I'm really just a pathetic creature crying into my shirt and sore from loving everyone too much.'

'Don't say that...' I got up and sat next to her. Putting my arm around her shoulder, I said, 'I think both Firoza and Scheher are brave and powerful. Firoza is strong in a quiet,

resilient way. And Scheher is loud and explosive with her
courage. That's all. And both these versions of you inspire me
a lot.'

She dipped her head, wiping her tears. 'Thanks for saying
that, Esai.' She got up and moved towards the kitchen, all
embarrassed. 'I've been so weepy off late. It really needs to
stop.'

'It will. Don't rush the recovery.'

She nodded. 'I don't know how to thank you for this, Esai.
I don't know how I'd ever repay you.'

'You don't have to.'

Scheher didn't look satisfied with my response. 'I want to.
Someday I will.' She strolled into her kitchen. 'Maybe I can
start by making you breakfast?'

She took out a cutting board from one of the top cabinets
and started cutting tomatoes with the dexterity of a chef. She
was making salsa. And when that was done, she proceeded to
make Parsi Akoori, something like scrambled eggs. The entire
time, she seemed lost in a happy place, one that I couldn't
access. She connected the speaker to her phone, and the room
sizzled with the harmony of jazz. She twirled me around,
dancing and laughing, and suddenly, everything felt all right. I
wondered if today was a good day. I wondered if tomorrow,
she would break again.

'Is this what you do once you're home?' I asked.

'Lately I've been cosying up to the idea of solitude,' she
said. 'I do a bunch of things. I reheat the tea throughout the
day, I smoke a joint, I read a book. I'm reviving my reading
habit, now that I've more time and peace of mind. I try out a
new recipe and I dust the house. I rewatch extended interviews
of Angela Davis and I go watch plays in Prithvi theatre. I drive
down to the outskirts to sit with the pre-monsoon fireflies over
the weekend. I dig my toes in the sand and I make new friends

and treat myself to street food. I do all the things that keep me warm. I'm finally realising I deserve a kinder life. I mean, there are days, really bad days when I miss him. But it's over. It's over for me.'

In that instant, she looked defenceless like roadkill. Only her smile was infectious and swollen with magic. The rest of her was limp and worn out, and I gave her a big, tight hug. 'That's brilliant.' I sniffed. 'All this is making me weepy. But in a good way.'

'Esai,' she said, shaking her head. 'I'm too young to be a sentimental old fool, and so are you. We've done our fair share of crying, now that's enough.' I pulled away, and patted her back.

By the time we spread out the table mats, it was eleven-thirty. 'This has become brunch,' Scheher joked, pouring coffee into two mugs that said His and Hers. One had a moustache on it, and one had bulky red lips. 'Please tell me these were gifts. I can't imagine you having such terrible taste.'

'My mother. She dumped a lot of stuff on me when she cleared out of our old space.'

'You talk about her a lot.'

She paused. 'She's all I have. And she's the only person who ever encouraged me to write and perform poetry. Everyone else keeps reminding me how lousy I am at it.'

I settled myself on one of the bean bags. Scheher's parents had separated when she was very young, and she'd only reconnected with her father recently, after her mother had remarried and moved away. From what I could understand, he smothered her with luxuries, but he did not call or visit her unless it was her birthday or the Parsi New Year. He did not know how to be a father, or perhaps, he did not want to be. Her mother, on the other hand, had provided for her as a child, but after she had found a new family, things had become a little strained. There was still a lot of love between them, but her mother's actions had made Scheher feel cast away. 'What does she say?' I asked. I was not sure how frequently they spoke. All I knew was that she was more in touch with her mother than her Baabaayi.

Scheher chuckled. 'Exactly what you say. She tells me to write about my own experiences. To get personal. But the problem is, I can't talk about it without crying.'

I shrugged. 'Then cry. Cry on stage. So what?'

She toyed with the idea of that. Finally, she said, 'I'll think about it.'

We spent the next few hours playing board games. I won at Cluedo, she won at Scrabble. And then she left to run some errands. I went to sleep, because I was still extremely tired. This time, the dreams were open skies. Snow falling. Pastures and tulip fields. Scheher's voice drifted in and out. I heard the scraping of chairs, and papers rustling. I heard the nib of the pen pausing and scurrying, and then it was all ebony black again.

When I woke up in the evening, the house smelled of essential oil. Scheher was sitting on the other bean bag, watching a movie on her laptop. It had started raining again. It felt nice to be indoors. I looked over at Scheher and smiled. 'I feel like I've been hibernating.'

'You still haven't told me what you saw near the lake.'

'A dream. It doesn't matter.' I didn't want her to think I had lost my mind.

She grinned. 'You know, we forgot to put our feet in the water. I'd have liked to be a mermaid for a day.'

I scoffed. 'As if you'd know how to reverse it after a day. What if it stayed?'

'So you actually believe me.'

'Shush. I'm just playing along.'

We spent the rest of the evening watching an old Sridevi

and Kamal Haasan film called *Sadma*, snacking on nachos and getting drunk on homemade wine.

Three glasses in, I stretched my legs over Scheher's, under the shared blanket. At some point during the movie, I dozed off again. In the middle of the night, when the lights went out, I sensed Scheher leave the room, and then return to put a thicker blanket over me. And then she was gone again, and I was by myself, flailing in and out of slumber to the balcony view of the crescent moon, under her glow-in-the-dark ceiling.

TWELVE

It was Friday night, two days since that dreadful party at Ira's house. In those two days, I had successfully gotten Scheher to eat properly, wake up and work out with me, and even go on a bicycle ride. We had watched more movies together, and I had taken her to her first therapy session. I knew it was too soon, but she did look like she was getting better.

And then everyone had gotten wind of the fight at the party. And they had started talking again.

'St. Margaretians live on drama, don't they?' I said, shaking my head. 'Something tells me you'll have a big audience today.'

'And it won't be for my poetry,' she added.

'You can call it off,' I said. She did not look like she could stand, let alone face a crowd.

But she insisted. 'If I cancel now, it'll seem like I'm running away. Like I gave up.' And so I made my way out of her house in the morning. I knew she needed time to practise by herself, and it didn't make sense to talk her out of doing something she loved so deeply.

But a part of me also left for a different reason, a more selfish one. And it was something I couldn't disclose to anyone because I didn't understand it myself. Ever since I'd had those visions in the lake, I couldn't help but want to know more.

And so, an hour before Scheher's show, I was there again, a missing piece of the serenade. Strolling near the lake, heady from its splendour. My fingers drew random shapes in the water, looking for the lost dynasty in its whirlpool. *Come on, come on, come on. Show me what happened to you.*

I searched my reflection for her answers. It had begun drizzling, but I still couldn't bring myself to leave. Only when I heard thunder did I rise, and that was when I saw the face in the water change. A sad, whey face. Eyes like rose leaves. She looked at me, blinked a few times, as if I was the reflection. As if she was on the other side, staring into herself, only to have found her features altered. As if to ask the same questions: *Who are you? And what do you want from me?*

And then out of the blue, she looked like she recognized me. She reached out to me, and out of the lake emerged a strong, feminine hand. Without another word, I took it.

As the hand pulled me into the lake, I saw bubbles float upwards. I'd only read about blue sunsets on Mars, but if anything came close to it, it would be this. I was fully submerged now, and everywhere around me, there were beautiful ultramarine lights. Sapphire dust lay hovering over it, and I eased into a world of colours, a world of wonders. I was walking through Iceland's crystal caves; I was looking through a kaleidoscope of cobalt. Dark, prickly ice lined my sky, lit my veins, filled my mouth. It transformed into liquid and then hardened again into a·cluster of glaciers. Meltwater coursed through my hair, slowly turning to frost, and I stood there suspended as the temperature dropped further. A split second of winter later, I was elsewhere.

In Minaxi's parallel universe. In my head was her voice again. That same deep sound, but this time, with a different interior monologue.

I often imagined the process of falling in love as a long essay in textbook science. A lover's skin, sugared wild mint. Adrenaline, I told myself. His hands, new motherland. Dopamine, I argued silently. His laugh, summer rain. Serotonin, I kept saying. See, hungry poets were always trying to justify sweaty palms and racing hearts in a desperate bid to make romance romantic. And I wasn't any of them, but I could still think of eighty metaphors for the butterflies and the stammering and my guts on his nylon carpet. That was what love did. I told myself, it's just chemical reaction after chemical reaction after chemical reaction. It's in the genes, in hormones, maybe in the limbic processes of the brain. Maybe we'd over glorified the affairs of Laila and Majnu, Sartre and de Beauvoir, Napoleon and Josephine. Maybe we were all just biology's avant-garde laboratory experiments. Maybe.

But try as I might, I couldn't make sense of this. I couldn't understand why I looked forward to him coming to class every day. I couldn't understand why eating together at the canteen unhinged me the way it did. I couldn't understand how just a month ago, I'd shown up with my big suitcases full of blouses and big textbooks with the sole intention of being a nerd, and now here I was, living a different life. The kind of life I'd seen people in films live. The kind of life that made my life seem normal somehow. I couldn't understand why the other day, when he touched my hand to ask me a question in the lab, I jumped. And ever since, my skin just couldn't stop tingling. He let me borrow his bicycle, and he invited me to his house to watch movies in his home theatre. There had been this one time, when he'd been so tired from extra classes that he'd fallen asleep during one of the movies. Watching him fast asleep, snoring on my shoulder, I imagined Marie Curie keeping a sample of radium next to her bed as night light.

Completely unaware that this would eventually kill her.

A hot summer, dotted with occasional cloudbursts, was beginning to sweep through the city of Bombay. In my little room, under the old, rusting ceiling fan, I did nothing but practise telling Lax that I liked him. I rehearsed what I would say a million times in my mind, and I found myself fumbling through each time. I, who'd never once been tongue-tied my entire life, suddenly found myself out of words when I saw him. There had even been times when I'd watched him so intensely as he spoke that he'd paused and asked, 'Are you all right?' and I had to make lousy excuses for myself.

I had never told anyone that I liked them before. I didn't even know if that was what I felt, or if I was just getting too close to a good friend. But how could it simply have been imagination and nothing more? The back of our hands brushing against each other? Or those moments when one of us said something a little too coy and brought in the awkward silence? Or even that evening in his house when we were watching a movie together, and he'd fallen asleep on me. When he'd woken up, he'd woken up in a lurch, and bumped his head on my chin. We'd sat so close then, and it had seemed as if anything could have happened.

But it wasn't just physical attraction. I knew he cared for me. Wasn't that why, on the day of initiation, he'd stood outside my hostel and yelled at me to come out?

'Lax! Please, just go away,' I had yelled back, angry at him for succumbing to the system. 'I made up my mind a long time ago.'

'You're too naïve, Minaxi,' he'd said. 'You don't understand! This is going to turn against you.'

He'd tried a few more times to get me to join him, and then realising he was getting late, shrunk back. 'Minaxi, I don't want you to get hurt. Please.'

'Why are you so bothered?' I had asked, looking out the window.

'Because I love you,' he'd said quietly. And then before I

had an opportunity to say anything at all, he had turned and walked away from me. I'd called out for him, but he'd already gone.

Because I love you. His words continued to ring in my ears. My face felt warm, and it wasn't the dusty heat that caused it. I sat on my rocking chair, pressing my head onto the cushion, and thought about it for a very long time. So this was what love felt like. This was what all those songs were about. I hummed one that came to mind, and I gently rocked myself into a lucid dream. Across me, the mirror gleamed. I looked at it carefully, and realised it wasn't my reflection there, but that of a dark forest. *Wait, what?*

Just then, the building began to crumble. Hands broke open from the oval shaped mirror in front of me, and it suddenly seemed as if the lake was on the wall. I got up and moved towards it, but as I did, I fell out of my own body. Turning, I saw that Minaxi was still standing there. And here I was, Esai again. Esai, intruding upon a dead woman's memory, being called to return. *No,* I wanted to scream. *That's it? Show me more.* But she shook her head and put a finger to her lips. Behind it flickered a small smile, a promise that there would be more.

Like the artwork of the man falling from a tower in Scheher's tarot deck, I began to fall. And as I did, I found myself plummeting into a new memory. I could see chunks of it, falling around me like confetti, until everything settled into one place, including me. I could hear echoes of students shouting, clapping, chairs screeching.

I was now standing outside Richardson Hall.

I watched Lax step down from the stool, and walk towards his classmates. He had not noticed me standing near the entrance of the auditorium. His attention was riveted on the applauding audience. I touched my skin and knew I was still her. Me. It was getting hard to differentiate. I was getting accustomed to this new body.

Minaxi's body.

I waited outside until the event was over. I felt uncomfortable when the seniors streamed out, because they looked at me critically. But Lax had just told me that he *loved* me.

And now I had to tell him too.

When he finally came outside, he was beaming. 'I did it!' he said, picking me up and swinging me around. I hugged him tightly, and said, 'I need to tell you something. Shall we go?'

Throughout the walk to his house, we held hands. I had a feeling he already knew what I felt. How could he not know? Even then, anticipation ate away at me. What if I didn't say it right? What if I jumbled up the words or spoke too fast or made a mess of myself?

'Laxman! Congratulations!' We both turned. I did not know the girl's name, but I knew she was in her third year, and was from the History Department. 'Can I talk to you for a minute?' she said. He nodded and walked towards her.

She took him to a side, and I waited impatiently, unwillingly. As she spoke, she kept looking over at me. What was she telling him that she didn't want to disclose to me?

'What did she say?' I asked him when he returned.

'Nothing.' We were walking again. But this time, he didn't hold my hand. I reached for it, but before I could, something hit the back of my head. We both turned, and I felt a heat wave rush through my body. Everyone was staring at me, but I was looking at the object lying on the ground.

A slipper. A red chappal with an intricate floral print.

I picked it up, and held it up in the air. 'Who did this?'

'Minaxi,' Lax said, grabbing my sleeve. 'Let's go.'

'Who did this?' I yelled.

'Please don't cause a scene. Let's go. Please.'

'Whoever did this,' I said loudly. 'You're going to be very sorry.'

People were laughing now. Lax was towing me towards his house like I was a mangled car that needed to be cleared off the road, and I could feel the hot tears on my cheeks and the subconscious slanting of my brows. I had never felt so insulted my entire life.

'Do you know who did that?' I asked, as we entered the living room. The house suddenly felt stuffy. I wanted to run back into the wild with that slipper and fling it at the person who had humiliated me with it. 'Was it that girl who spoke to you?'

'What? No!'

'What did she say? Tell me what she said!'

'She just told me that I should spend time with them instead of...'

'Instead of?'

He looked down. 'Wasting it on you.'

'I knew it was her!'

He shook his head. 'No, Minaxi. It wasn't her. Or at least, it wasn't *just* her.'

'What do you mean? Just what do you mean by that?'

He looked up. 'I told you people wouldn't like it if you skipped initiation. Why do you think I stood outside your window begging you to show up?' He sighed. He locked the door and crossed his arms. 'Never mind.'

'Easy for you to say. Nobody threw a slipper at you!' I ripped my bag open, searching for my bottle of pills.

'I know, I know. I'm sorry. That was an awful thing to do, I agree.'

'Find out who did it. You've got the influence.'

He looked uncomfortable. 'I mean...'

'You don't want to, do you? Because we both know it could've easily been one of your friends.'

'Minaxi...'

'If it was one of them, would you still stay friends with them?'

He rubbed the back of his head. 'I don't know.'

'Wrong answer.'

'All right, no.'

'Sure?'

A pause. 'Sure.'

He touched my arm gently, and I turned away. 'Where does it hurt?' he asked, palm on my scalp. I shook my head. 'Forget it.'

'Shall I make soup? Will you feel better?'

'Do whatever you want.' Nothing could make me feel better after what had happened. I paced the floor for a few minutes, feeling restless. And then I finally sat on the sofa, and stretched my legs. Lax cast a sidelong glance at me and grimaced. 'What?' I asked.

'Please keep your feet down, Minaxi.'

This was just not the time to berate me on something so trivial. I glared at him, and then slowly dragged my feet to the ground. I didn't want to speak to him or anybody for the rest of my life.

But then, as I listened to him singing to himself in the kitchen, wearing an ugly old apron and trying his best to make small talk, I found myself warming up to him again. Minutes ticked by, and then half an hour, and it was surprising how a good bowl of soup could be life-altering.

And so, life felt normal again. In that moment, everything around me conspired to make things better.

The steaming pot. The pleasant house. The smell of laundry. The boy sipping from the ladle and then adding more salt. The big, magenta window. The meshwork, holding a sky the colour of crushed cranberries between its spaces. The ordinariness of a day in. The abundance in simple, mundane moments.

The gratification of not knowing how bad it was about to get.

'Is the soup all right?' he called out.

'Yes,' I said. But for some reason, no sound came out. Lax turned to me, and as he did, he broke into a spasm. I screamed, but I couldn't hear my own voice. I began to see the bubbles again, and the lights shot past me like a laser show. I was hurtling once more, into a tunnel lit by blue gemstones, and I felt my body shrink. I could see the forest again, and I could see everything that belonged to it. The fractured snail shell, left to rot between the weeds. The hummingbird and its tiny, agile wings. The rings on tree trunks and the whitish worms in the soil. The ladybird on the fading leaves and the lost bottle cap pressed into the dirt.

As I hauled myself down onto the ground like a feather, I felt the cool dew on the grass. Everything around me pulsated, as if it had a breath of its own. My surroundings appeared in high definition, like an eagle that had long-distance vision. I heard laughter, but I wasn't sure where it came from. I reached out for my watch, which lay a few inches away from me, and looked at the time. A lot of it had passed, even though I hadn't realised it. I pulled myself up and dusted the grass off my pants. I stood there for a while, willing the lake to move again, but it was still, lifeless, guarded. There was no going back now. And even if I could, I wouldn't be able to sacrifice my other commitments.

Sullen, I looked at my watch again. I could still make it for Scheher's show, if the traffic wasn't too bad. I hoped it wasn't, but that was too much to ask for from Bombay. I briskly walked past the trees, and stepped into the bright, open ground of the campus. Slipping out through the back gate, I found a rick to get me to the Bombay Comedy and Music club.

The club was jammed. It wasn't the usual crowd. I scanned

the room for faces I was acquainted with, but from where I stood, I could only see strangers. And then I spotted Joshua and Anisha seated at the front, and sighed. They were hell-bent on giving her a hard time.

But it wasn't just them. The more I observed, the more I realised it was a much larger crowd than the last time. And a lot of the unknown faces belonged to seniors. They were here for a spectacle.

I moved into the audience and made my way towards the back. There, I found some of our batchmates, and I pushed them forward. 'There's space at the front, go stand there,' I said, and they hesitantly shuffled towards the front. Scheher, who was watching from the side door of the green room, shot me a thankful smile.

More people thronged into the club, this time, older, probably not even from St. Margaret's. The lights dimmed, and the spotlight fell on the stage. It was show time. *Good luck, Scheher*, I thought. I hoped she wouldn't be intimidated by the seniors who sat at the front. I had considered telling them off, but it would have only made things worse.

Scheher blazed in; a winged, warring thing. Everyone watched, mesmerized for a second. She had on a navy blue suit, and held the cigar in her hand like an accessory. She held the mic elegantly and began to speak.

'I know why you're here. You're here because you're curious. But today, you're going to find out more about yourselves than about me. Because that's what art is about.'

There were whispers in the crowd. Too obscure for me to catch.

'Art is my way of daring the world to get fiercely vulnerable with me. It's my way of ripping the band-aid off. My way of finding myself again.' She looked straight at the people sitting in the first row. A vulture-like gaze. 'So come at me, see if I care.

I am whole beyond repair. So whole that if those who broke me lay in battlefields wounded, or on their deathbeds in hospitals dreaming of life, I would show up. I would declare, here, take my blood. I have all this to give and more. Nothing can deplete me anymore. I have mastered the alchemy of creating myself over and over again. I know bone work, I know to stitch skin back. I know nothing can stop me from being alive. Nothing can stop me from thriving.'

Scheher paused, and the pianist began her set. The music reminded me of the lo-fi playlists I used to listen to at night while trying to study for exams. It made me wistful, and hit me with a longing for solitude.

Like a falcon, Scheher swooped back in.

'I will never know if any of this is beautiful. How I wasted time turning into a jungle and growing into the ground and bathing in waning moonlight and wandering and growling and sobbing; if I'll ever be more than burnt mouths and hip hop in lit streets and sober eleventh hour candy receipts and daydreams in unmade beds and three-day-old lemonade and sore legs; if writing myself back to life in heroic verse and slicing myself open to look for rose quartz on nights I couldn't sleep were ever worth party small talk or first date conversations… but I did whatever I could with this body. Whatever bruised, glowing, fragile, daring, warm, wildling-skinned mess stumbling out of its girlhood I was, whatever the hell was left of me, I drilled light into it molecule by molecule.

I sculpted my pulse into dawn.

I kneaded myself into a trembling, brave thing that still runs in the dark, plays with the moss. I am teaching it that it is allowed. I am teaching it to make voice from a spinning wheel.

I am teaching it that it is distant stars and cookie jars,
baby parrots at golden hour and cherry blossom festivals
and midnight carnivals pulsating to mothers singing
ancient folk tales left behind by their female ancestors.

It is hour-long phone calls with old friends and dresses
the colour of peacock feathers and

peaceful protests and children awakening to their rights
and glorious internet detox weekends

and colour pencils and notebooks and poetry gigs and
new make-up looks and ink ballet shoes

and bangles and platonic hugs and raspberry lipstick and
banana peanut butter milkshake and

that disco lights rick and homemade carrot cake

lace underwear and the local zine fair and balloons, lots
and lots of balloons

and the moon and moonlight and black irises turning
brown in sunlight

and windows with mountain views and lakes and treks

hotel rooms and bathrobes and free shampoo and hot
showers and cat cuddles

libraries and poems and candles and clean days and
healing.

It isn't just grief, it can't be. My life...is not my grief.
Your life is not your grief. Your identity is

not your grief.

You are not your grief.

So please, let go of that belief.'

There was no clapping. There were only thunderstruck faces.
Adam's apples rising up and back down. Eyes that forgot to

blink. The room was frozen, as still as a painting. What were they thinking? What was Scheher thinking? I had to knock them out of their stupor, I had to get them to show her they were stunned.

I snapped my fingers loudly. I'd seen people do that in videos of poetry slams. Less disruptive, perhaps, and yet such a wonderful way of showing appreciation. Slowly, everyone else began following suit. The snapping intensified, but Scheher didn't smile.

When the snapping ended, the next poem began.

'Those who break me will one day bow to me.'

At the front, I saw Anisha scoff. Some of Joshua's friends were rolling their eyes. But I was the only one who noticed them. Everyone else was enraptured, waiting for her next line.

'Join me,' Scheher said, holding her hands high up in the air. 'Those who break us will bow to us.'

'Those who break us will bow to us,' the crowd murmured.

'I did not come this far to fall here. This is not my calling. After all these years, to be a stranger to myself,' she said. Someone at the back whistled loudly. Someone else hooted and clapped. 'Those who break me will bow to me. Say it. Those who break us will bow to us.'

'Those who break us will bow to us!'

'Those who break us will bow to us!'

'THOSE WHO BREAK US WILL BOW TO US!'

Scheher moved closer to the mic, and when she ended the poem, tears were streaming down her face. Her cheekbones looked more outstanding from the dampness. She allowed the audience to snap for her, she even nodded at someone who screamed her name. When she began her next, her voice quivered for a split second, and then smoothed over everyone like champagne. *How Foolish of My Beloved*, she called it.

'How foolish of my beloved to think he can spit on the sky.

How foolish to believe I am not the sky?
I am the mountain; I am the sea. I am not the lovers who
tried to destroy me.'

A girl I'd seen sitting in Bagchi's class the other day began
weeping too. Everyone noticed her, because as the poem
progressed, she began whimpering uncontrollably, unabashedly.
Before I could go up to her, her friend came and stood next
to her, wrapping her arms around her. They held each other
and watched, and all at once, the energy in the room was
transformed.

Scheher broke down into gut-wrenching sobs in front of
everyone. It was like watching the ultrasound of an unborn
baby. The secret was out in the open: she was soft at the
core. The piano slipped into a pensive symphony, and Scheher
swayed to it. An odd sense of despair shot through the room.
She paused in between for a few sips of water, and then she
informed the crowd that she was now performing her shorter
poems. 'They're not exactly haikus...' And for the first time
since getting on stage, I saw her smile a little. 'I don't know
what they are. But I think you'll like them.' She looked at the
people at the back, and then the ones to her side. She steadily
maintained her eye contact with everyone throughout the piece.
She was sometimes shy, sometimes confident, but mostly, she
was unapologetic.

'Shaky heart, tied like a tooth
on a string to you.
Bam—the door slams shut.'

There were hushed tones. Recognition clouding in the air.
Some were nodding at one other, some were staring at Scheher,
heartbroken, feeling things they never knew they could.

'Lost my beloved
found him like a blanket spread—
in another's bed.'

She howled into the mic, eyes shut tight, her face wet and shiny. The saxophone took over, developing its own sorrowful style. Almost everyone was crying now, as if it were a mass mourning. I could feel my own throat swell and close up as she kept repeating, 'Maybe my heart is just a mistake.'

'This last one…Okay, if I cry, don't judge me.' The audience looked on, intrigued. She looked straight at those who were sitting in the front row. At Anisha. At Joshua.

'When I was alive again, I looked for you.

I stood outside your door, a consequence of our past romance.

A cold body in an old mortuary.

You once said you were family

so how come you never came to identify me?'

There were more cries from the onlookers, more tears shed mercilessly.

'And now you ask me why I don't come to class anymore

I tell you the tapes on my veins don't let me off the floor

I mean, you can't just say it's over

and then expect me to stay sober…'

The hurt in her voice stung. The whole place throbbed with it, burned with it, ruptured to it. Her face crumpled, like every word was tearing her apart, like she was fading to her own song, disappearing into each guttural whisper of a note. To anybody else, she was a woman trying so hard to be strong, but finally giving up and dwindling into a lullaby. To me, she was Scheherazade, a warrior. Soothing, shattering, leaving nothing but ashes at her wake.

At a carnival, years ago, while watching a woman walk on a tightrope, Jolly had warned me never to fall in love with danger. As the sheer chiffon-like light clung to Scheher's hair, I thought about how she had to learn that the hard way. To swallow fire and not die, what was that like? To sleep on a bed of nails, to live in a pit of lions? To sit on someone's roof, watching the moon with your legs stretched, last cigarette burning, sky slowly swinging into dawn the colour of pink tulips, only to have them turn into a monster—how did one deal with something like that?

I thought about Pipi reading me the news about the ropewalker who had crashed to the ground and cracked her skull on the cement. But Scheher, Scheher wasn't her. Scheher was the girl who went looking for magic in a boy who had only darkness to offer. Scheher was the girl who stole the limelight from his ridiculous disappearing act and became a star overnight.

Didn't the past always call like an old friend passing through your town? *Let's catch up, let's catch up, let's catch up.*

Her poem left me thinking of last kisses and bullets, heather and missed trains. Stumbling in the streets, dressed to kill, looking for soulmates to spend the night with and forget in the morning. In that instant, the effect she had on me was profound. Melancholy walked through my body, holding an oil lamp. A hooded, sallow figure, cascading through my veins like they were tunnels. Finding a path to my eyes. Leaving my insides rotting.

Everyone now knew there was nothing to be laughed at or pitied. Because here was a tigress coming apart at the seams, opening her wounds to the world, asking it to hold instead of prod. Here was a girl with her outrageously confessional poetry, offering herself up to be loved.

How could anyone not love her?

And so, when it all ended, the crowd gave in and erupted into applause.

THIRTEEN

After the show, newly born fans huddled around Scheher to talk to her with stars in their eyes. I waited by the corner, giddy from the sudden shift in dynamic. Just two hours before, they'd hated her. And now here they were, cheering for her, celebrating her. It was scary, it was dangerous, the way things could change in the blink of an eye. How you could build and break a person with love and the absence of it.

When Scheher was done, she waved at me, and tipped her head towards the door. Together, we walked out with looped arms. The hosts locked the auditorium, and thanked Scheher for bringing in so many people. They'd sold a lot of drinks, and they were planning on making her next event ticketed.

'Do you think people would pay for it?' Scheher had asked them, surprised.

'We can start small, we can try it out,' the manager had said.

On our way back, Scheher danced by herself in the streets and smiled at passers-by distractedly. She'd recollect something from the show, and then go over it again and again, savouring every detail. Her speech was getting faster by the minute, and her voice was rising in its pitch. I had never seen her like that before. 'Sick, isn't it?' she said breathlessly. 'It was a good crowd; they were really responsive.'

'It was a good show, that's why,' I said. 'You did good, Scheher.'

'I was really feeling it,' she said, twirling me around. 'I was crying, wasn't I?'

'So was everybody else.'

'I saw that. This girl came up to me and cried on me. Jewel or something, goes to our college. God, she cried so much, I felt terrible. And then she told me she wanted to tell me something.'

'Tell you what?'

'That's the thing. She was crying so much, she couldn't get it out. It was weird for me, but it was also...I don't know. I'm not good at consoling people. You are,' she said, looking up at the sky. It was raining. The roads were as wet as fish.

'It's beautiful, what art can do,' she whispered in awe. She sang a bit more as we walked. 'I don't want to go back to my apartment yet,' she confessed. 'I don't want this dream to be over.'

'Come home, then,' I told her. 'We'll do karaoke. All the way into the night.'

'Oh, that would be amazing.'

We got into a rick. In the fifteen minutes we spent inside it, she taught me how to use her pipe. I was a fast learner, but realized it wasn't for me, so I gave it back soon enough. The incense in the vehicle lulled me, hushed all the chaos outside. I leaned my head on Scheher's shoulder, and she played Mazzy Star on her phone throughout the ride.

Just as we stepped out, Scheher began to cry. She wiped her nose on her sleeve. 'Oh God, today was extraordinary. It really was. But it was also so exhausting.'

'Of course it was. You were on stage for a whole hour. And you were shouting, so...'

She shook her head. 'No, not that. I meant...just talking about all that's happened. I don't know if it's healing me or harming me more. I know I'm addressing the pain, but it's also reminding me of it. It was like standing very close to the wound and looking it in the eye.' She shuddered. 'And then people came and told me about their wounds...and that was so hard to hear, Esai.' She allowed one last tear to fall before containing herself. 'Anyway, forget it. Let's just go to your place.'

When we entered the apartment, the smell of jasmine tea hit us hard. 'Mmm...' Scheher sniffed the air and put a hand over her chest. 'I want some of that,' she said brazenly, and Jolly quickly came out of the kitchen to see who her guest was.

Jolly was wearing an apron and a top bun. Everyone who knew her had the same thing to say about her: she had the kind of smile that lit up the room. Nothing could compare to Jolly's excitement about the smallest things, nothing could live up to her optimism.

'Jolly, this is Scheherazade,' I said. 'My friend from college. Scheher, this is Jolly, my aunt. And that,' I said, pointing at Pipi, who was sitting on the couch watching cricket. 'Is her husband, Pipi.'

'Priyank,' he clarified, as if he was suddenly conscious of the pet name.

'Jayalakshmi,' Jolly said, imitating him.

'Nice to meet both of you,' Scheher said politely.

'That is my little cousin, Tendral,' I said, as Tendral waved from the chair across Pipi. 'And that's Raza, her boyfriend.' Scheher nodded in acknowledgement. 'Come on, I'll show you my room.'

Jolly patted Scheher affectionately. 'I'll bring the tea once it's done.'

In my room, Scheher sat on the bed and fiddled with a loose blanket thread. 'Sweet family,' she said wistfully, as if she wanted to be a part of it too. Now that I knew how her parents treated her, I understood why she felt that way.

'I met a girl today, after the show,' Scheher said. 'Remember the one who was sobbing like her heart would fall out any second?'

'Jewel?'

'No, that girl cried on me after the show, when she came to talk. This one did while I was performing, and her friend came running to hold her. Remember?'

'Oh, her. Yes. It was hard not to notice her.'

'So she told me, when everything was over, how for the longest time, she couldn't forgive her parents for being in a cult and raising her in one. Sometimes our parents really mess us up without even knowing it. There's no way around it, really.' She looked like she'd been whisked away by an old memory she'd tried to bury. 'By the way, did you see Anisha and Joshua in the audience?' she asked me.

I balled my fists angrily. 'God! How could I not? They were right there at the front.'

'He made me nervous,' she said. 'I still miss him sometimes. But I'm glad he ended it.'

'Are you?'

She nodded. She rolled her sleeves up till her arm and showed me old, dried up bruises. 'Cigarette burns.' I pulled the sleeve back down and shook my head. 'Don't.'

'I shouldn't even be missing him. Not now, not ever.' She frowned. 'You know, I think he even took a photo of me sobbing.'

'Who cares? There are people who took happy photos with you. They're probably already telling everyone else about how great tonight was—the way things spread around here.'

She smiled. It felt really nice to see her in a good mood after all that she'd been through. I couldn't remember a time when she hadn't been moping around—up until now.

'Let me do a tarot reading for you. I know, I know. You don't believe in all that, but it's fun. Ask me anything.'

I grabbed the opportunity. 'Tell me about Vikas sir. That day, you told me he was into money laundering.'

'Oh, that. We don't need tarot for that.'

'Tell me anyway.'

'Well, it's not just him, it's the whole Cabinet. During the annual college fest, Solstice, they get big sponsorships from brands, and then eat up half the cash. I know Vikas sir bought himself a shiny red car the last time it happened. Joshua told me.'

'How corrupt!'

She shrugged, as if it didn't surprise her anymore. 'Now ask me something else.'

I didn't believe in her tarot, but I yielded, only because she looked so childlike, so precious as she sat across from me, cross-legged. 'Okay. Tell me something about Bagchi,' I said, trying to look aloof. For some reason, I'd expected him to be at the show, and it had galled me that he'd failed to turn up.

She picked out a card for me that looked like a man being hanged upside down by his ankle. 'The Hanged Man,' Scheher whispered. 'The ultimate surrender.'

'I'm not surrendering to him. He needs to reach out first and apologize for being an abuse apologist.'

'I don't think the cards are talking about the quarrel at the party. I think we're onto something else here.'

'Like what?'

'Well...' She carefully collected her thoughts before she spoke them out loud. 'It's asking you to...er...surrender to your *feelings*.'

I shook my head. 'There are no *feelings*.'

Jolly chose that moment to enter the room. She bustled in with a tray in her hands and announced, 'Tea is served, girls.'

'Thank you so much, aunty,' Scheher said, hurriedly picking up her cards from the bed and stacking them together. 'Wow, I love elaichi in my chai. Just like I make it at home.' Jolly smiled graciously and then carried the tray with the remaining two cups to Tendral's room.

'Speak of the devil again,' I said, looking at my phone, when I was sure Jolly was out of earshot.

'What?'

'Bagchi texted me just now.'

'See! The cards got him thinking of you.'

'Bull,' I said. 'But listen to this. Apparently there's talk among professors to suspend Joshua. I mean, there's going to be an inquiry.'

Scheher leaned forward. 'What are you saying?'

'Your poetry has been doing rounds already. Some students showed up outside the principal's office and caused a ruckus, screaming abuse.'

'At this hour?' she asked, dismayed.

'I know, right? How'd they let them in? Apparently it started with someone calling up the dean and complaining to her. But anyway, to say the least, you've got a lot of new fans. Look,' I said, waving my phone. 'Bagchi's sad he missed out on the show.'

'Oh, please.' She shook her head. 'He's sad he missed out on seeing you. He's not my fan, he's yours. It can't get any more obvious that he's got it bad for you.'

'Really? Is that why he's with Ira?' I asked.

'Frankly, I think they're an odd pair. She's rich and conceited, he's middle class and hardworking. I'm sure the principal hates him, people like that always think nobody's good enough for their perfect little daughter.'

'You should write a soap opera,' I said, sniggering.

Jolly knocked on the door again, and we jumped. I got up,

and grabbed hold of the mugs. 'Karaoke's getting started,' Jolly said. 'Are you two ready to join?'

'Yes,' we said in unison.

Outside, I could hear Pipi already yodelling to his favourite song. I sighed. 'That's not how he sings, by the way.' Scheher looked flabbergasted. 'He's using his Shakira voice.'

'His Shakira voice?' Comprehension dawned on her face. 'Oh, I get it.' She burst into laughter. 'Oh no, that's the wackiest thing I've heard today!'

I was laughing too, by the time we reached the hall. Pipi was jumping around wearing a curly wig, something he had gotten online from a shady seller. He'd ordered a brown one, and received it in ginger instead.

Scheher was fascinated by his bizarre avatar. 'There's no competition, Pipi, we salute you,' she said, shaking her head in incredulity.

Pipi looked at us, tweaking his moustache. 'I'm going to impersonate Britney next.'

Jolly shut her ears with her hands. Tendral clapped in support of him, and Raza looked a little ill.

'This is much better than my show,' Scheher said, moving to the beat and Pipi's off-key tune. 'He's a mastermind.'

Like an accomplished map-maker, Pipi led the way and grooved like he was the star in a concert. It was adorable, and we couldn't help but spin with him. Scheher joined Pipi in a duet on the one condition that he let her borrow his wig. He succumbed, and they sang to the Lion King. Pipi's pace kept betraying him. His two left feet were his biggest enemies. But we loved him, and we wouldn't have traded the night for anything else. I sank into my armchair and rubbed my toes, as Jolly poured all of us a glass of wine each. The songs slowly turned into acoustic covers to avoid the neighbours' wrath, and by two-thirty, with the close of one last acoustic cover, we were ready to turn in. The world was going too fast, and I'd soon find out things were about to change drastically, but that night, in the comfort of our tiny space, everything had slowed down. Just a little bit. Just enough to remind us we were happy, in our own strange ways.

FOURTEEN

The crowd at the National Centre for Performing Arts was terrifying. It was Scheher's highest attended show. I stood in front, and the roar was deafening. People had arrived from cities outside of Bombay to watch her perform. They had tattooed her words on them, worn t-shirts with her quotes, lit up their cell phones to sychronize with her popular poems. After that night at the Bombay Comedy and Music Club, her world had flipped.

A month had passed since then. Scheher had experimented a million times with her look, and had now decided on a high braid, her intense eyes tapering into glitter and gold wings at the sides. There were healing stones on her wrists, sent by a reiki healer she'd met on some forum, which had become an obsession lately.

Spirituality was her new lifeboat. She'd thrown her money at some of the most expensive therapists in the city, and then sworn at them and walked out of their clinics. She'd pored over the copy of Sylvia Plath's poems that I'd bought her, and then she'd gone and bought some more. She'd discovered a book on Neopaganism last week, and now her whole universe revolved around trees that talked and turned into oracles and churned out prophecies.

She was fragmenting. But I didn't know how to point it out without hurting her feelings.

The other day, she'd stood in front of the blackboard with a piece of chalk and voluntarily spoken about manifesting to the whole class. 'This is how it works,' she'd said, scribbling Vikas sir's name on the board. 'Vikas sir is not coming to class today. Repeat after me.'

They had all mumbled it, and she'd written it a couple more times on the board. Just as she'd been about to write it the fifth time, Vikas sir walked into the class and she'd slunk back into her seat, looking cross. 'It doesn't always work, I guess,' she'd said. It would've been funny if Vikas sir hadn't looked so furious.

But who could blame her for trying it all? I still remembered that time Anisha had deliberately stood outside her class so she could heckle her when she walked by.

'She doesn't have any friends,' she'd remarked, shaking her head at the girls who had accompanied her. 'Why is she wearing all that make-up? Joshua's clearly not going to look at her anymore.' And then this other girl had said, '*Accha*, probably doing her face up to hide all those punches and slaps.' God, how it had infuriated her. She'd gone home and drawn the kohl thicker. And every day since then, someone had something to say to that as well.

'You look like a terrorist.'

'What's happening to you, where's all this goth coming from?'

And then, the look became iconic. Everyone began to overdo their eyeshadow, everyone looked like they were in a boxing ring. Everyone wore thick boots and leopard print shirts and rolled up their sleeves and painted their faces.

The fever had caught on.

During her break, I met Scheher in the green room. Half her set was over, and she had another thirty minutes to go. I'd brought in some snacks for her, and a packet drink. 'I loved the second to last one,' I said, leaning against the wall. 'A body's worth of earth to lie in. I want to die for a year and come back only when I'm ready to live again,' I quoted her. 'It really touched my heart. Oh, and by the way, I also saw a lot of agency people in the audience. Overheard one of them saying they were going to book you for some show next month. And...I got you this,' I finished lamely, handing her a bouquet.

'Oh, how pretty! Thank you, Esai. Where are we going for dinner after this?'

'You won't be tired?' I asked.

'I'll be hungry!'

She walked back onto the stage after five minutes. The crowd went berserk, and then settled into curious silence. I held up the banner I'd made just for her, the one with her name on it. She laughed when she saw it, and then her face turned grim, ready for the new set.

The women behind her began to sing. She'd been collaborating with a lot of new and upcoming artistes lately. Their voices spread over one another sweetly. Each alto, tenor, bass wafted into my ears, sprouting wings, learning flight. Uniting and splitting like light through a prism. And then Scheher joined in as the acapella faded out slowly.

'I bled hope into the hollows of strangers' bodies.

When I was done rebounding on them, I gathered my bones again.

I combed the cobra forest of my hair.

I pleated into my ribcage the ghost of a heart...'

NCPA was a success for her. By the end of the show, she'd already been approached by four talent managers, massive

brand collaborations and a six-figure book deal. She'd said yes
to the book deal, and she'd accepted the business cards of the
managers. Some people even asked her to sign their diaries and
write notes in them for their partners.

All the way to Marine Drive, I kept telling her it was no
real surprise, but she was floored by the reaction. 'You don't
understand, Esai, there are a lot of people out there who hate
my art.'

I remembered the first time she had performed. I'd been
one of them. She'd looked deranged that night, with all the
hand flinging and shouting. But things had changed now. I could
see how much she'd grown, how far she'd come. She practised
diligently, day in and day out. She enrolled for vocal training
classes and theatre workshops. She took her art seriously, and
she took herself seriously. I didn't know if I was biased because
she was my friend, but I did see the transformation. I did notice
the glow-up.

She was walking ahead of me, looking like city traffic, drunk
on midnight. She unfolded herself on one of the stone benches
and stared at her feet aimlessly. 'Ever since things began blowing
up for me, I've also been hearing a lot of bad things.'

'Like what?'

She got up again. 'A lot of them are like, she's capitalizing
on her trauma. Or worse, she's faking it. It makes me feel like
an imposter.'

'But you're not.'

'I know, but it gets so noisy at times and I can't seem to
hold on to my identity. And then a lot of them are like, how is
this even poetry? It sounds like talking or rapping or something.
They say I'm basic.'

'But Scheher, that's why it works. Because people understand
it.'

'But maybe it's not literature, you know?'

I stopped in my tracks.

'What?' she asked, stopping with me.

'So what is it that you want? You want to write the kind of poetry that gatekeepers do? You want your listeners to hold a dictionary in their hands while you perform, looking up every word? Poetry isn't about showing off your vocabulary. Poetry is simple, like mother tongue. Like...'

'A weapon made of flowers,' she added. 'A friend who holds your hand through the sleepless dark.'

'Exactly. Poetry is the closest we get to our own hearts. Your purpose, Scheher, isn't to vomit pretty words and frame them in a museum for aristocrats to see and applaud. Didn't you say you were here to dare the world to be vulnerable with you? So dare the world. Don't question yourself like this.'

She toyed with her high braid, pensive. 'You're right. Poetry is meant to be shouted in the streets, not offered like biscuits during high tea.' She laughed. 'Damn, Esai. Look at you.'

I bowed like she had earlier, when the crowd had exploded at NCPA. 'Says the great Scheherazade herself. Oh, what an honour.'

Marine Drive was jammed, but we found a spot, somewhere between two young couples, offended by our interruption; by our loud, magnificent, almost-drunk laughter. Scheher began looking for constellations and identifying them, and I observed the joggers passing by. She tilted her head back and sighed. 'Once I get home, I'm rolling one.'

She gazed at the sky, disappearing into it for a while. We sat there for what felt like a lifetime, until I said to her, 'Are you feeling all right though?'

'Don't worry about me, Esai,' she said. 'You've done your best. Now relax.'

Had I? I could never tell.

I'd taken her out often. I'd even stayed over at her studio.

We'd dressed up and taken so many mirror selfies till my phone began to hang. We'd binged on rum and vintage Bollywood and window shopped and bar hopped. She'd kept saying through it all, 'Esai, you're saving me. Esai, I'll do anything for you. I'd risk my life for you.' But I wasn't trying to save her. I was just being her friend. Our friendship had become a hiding place from campus politics. Between us, there was no politics. It was something very pure and sacred. Scheher had her flaws, and they were evident. She overshared a little too much, she jumped from one thing to the next. One moment she was going to church with her fans and discovering new religions, and the next, she was turning to angel numbers and asking for signs from the universe. I understood that. She just wanted a life she wasn't trying to escape. And she was trying her best to do everything to get it. And I knew she was strange and came with a lot of extra baggage that she couldn't cover up, but I didn't mind. Because by the end of the day, I loved her honesty and innocence. It was such a breath of fresh air. It was inspiring to see how she still held onto herself despite having been chewed and spat out by St. Margaret's. It was rewarding to see her turn that around and make the city love her again. I wanted to be here for it. And I wanted to be here for every road trip to the outskirts of Bombay, every weekend at Powai Lake, every night out discovering one club or the other. Our friendship was the only good thing I'd found in such a hostile campus, and I wanted to dog-ear every moment of it. I wanted to come back to its pages much later, even after the book was closed.

The strangers in Marine Drive were being replaced by new strangers, and the roads were getting thicker with cars. We sat there for a bit longer, and then climbed into a yellow taxi, caught in a silence of the same frequency.

We made our way to Leaping Windows, ordered our food, and sat in their hip underground library. It was sixty rupees per hour to browse or read, and we rummaged through the shelves of Buddhist tales, Naruto, Dragon Ball and the cyberpunk post-apocalyptic manga volumes of Akira. Posters of Star Wars and Calvin and Hobbes were stuck to the back wall. We found a nice cushioned corner with good lighting from the yellow bulbs under black, magician's hats. Old files, unused notebooks, colour pencils and enormous cartons of beer bottles rested under the staircase. When dinner was ready, we walked back to our table upstairs, and gorged on it. Across me, an aspiring actress was sitting with a reasonably well-known director and silently reading a web series script. A little boy was hitting his mother with a balloon stick as she heatedly engaged in conversation with her female friend about her husband's lack of co-parenting skills. A girl sat by herself with her earphones on, studying and making notes. I watched her bite into her cutlet absent-mindedly, spilling cubes of beet onto the ceramic plate. An unfinished lassi stood isolated on one of the tables. I was looking at one of the posters of a popular comic book character when something else caught my attention.

'Scheher, look!' I said, pointing excitedly.

Her eyes grew moist. 'Oh, wow.'

Someone had scribbled a line from one of Scheher's poems on the walls. It said:

You will always find me
in a state of heroic vulnerability.

'It's beautiful,' she said, turning red. 'It's all so beautiful.' Her hands were quivering. I made my way to her side and put an arm around her. 'It is, it is.' We stared at it a few more minutes, but then recognized the possibility of being blamed for it. What if the owners thought we'd put it there? We wrapped up and took off in a hurry.

It was night, but sleep evaded the city. Women ate ice cream on the streets. Children played badminton in their uniforms.

Lovers rode on bikes. Old men slept on the benches of bus stops. Traffic jams turned highways into car parks. Security guards of gated communities gave in to midnight snacks. Dogs picked fights. Cats watched from afar. Friends caught up for a smoke. Bombay was juxtaposed with honking and cheap lighting.

Scheher crashed at mine that night. Nobody was home. We spoke for so long, we got hungry again. So we took over the kitchen and made white sauce pasta. It felt so nice, cooking with her again, for this had somehow become our rite. We took our plates to the room and called it a night. Scheher stepped out with her last Marlboro, and I switched off the lights. From the window, I watched her smoke in silence, and then walk back in after a few minutes.

I pretended to be fast asleep, and she cried herself to sleep.

FIFTEEN

Solstice, the annual college fest, arrived with colourful ribbons, kulfi stalls and graffiti. It sunk its teeth into everyone, it put us all to work. The Cabinet members were suddenly everywhere, carrying banners to different venues on campus, testing the mics at every stage, and micromanaging every team. I saw Ira walk past me at least four times, phone in her hand, co-ordinating with the speakers and the cabs that were sent to pick them up. She had listened to my suggestion of booking a band the students wanted, and because it had been received well, she had consulted me on other things as well. We had spent hours together discussing lantern colours, gifts for the chief guests, and designs for badges and passes.

Meanwhile, Bagchi and Joshua were working together to ensure that all the literary events happened on time. Classrooms were turned into green rooms, and labs were locked so that no accidents happened. Even Vikas sir, whom I'd not seen do anything at all, was standing near one of the smaller stages, a walkie talkie in his hand. When he saw that I was watching him, frown lines appeared between his brows. While he wasn't like Joshua, there was still something about him that threw me off balance. He always made me feel like I'd made a lot of enemies after coming here.

I walked away as soon as I could. Today just wasn't the day for another argument about *Funny Boy*.

I was assigned the backstage with Soha, one of the nicer seniors in my department. I'd never experienced an event on such a grand scale, and there was something about being in the woods that made Solstice wild, feral, so bestial. You could see it in everyone's eyes, in their body language, how the forest had crept into them. The music was loud and felt like a whiplash. Every time the lead singer jumped around and the energy of the band escalated, Soha bounced around in excitement too. Scheher was also on the list of performers, and she was reciting her spoken word poetry on one of the smaller stages.

Just as it was my turn to go grab tea from the counter, I heard a familiar voice barge in. 'Soha, can I borrow one of your juniors to help me out for an odd job? Oh, that one would do.'

I swore under my breath and turned around. Bagchi stood there, hands in his pockets, grinning.

'What's the job?' I asked, five minutes later, marching alongside him as we made our way towards the campus houses. He had on a green tag, the one that third years were given, and a special badge for those who were on the core committee of Solstice.

'We need to get alcohol from Sahaj's place. He lives on campus; his mother's the Head of Department for Visual Communications. Morning batch.'

'Couldn't you have asked just anybody to accompany you in this silly job?' I asked Bagchi. He was walking too fast, and it was getting hard to catch up. Moreover, it was terribly humid, and I was getting grumpier by the minute.

'I needed the eye candy. It's been such a tiring day, and it's still not over. We need some kind of beauty in our everyday life to move ahead, don't you think?' he said, turning around suddenly. I bumped right into him, and the impact left us feeling slightly breathless.

I was the first to speak. 'Apparently you think I should be honoured.'

'Of course.'

'You just called me eye candy.'

'Nothing's a compliment with you, is it? You've always got to argue.' But it didn't sound like he was complaining. He said it as if it was something so very delightful to him.

'How is that a compliment? It's demeaning,' I said.

'How about you relax and let me flirt with you?'

I raised an eyebrow. *So you feel it too, don't you?* I thought. We had begun walking again, but slackened our pace. 'How about you go get some flirting lessons?'

'How about you teach me?' He was grinning now. I realised we had arrived at Sahaj's house, because Bagchi began pulling the gate open.

'I charge ten rupees a minute.'

We were in the front yard. 'Phew. That's expensive.'

Once we reached Sahaj's doorstep, Bagchi took out a key from his pocket and jammed it into the keyhole. It didn't open. 'Wait, this isn't...' And then he began laughing when he realized there had been a grave mishap. 'That silly boy, he's sent his car keys.'

Annoyed, I stood on tiptoe and looked through the window. It was too hot to go back and get the keys. 'Let's break in,' I said.

He looked at me in surprise, and then began laughing harder. I ignored him and pulled out a pen knife from my bag.

'Whoa, girl.'

I looked around to see if anyone was coming, and then slid the knife between the two sashes to force the latch open. Just as it did, his mouth fell open too.

'What? It's a sash window with a basic latch. Of course, it's going to come off.' I climbed through it, and tried to jump onto the other side. I'd done this so many times at home. Jolly would never let me go out after dark for obvious reasons, but I had always been an adventurous child.

He put his hands on my hips and helped me up. My feet hit the soft carpet floor.

I gave him a thumbs up to signal that I had landed safely. I watched him clamber in after me, a little dumbstruck.

It took him longer, because he was taller, and he kept hitting his head. 'Where's the alcohol?' I asked, looking around.

'It's not for you,' he said, folding his arms.

'No commission?'

'No commission.'

Shrugging, I moved towards the storage. He was right behind me, observing, willing goose bumps on the back of my neck. I passed one cardboard box to him, and took hold of the other. Unlatching the front door, we walked straight out, and never spoke about the broken window again.

'Where do we take this now?'

'The Cabinet office. It's been open for the seniors to party.'

'Good for you.'

I'd never been to the Cabinet office before, but I was nonetheless impressed by what the Solstice mania had done to it. The seniors had put up colourful party streamers and balloons all over the place, and the speakers had come out. They were sitting in a circle, distributing cards and jamming to Coke Studio. It was a welcome change to having EDM on blast the entire day. I recognized none of the students there though.

'I know it's called the Cabinet office, but you won't find any of the cabbies here, Esai,' one of the boys said. I didn't ask him how he knew my name. He had a friendly face and a genuine smile. He reached forward and held his hand out.

'It's Harsh, by the way. You've been notorious ever since the whole initiation debacle. As I was saying, ever since Joshua was temporarily dismissed from the Cabinet after the inquiry, they've been under fire. The management has been questioning them and they're dying to prove themselves. So they're out there, slogging their asses off. They'll join us later, when the last band starts playing.' He looked at Bagchi. 'Bro, why are you just standing there? Join us.'

Bagchi shook his head. 'I always lose at this game.'

I crouched down. They were playing poker with real money. Harsh looked at me as if he was issuing a challenge. I took it instantly, and sat down next to him.

All eyes were suddenly on me.

'Don't take her seriously,' Bagchi felt the need to say. 'Do you even know how to play?' he asked, crouching next to me. Everyone ignored him.

'Place the blinds.'

Harsh slapped two cards in front of me. I quickly checked to see what I had.

A few minutes into the game, I raised the bet. Bagchi looked at me like I was deranged, and then tried to peep into my cards when he realized I knew what I was doing. In the final showdown, I was on fire. I put my cards down, facing the ceiling, and they all moved in for a closer look.

'*Kya baat*. A straight flush.'

Bagchi's face had taken on the most satisfying shade of blue. I smirked. 'All this money, it's mine?'

'Look at that greed,' Harsh said in admiration. 'Did you see the look in her eye? Yes, Esai, it's all yours.'

I got up from my seat, picked up a beer bottle from the box, and bowed. They clapped for me and tried to pull me into another game. But I looked at Bagchi and said, 'Let's go.' Bagchi grabbed a bottle for himself and followed me out, still reeling from all that had happened.

'Where are we headed?' he asked, pushing his hair back. It flopped back down again, too wilful to listen to him.

'We? I was thinking of seeing the bonfire they've put up outside the evening canteen.'

'They've got barbecue. I'm coming.'

There were people singing and dancing around the bonfire. Mats had been left for anyone who wanted to sit, huddle and eat. I absolutely loved the vibe. It seemed so cosy, like a civilisation of its own. We found a spot under a Banyan tree, and settled there with our corn on the cob and kebabs. I could hear Scheher's voice from the Mehfil stage, and pride engulfed me.

'She sounds amazing,' Bagchi said, noticing my expression.

'Yes, yes she does,' I said proudly. I was surprised that they'd still allowed her to perform in college. A fortnight ago, Scheher had gone on to create a weekly zine called *Our Bones in Your Throat*, and it had all these small columns contributed by young writers who wanted to expose the college. They spoke about bribes being paid for admission. Exploiting donations. Delays in scholarship funds. Unfortunately, these couldn't be proved, and so nothing could be done about it. Nonetheless, it had made everyone apprehensive about the system. A section was dedicated to St. Margaret's Confessions, where students anonymously spoke up about things they'd seen or done. I heard it later turned into a place to ask someone out. With time, it went from being a dating thread to a dating advice section. Even then, it had been a good initiative, one not a lot of people would have had the nerve to do.

'She reminds me of Sekhmet,' Bagchi said.

'Sekhmet?'

'You know, that lion-headed goddess in Egyptian mythology. The goddess of the desert sun, the plague, the war, and of course, healing. They believed she protected pharaohs. In her calmer state, she became a cat.'

'Sekhmet, indeed.' I thought of Scheher's winged liner and sharp, marble-like eyes. 'You know, it's like she was born for this. And I love her base voice. She switches to this low, menacing tone after the shouting, I don't even know how. But it's like she's growling, and it's remarkable.'

'Word's been going around that she's in talks with big labels. That she'll be signing a record deal soon. Is that something she wants to do? Make an album?'

It was. 'I mean, this is the right time too, because everyone's so curious about her work. And she's been performing at a lot of places these days, she's been really consistent. I think performing poetry has been very therapeutic for her. I know she's been writing a lot of it.'

'And she put out that lyric video recently. That protest poem about the environmental apocalypse.'

The Aarey colony protests had inspired the poem. The colony, with its vast thirteen thousand hectares of land, was the natural habitat of many animals, birds and plants, as well as home to multiple Adivasi villages. Recently, the city's metro rail corporation had received permission from the tree authority to chop down the trees in Aarey. The chief minister and his deputy had announced that a car shed for the metro would be built. It had led to a lot of shock and agitation. Non-profit environmental NGOs and Green activists weren't the only ones who'd protested this deforestation. Hundreds of people including big stars arrived at the spot to voice their disapproval. Scheher had gone as well. I'd found her reading the newspaper one morning, shaking her head, and by evening, she'd been fuming. 'I'm tired of power dynamics everywhere. I'm tired of people walking over the underdog,' she'd kept saying.

'I remember the first time she performed the poem live, somewhere in Khar. She had this tiny monologue right before it. What did she say? Oh, yes.' I smiled. 'I don't give a damn about hot girl summer. I'm more concerned about hot summer. A very, very hot summer because of what we've done to mother earth.'

'I saw a review of it in an arts journal, it was a rave. The editor called it one of the most gripping anthems of our times.'

'And they called her the voice of our generation. We read it together, actually. I asked her how she felt about all that, she told me it was scary. She always feels like an imposter. She keeps saying that, I really don't know why.'

He stretched his legs and leaned back. 'Everyone loves a tragic hero,' he said, after a while.

'She literally said the same thing.'

'Oh?'

'She has these moments when she realizes what's going on.'

'And what exactly is that?'

'Just what you said. Everyone loves a spiralling girl in the spotlight. You know, nobody ever asked her if she was okay when she was going through all that pain. She wrote trauma poetry and she started getting a lot of attention. And now everyone's telling her they love her for her rage and grief. It's going to mess with her head. She's going to think she has to be angry or sad all the time to be loved. She's not going to want to let go of all that hurt. And she's going to be afraid of being happy. I don't think it's healthy for an eighteen-year-old girl. I'm genuinely afraid for her.'

He looked shocked. 'But it's her resilience that people love. Not the pain or fury. She knows that, right?'

I wasn't sure if she did. So I merely shrugged.

'Well,' he said. 'I still think it's all really cool. She blew up, she's doing great, and it's best not to overanalyse these things. After all, there's so much in store for her. She's just getting started.'

'She's just getting started,' I agreed.

'It's mad, how people's lives change so fast.'

I knew he was referring to Scheher, but I thought about Minaxi and how everything had dissociated for her after initiation day. How one decision had marked her an outlaw and had haunted her through the rest of her time at St. Margaret's. People's lives did change in a day, in a second, for better or for worse. And there was nothing you could do about it.

'It changes badly sometimes,' he continued, reading my thoughts. Our shoulders were touching, igniting. I had a distinct awareness that I had entered a world similar in loneliness to mine. The world of a young boy who had been prey to life's merciless circumstances. I inched closer, unsure of how I could provide comfort. I wondered if he sensed it too, the succulent warmth of our thighs overlapping the soil near the roots, the impression of his toe on my denim. The feeling of sharing something so personal with someone as your bones settled into theirs for a while.

'Who left?' I asked. I sat up straight, and stared at him with rapt attention. My gut told me he was about to tell me something deeply personal. And I wanted to be fully present.

'My brother.'

'I'm sorry.'

Bagchi's eyes focused on the bonfire and the people dancing around it. For a while, he looked like he'd been transported elsewhere. And then he began. 'My younger brother started falling sick when he was nine...' He turned to me, and I nodded in support. *I'm listening. You can talk to me.*

'We had to get him out of school. Papa spent all the money on his hospital bills, and that went on for a few years. I still remember, towards the end, he had all these bed sores on his back, and tubes running through his nose. I couldn't even recognize him, that's how thin he'd become. He didn't make it. By the time it was all over, we had a lot of loans to repay. A lot.' He squeezed his eyes shut. I wanted to put my palm over his, but I wasn't sure if I would be overstepping a boundary. So I simply sat there, waiting for him to pick up from where he left off.

'We were...poor. Papa never studied past standard twelve, so he was working as a security guard. I did a lot of random jobs, helped load timber on trucks, worked as a cook in rich people's houses, learned to talk like them. I went to school as much as I could, and I wasn't doing as great as I could have, but I made it into higher secondary, and found work typing and sitting at desks as a receptionist, and the pay was suddenly higher. A friend taught me Photoshop, another gifted me article editing skills, and because of that, new work began coming in. We got by.' He looked at me, his eyes a little moist. The fire and the people and everything around us turned indistinct. Bagchi's face fogged up my entire vision. I could feel myself moving closer and putting an arm around his shoulder. 'I am proud of you,' was all I could manage to say. He lightly bumped the side of his head against mine and smiled. 'Thank you. My parents are not dependent on me for money anymore, but I still send something every month. It's become a habit.' He suddenly realized we were sitting a little too close, and pulled away. My hands continued to prickle. 'I've never shared that with anyone. Not even with Ira.'

'That's okay. I've had a lot of people tell me it's easy to open up to me.'

'It certainly is.' He looked down at his hands, traced his lifeline distractedly. 'The thing with Ira is...she'd never understand any of it.'

'As in?'

'She's never had it rough. I know I can't say that, I mean, everyone's got their own baggage to deal with, right? I know her father is really overbearing, that he really expects a lot from her. That whole family is like that, has been for generations. It's probably what made her so emotionally unavailable anyway. I don't doubt for a second she hasn't got her own issues, that's what I'm trying to say. But...' He scratched his head, trying to understand how to put the words together without sounding critical. 'She'll never know what it's like being poor. She's had the privilege of not being the breadwinner of her family. Since she was a little girl, she's had the luxury of vacationing in Paris. Istanbul. Hong Kong. Wearing brand new clothes. Branded clothes. Eating all the chocolate in the world. I sound stupid, don't I? We're not children anymore, none of this should matter...' he trailed off. 'Especially chocolate.'

'Chocolate always matters.' I smiled. 'Don't feel guilty about this. Sometimes our inner child still craves those things. Or at least remembers the absence of them.'

'Maybe. We always remember absence.' He looked away. 'I'm doing good now, but those old wounds never seem to go away.'

'I know what you mean. It's like the past is always lurking.'

'And there are people in the present who remind you of that. Who make you feel as horrible as you did at your worst. Ira's father thinks I'm not good enough for her. He's always treating me like I'm trash. Like she could do so much better. I always get this feeling that I'm just around. Like I'm the filler boy.'

'Filler boy?' I asked, taken aback.

'Like I'm a placeholder till the real deal comes along. She'll find some rich businessman to marry years down the line, when I'm still working to repay the last of my family's loans.'

'Ouch. Have you talked to her about it?'

'Would you?' He looked at me sharply.

'I'm not dating the principal's daughter.'

'I can't ask her if I'm just a substitute for her dream man. That would be a little too much.'

'Why? It's just honest communication.' I leaned forward and hugged my knees. I had no business interfering, but he sounded so sad, and I would have done anything to make him feel better. 'Like right now. You could tell me anything you want and not feel stupid, right?'

'That's...different. It's different,' was all he could say.

Cool blue swirled above us like an overspread. Tucked under the tenderness of dusk, we drifted towards and away from each other, conversing seamlessly and then choosing to let go, as if we were a kiss shared between two enemy countries. As if anything between us was soap scented live wire.

He placed his palms on the ground and looked up at the sky. The music and the bonfire added to its beauty. 'Man, what I'd give to be closer to that,' he said, caught in a dreamscape of his own.

'That's easy.' I got up and offered him my hand. He took it, but didn't get up immediately. 'There's a spot in the woods where the sky looks like a parallel universe. You feel so sucked into it,' I said.

'Really?' Interest flashed in his eyes.

'When you sit there, you feel all of existence. You feel... excruciatingly alive. Right under the stars, all your energy points exploding. All at once, you're everything and nothing. I'll show you. Come on, I'll show you.'

And so, downing the last swig of beer, I led him into the forest.

SIXTEEN

'What did you think of Girish Karnad?'

It was pitch dark now, and I could barely hear the EDM from the main ground. Even the chatter near the bonfire had quietened, and the clicking of beetles had taken over. We walked past the two striking white frangipani trees near the sports ground, doubling as a habitat to a three-legged squirrel. The marigold, orchid and chrysanthemum amidst the shrubs. The army of grey parrots crowding near the deserted swing. I could hear cuckoos competing with one another, and a rare, elusive peacock slipping into the shadows. The whisper of a waterfall beckoned somewhere near the infamous lake. The forest watched us discreetly. If I slit its chest, I would unearth richness, radiance and dirty, messy things. A bygone culture of beauty and bullshit.

'The female protagonist reminded me a lot of an old St. Margaret's student,' I said. My heart accelerated, knowing it was about to enter uncharted territory.

'Who?' Somewhere, a dog howled. An eagle watched with its sharp, round eyes.

'Minaxi,' I said. We'd never spoken about this. He'd

mentioned it in passing that one time I'd caught him near the lake with Ira; and even then, it had felt like a closed chapter.

'Minaxi?' *Let's not go there,* his eyes willed. But I wanted to, I would.

'All that loneliness, the emotional need to be loved.'

'I don't know what you mean by that.'

I hesitated. Could I tell him what I'd seen? The changing lake that was sometimes a mirror, and the music and the romance with the man who now owned St. Margaret's? About how she'd rejected initiation and in turn, they'd made her out to be an exile? About Nanda sir's morose story of Katharina Kepler and how eerily similar it sounded to Minaxi's fate? What would he think of me? Perhaps that I was insane. Or if he didn't, he would still chastise me for being where I shouldn't have been. No, I wouldn't tell him. 'I just feel like she's not as horrible as people have made her out to be, you know?' I said.

'You're feeling bad for her? Esai, this is the same person who tried to drown a child. And probably killed it.' He looked disappointed. 'I don't get you at all.'

He wouldn't understand. Nobody would unless they'd seen what I had. I had half a mind to take him to the place where I had seen her dreams. But what if she wasn't even there this time? Or what if she refused to show him what she'd shown me?

I looked at the path towards the lake. Pitch dark. Pin drop silence. Not a single leaf swayed. No bird sang. No, she'd made it clear. He wasn't welcome.

'No. I mean it,' I said adamantly. 'How do we know if any of that's true?'

'How do we know it's not?'

I took another route. 'I've heard a lot of ugly things about people since I got here. To the point where I just don't know what to believe anymore. But I'd like to believe Minaxi was innocent.'

He looked at me carefully. 'Is there any reason you would say that?'

'Because when I heard people say terrible things about Scheher, I didn't believe any of them. I'm glad I knew her enough to fight the lies. You know what I'm talking about.'

He didn't argue with me about that. 'I know. I was there half the time they were discussing things about her in the boys' hostels.'

'I don't want to hear any more of it. Even in the midst of it, I avoided it.'

He nodded. 'It made me uncomfortable too. It wasn't right.' He stepped on a branch and it cracked under his weight. 'So you're saying people did that with Minaxi too? Now that we're actually talking about her, there's something I want to confess. I wouldn't be surprised if she didn't even exist.'

'Oh, she did,' I said darkly. I couldn't tell him everything, but for the time being, I would at least tell him about the research I'd done. He couldn't be upset with me over that, could he? I wasn't putting myself in any danger. 'There's this tiny article about her in an old newspaper. It's very brief. College student drowns in a lake. Not a lot of information there. But she was real.' I had found that article in the archives while browsing for old newspapers on the library's computer. I had to leave on an advanced search, and yet I hadn't been able to find anything more. The black and white photo of the girl in braids had been nothing compared to what I'd seen in my dreams.

He scratched his head, still flummoxed. 'All right. So she was real. And then people just made gigantic rumours about her until she became a myth?'

I nodded. 'People like tea.'

'But something as atrocious as baby sacrifices and water ghouls?'

I didn't know why, but I thought I heard footsteps behind

us. 'They'd lap anything up,' I said, a little alert. 'It's all about presentation. About narrative, good storytelling.'

'As in?'

'Well,' I said. 'Think of what you said about Scheher. Everyone likes a tragic hero. In fact, everyone loves it. They love theatrics, they love drama, they love things that are hard to believe. That's why folktales work. They've been around since forever, why aren't they extinct yet? Why do we have ghost stories and why do we believe all the boys who said they screwed Scheher? Because that is exactly what we want to hear. The juicier it is, the more interested we get. Ordinary tea dies out. It doesn't make the cut. For tea to be worthy of being spilled forever, it needs...'

'Flavour.'

'*Flavour.*'

We looked at each other for a fleeting moment. 'You add a bit of ginger.'

'And then someone comes in and adds cinnamon.'

'Tulsi. Jaggery. Cardamom. Tea is served. Tea is spilled.'

'For years and years to come.'

'We made it together. We all pitched in.'

'Fun, isn't it?'

We looked at each other and burst into laughter. 'So that's how it goes,' Bagchi said.

He had such a friendly, approachable face. When he smiled, I was reminded of the sun sifting through the trees on campus. His eyebrows were thick and shapeless. He had one pointy vampire tooth on the left. His dimple was a little too deep. Even when he spoke, it showed. His hair was a tad bit too choppy. But all these imperfections only added more character to his face.

'What're you staring at?' he asked.

I shook my head, embarrassed that he'd noticed. 'Nothing.'

He didn't look like he believed me, so I quickly added, 'Now you know why I think Minaxi wasn't a witch.'

The moment I said her name, I heard the footsteps behind us multiply. I quickly spun around. There was nobody there.

'Esai, what's wrong?'

Did you hear that? 'Nothing.'

'Hmm.' He stroked my head. The eerie sound of anklets stopped, and I felt myself skidding into the comfort of his touch. 'You have a big heart, Esai,' he said. 'You see the best in people.'

'And you don't?'

He shook his head. 'I'm not saying I don't believe what you're saying about all that lake nonsense. They probably built something up when it wasn't there in the first place. But with people, it's so confusing. It's hard to see the best in them, and sometimes they don't even deserve it. I'd be a loser to expect goodness in such a wicked world.'

'You've been surrounded by the wrong people in life, then.'

He raised one eyebrow. 'Oh? Is that so?'

'Damn right, it is.'

'I'm mending my ways. That's why I'm hanging out with you.' *That's why I'm hanging out with you*, I thought. I couldn't have cared less about the Cabinet had he not chased me to help them out. They were all egoistic, power hungry and patronizing. But they were Bagchi's friends. And Bagchi was my friend.

I smiled lopsidedly. 'And here I was, thinking that it was because you liked me.'

'I like you,' he replied curtly, and all at once, the lightness evaporated, like changing seasons. I was left with my own obsessive thoughts again. What did he say? He *liked* me.

But not as much, I thought. Not enough.

And there it was again, a ghost between us, an uninvited third party; looming above our heads, inserting itself in the space that separated us, like an accusation. If he was with Ira, what was he doing here? And what was he doing with Ira anyway? She was always going to look down upon him, laugh at him with friends like Joshua, make him feel like he belonged nowhere. But he'd said it himself, he was with a woman who never had to work for a single thing all her life—because the world had already belonged to her from the very moment she was born.

'Here's the spot,' I said, looking up. I swayed a bit as I gravitated towards him and pulled him forward.

'The oak tree?'

I put one hand on the bark and nodded at him. I wasn't yet sober enough to do this, but then again, neither was he. Fool's courage took over again. 'Come on up.'

'So you play poker and climb trees? What are you?'

'A leprechaun,' I said friskily. 'Loosen up, *kid*. When was the last time you did something like this?'

'When I was eight.'

'And now you're eighteen.'

'Don't make random things sound significant.'

I giggled. 'Just trust me.' His eyes deepened with questions. I held out my hand and he took it.

I helped him reach the top, and we sat on one of the sturdier branches, our legs dangling in mid-air. 'Aren't you scared of anything?' he asked.

I shrugged. 'The only thing I'm afraid of is being a coward.'

'Fair enough.'

'Look up,' I said, pointing at the stars. A beautiful smile spread across his face as he did, and I let myself steal a glance. There was something so sincere about him. He reminded me of second-hand bookshops and old guitars. Children's fiction by the fireplace, bare feet on a carpet floor. And here I was, leaves sticking out of my hair, brutal to the bone and knee-deep in catastrophe. In a way, I was just as wrong for him as Ira was. He needed someone merciful, someone he could trust to keep his heart safe.

'Look!' he said, and my head snapped up. Red, blue and green erupted in the air, dazzling me. 'Fireworks? Fireworks!' I screamed.

'They do this every year during Solstice,' he explained, pleased to see how thrilled I was. The colours cast a red hue to his eyes. His face was illuminated. I was so caught up in the sight that I didn't realize he was looking at me.

'Your hair looks so wild in this light,' he said, thumbing my cheek like a delicate brush stroke. One finger traced the coastline of my neck, making carvings more sacred than Egyptian hieroglyphs. 'Pretty.' He looked at me hungrily, and I nodded. 'Yes,' I whispered. I slowly took his hand and dipped his fingers into my collarbone. And then I dragged them along the buttons of my shirt. His eyes widened.

Everything stilled. Everything moved. The buzz from the alcohol had disappeared now. All at once, it was replaced by something else. The stars were everywhere. Glow worms stopped and stared.

Could a kiss go from ghost to full flesh, full blood? Breathing, heaving, thriving? He leaned in, and I thought the world was combusting.

He placed a thumb and index finger on my chin. Tilted it up slightly to face him. And then he rested one hand on my cheek. I turned into it and pressed my mouth onto his palm. Seconds passed. And then a leaf fell on my shoulder, and I jumped. He quickly grabbed my arm, to stop me from falling. 'Esai,' he said, his voice a little hoarse.

'Yes?'

'Let's head back. This is dangerous.' I wasn't sure if he was talking about sitting on a tree or what we'd just done.

He led me back down the tree, and I followed. As we were about to reach the ground, I almost slipped, and he caught me by the waist. He had one arm on my back, exactly over the hook of my bra. The other hand had slid to my hip, and for a moment, we stood like that. Was he contemplating? Was he about to change his mind? I didn't know. All I knew was that the eye contact was killing me, and I could feel electricity bills rising with tension like this. 'Bagchi,' I said. Even my voice sounded strange to me. He didn't respond. Our faces were so close that our lips were almost brushing against each other. 'Are you going to kiss me?' *I want you to.*

He circled my wrists and pinned them to the bark of the tree. I felt myself being driven into it like a nail; being lifted, my legs over his torso. We were kissing now, and my top was rolled up, stripped off like an orange peel. I could hear the sound of our breaths, and it was suddenly all I could hear despite the crickets and the faraway laughter and the leaves in the wind.

I clutched the front of his shirt, felt a fistful of cotton crumple against my skin. His hands were on my waist, and mine were in his hair. Deftly exploring. An eager nomad to the curls.

He caressed my face. He pulled at my lower lip with his two fingers. He licked my ear.

I had the urge to run naked, shouting eureka like a maniac. Like him and I were some monumental discovery whose dynamics we were yet to figure. Like he was light, and I was all kinds of heliotropism. Like I'd just chanced upon photosynthesis.

It was the sound of the second fireworks show that snapped us out of our delirium. He came up for air, and then took a step back, still swaying from the impact. His hands were in his pockets again. I picked my top from the branch and put it back on. He watched me dress. I took my own sweet time so that I could watch him watch me. The two of us had this scorching look in our dilated pupils, a pounding, clandestine glory. I was convinced by the flecks of gold in his eyes and every possibility of history repeating itself, that it was the same look our ancestors had, millions of years ago—the night they stole fire from the Gods. So why had he stopped?

'We should really go back now,' he said.

No, I don't want to.

'Esai?' he said, confirming with me. I nodded unhappily. 'Sure. Let's go.'

After that, all the way to the bonfire, we barely said a thing. There had been nothing left to say. Was he thinking about Ira? Was he feeling guilty about what had happened? I could feel the warmth from his body, still intact, despite the calculative distance from me. But there was nothing I could do. I was disappointed, but I wasn't going to let him know.

We were about to reach the main area, when I saw her again—the Lake Woman. My heart swerved, crashed. Had I not turned, I would have never noticed her. But I'd heard the humming again, and the farther I got from the woods, the louder the cry for help became. She was standing near the trees and staring at me, not moving an inch as if she wasn't allowed. As if the lake was her harbour, her grave. As if the forest had drawn an unforgivable boundary for her own safety. She was in her wet white gown, and suddenly, all I could hear was song, through and through.

I squeezed Bagchi's elbow. 'I'll be right back.'

'Wait. Where are you going?'

I didn't reply. I ran straight back into the forest.

SEVENTEEN

Only when I reached the lake did I realize I'd been lured. At some point, I fainted. At some point, I was floating on bioluminescent water. Rubies and diamonds glistened against my skin, and I crashed into oblivion.

I heard shouting, and I followed the voices. There was a door held ajar, and I walked right in—into a woman slightly taller than me, and suddenly, the anger in her voice came over mine.

'You stood with them!' I cried. I was long-faced again. My shoulders were broader; my torso was wider. I was in a nightdress, and my hair was all scrunched up. My whole body was shaking in fury.

'I didn't, Minaxi! I had to say something to escape, didn't I?' the boy standing opposite me said. I rubbed my eyes. I knew him, I knew him.

Laxman Dalvi. The younger version.

I couldn't focus. My heart was racing, and I could taste the blood in my mouth from gritting my teeth too hard. With shivering hands, I opened the bottle of antidepressants and held one in my palm.

'So you go and say, yes, Minaxi's crazy, I've seen her take medication for it?'

'*They* said you were crazy,' he cried. 'I mean, they didn't know about the medication...'

'And you offered them that information. Yes, Laxman?' He hated it when I used his full name. Only his father called him *Laxman*, and it was always in that tone.

'I didn't know you were trying to hide it. You never told me not to tell anyone,' he mumbled, defensive about being caught.

'I hide it,' I said, closing my eyes. 'Because instead of trying to understand my condition, insensitive fools like you and them call me *crazy*. And that does not help me.'

He didn't say anything to that. Instead, he said, 'You should've agreed to the initiation. You should have just gone through with it.'

I couldn't stand that he said that. But this was something else entirely. This was what traitors did.

'So all this is my fault because I didn't go through with it?' I said. 'Right, right, I should've seen it coming! Them isolating me and turning everyone against me and calling me...crazy? Because I broke down in public? They destroyed my project, Lax! They drove me to the edge.' I rubbed my forehead. 'And now you've confirmed their suspicions. You've gone ahead and told them I'm on pills for my crazy. Don't you see how you've made everything worse?'

We were standing in the middle of the hall, in his big, Viking house. We couldn't stop shouting at each other. This wasn't the first time. Ever since initiation, we'd been in a bad place. Our ideologies didn't match. He had tried to persuade me to join in, and I'd tried to get him to miss it. Why had he done it? Out of fear? Now that I knew him well enough, I could tell that his entire life had been dominated by that same pattern: being afraid of what people would say. He blamed it on his father raising him with harsh discipline, but the way I saw it now, he was just choosing to be a coward.

What a pity. He'd told me he loved me a few hours before they'd initiated him. And I'd told him I loved him back after he got off that ugly chair they'd made him stand on. The chair, a geographical reference line; splitting us into two time zones. How could we possibly think we could be together? Of course, for the first few weeks, everything had been rosy and perfect. And then Lax had become friends with more seniors, and I'd had none. And somehow, their approval of me had meant everything to him. And because I hadn't been good enough in their eyes, he'd begun to avoid being seen with me in public. I'd hated the hypocrisy, and every time I'd tried to leave because of it, he'd stormed and thrown a tantrum and then begged for me to stay. *They don't know me like you do*, he'd said. *I can't talk to them the way I talk to you.*

Well, I wasn't going to put up with it anymore.

'Don't talk to me. I don't want to be friends with you anymore,' I said brashly.

'What do you mean? I'm literally your only friend,' he said.

That hit a nerve, but I didn't show it. 'It's fine. I'll survive.'

He sat on the chair, looking devastated. 'I won't.'

I looked at him quizzically. 'Our whole batch and a lot of the seniors are friends with you. What more do you want?'

'It's not the same,' he said. 'I mean, it's nice to drink and party with them, but there's nothing to talk about. The conversations don't feel real.'

'You make me sad, Lax.'

'This isn't what's bothering you,' he said, on the defence again. 'There's something else on your mind, and it's eating you up, isn't it? I can feel it.'

There were many things on my mind, in fact, that were eating me up. But I couldn't bring myself to tell him about what Diksha from Biology had told her boyfriend when I was passing them by. They thought I hadn't heard, because I'd been wearing headphones. It was what I did, every time I had a feeling someone was talking about me. I'd pretend like I was listening to music so that I couldn't be so obviously, publicly shamed. But I knew every single word that came out of their mouths. It punched me in the stomach, it choked my soul. At rock bottom, I heard their voices over and over again. Telling me I was pathetic, eating alone in the canteen like that. Telling one another, *oh, Minaxi is such a waste of space. That's what happens to people who aren't initiated.* I couldn't bring myself to tell him I had stopped writing to Marie Curie, stopped following Science journals, stopped doing anything I loved.

Not being old enough to die, but being old enough to know what dying felt like. It was happening to me, this slow decay, and I wasn't even fighting it anymore. When was the last time I'd actually tried to look beautiful? Combed my hair, looked into the mirror, been an actual person? When was the last time I'd felt good about myself, happy about my life? I barely remembered.

Staying afloat—when did it become this hard?

'What is it?' he asked again, a little impatiently.

I opened my mouth to say something, and then shut it hard and tight. 'Nothing. Just the usual.'

What is it? What is it? What is it?

It was Riddhi locking me up in the bathroom with her and asking me college facts I refused to answer. It was Riddhi slapping me every time I got it wrong, and then hissing, 'Why can't you just do it? We all did it, what makes you so special? You're so arrogant. No wonder the seniors hate you.' It was Bharat chasing away the only friends I ever had and forcing them to stop talking to me. Threatening to isolate them from the rest if they stood with *vipers* like me. It was the Science experiment mess and the agony and the rage I made the mistake of feeling. It was the damned chair I threw, it was the way Shyam and his friends accosted me one day on campus and made me cry so bad I thought my insides were damaged. I'd been walking, I'd been by myself, and they'd all appeared out of nowhere, yelling. I'd crumpled to the ground, and I'd covered my head as if the sky was falling. It had been sundown by the time the dean, Sonali ma'am, saw me and dispersed them. She'd taken me to the day cafe, she'd bought me some filter coffee. The compassion had only ruined me more. Sometimes the worst thing that could happen to the broken was a stranger's empathy. When they looked right into you and treated you the way you should have been treated all along, it hit you. You knew you were too far gone to even understand it, but it still found its way to you.

It was all of it, and how I was on the verge of losing it. It was the professors, and how they closed their eyes when you needed them the most because it was easier that way. It was how people older than you kept telling you to open up to them, but when you did, it was always your fault.

And last, but not least, it was Laxman. Laxman, and how I could no longer tell if he was really being my friend, or if he was taking advantage of what a train wreck I was. Kissing me just because he could. And all I could do, all I could do was hope to God he wasn't stringing me along.

I had to get myself to trust him. He was all I had.

Sighing, I said to him, 'Tell me again what happened? Maybe it wasn't such a bad thing, after all.'

He was unbearably thrilled that I'd given him a second chance. It wasn't his fault, he kept saying. Gokul, that big, tall third year from the Social Work department had stopped him and told him to stay away from me. I didn't even know Gokul. And yet, he had decided to make my life difficult for me.

'He said, now that you're initiated, you shouldn't be with Minaxi. I told him that we just talk, that we aren't very close. You know, right, that I had to lie to him?'

No, I didn't. And I didn't hear half of what he was saying either. His voice trailed off, and I found myself in a different place. Back home, with my sister, as we played kabaddi with the other children. Buying my first birthday gift for her, after receiving my first salary from a side job. It had been a pen, nothing elaborate, but she had been so happy. I'd been happy.

St. Margaret's had turned me lonely. And because Laxman really was the only friend I had, I forgave him.

I had disappeared so deep into my thoughts that I hadn't even realized he'd asked me a question. 'What?'

'Why are your hands bruised?' he asked me, pointing at the blueness of my knuckles.

I told him about the girls in the hostel who had locked me inside the bathroom while I was showering. They'd heard me humming, and known it was me.

'I was thumping, banging, trying to knock the door down until I got really anxious. I ended up fainting,' I said.

He took my hands in his and massaged them. 'You should complain.'

'I wrote a complaint letter to the warden, but she likes those girls. She doesn't listen to me.'

'Don't stay there, then. Get out of the hostel.'

He made it sound like it was such an easy option. Where could I go? I didn't have parents I could live with. I only had my sister. And how could I even ask her to come stay with me? I'd left her in boarding school, and that had made me feel bad enough. How could I uproot her from there, ruin her studies, her future, just because I was miserable?

I looked at him desolately. He noticed tears springing up in my eyes. 'We'll find a way, okay? Once we're done with college,' he said hastily. 'We'll get jobs, and then we'll get married, and then, you know the rest.'

'No, I don't,' I said, smiling. I wanted to believe him so badly, because a part of me loved him so much. I was empty and he made the bad days bearable. It wasn't a good reason to love someone, but I couldn't help feeling what I did. I wanted to be the one who smoothed the creases on his forehead, I wanted to be the one who made his bed. I wanted to read classic novels and wear woollen socks and exchange sweet nothings and share grocery lists for the rest of my life with him. I wanted to snuggle in the daylight with the curtains closed, I wanted it all. It sounded like a good life, a safe life.

Did he really mean it? Or was he saying it all in a state of passion? Was I allowed to hope for something real? God, I was so ashamed of the way I felt about it, how much I hinged on him for my happiness.

I put my palm on his thigh, and for a moment, I had this odd feeling that he flickered. Almost as if he was a hologram, a glitch from another time. He sat there, motionless, as I tried to make sense of what was happening. Somewhere, in the distance, I heard someone calling out for me, but it sounded distorted.

'Do you hear that?'

'What?' His voice sounded distant. I walked up to the door.

I turned the knob and looked outside. It was drizzling, and the forest felt like it was asleep. As I stepped out, the cold wind hula-hooped through my night dress.

If it was a dream, it was lucid. I stood there, eyes closed. Trees were starkly set against strips of lilac sky. Spring was around the corner, I was sure. The clouds teased one other, fleecy white crystals drifting into a storm. Somewhere, thunder purred, and a flash of lightning somersaulted into itself, cleaving the atmosphere before disappearing again.

There was a girl running towards me somewhere ahead,

and she was me. Or maybe I was her. I didn't know if I was supposed to turn back and shut the door on her, or move in her direction.

'Lax?' I said, my throat parched. But he wasn't there.

She was now right in front of me. 'Let's go,' she said. 'Let's go, Esai.'

'Where?'

She didn't reply. Instead, she put a hand on my chest, and all at once, the world was a big, gaping hole. I woke up in a pile of leaves, and then my bed.

EIGHTEEN

✿

The morning after Solstice was hell.

I was late for class, but I had a feeling so was everyone else. Our most anticipated college fest had officially ended, and I'd woken up hungover, with whisker burns on the outskirts of my mouth and Tibetan singing bowls vibrating in my chest. I tried calling Scheher to ask her if she was going to class, but she didn't answer.

There was a rumour going around that Bagchi had gotten so drunk with his friends after I'd gone back into the forest that he'd passed out near the fire and almost burnt his foot. Another one went like this: he'd been caught with his beer buddies by Vikas sir in a forbidden part of the campus, and they'd been causing quite the ruckus. Vikas sir had yelled at them for almost half an hour, and when he'd been done with them, most of the boys were reduced to tears. 'No more messing around,' Vikas sir had ordered, and they'd all nodded.

And then Bagchi had slurred in the most comical way, 'Sir... did you say something?'

The boys could have killed him.

In another version, they actually did. I thought he would've looked pretty on a stake.

When I was done with my shower and went down, I saw Jolly sitting on the floor and applying henna on her hair. 'Wait, wait. I'm making upma for breakfast,' she said. But I was already running late, so I had to skip it. She called out to me, despairing at how this was becoming a habit, and I promised I'd come back and eat all of it.

I entered through the back gate of the campus, and sprung past the magnolias and starved crows staring at me unflinchingly. What was this stillness? When had the place been turned to stone? I was just about to move into the Arts block when I saw from where I stood, the gathering of a big crowd near the main stage, where Solstice had taken place last night. They hadn't taken down the huge banners yet, and if not for the muffled shouting, I would have easily assumed that the students there were volunteers undoing the set-up. I was about to make my way towards the flock, when Bagchi called. It sounded urgent. 'Are you on campus? Come to the Student Union, please?'

Curious, I went.

The Cabinet members were sitting in terse silence. The first pair of eyes that met me were Ira's. She was standing at the end of a long table, the kind that reminded me of The Last Supper painting, and the other Cabinet members were seated in their respective places, all looking grim and ashen. 'Good, she's here.' And then I saw Bagchi, who looked just as hungover as I was.

'We usually don't have meetings right after Solstice, because we're all very tired,' Bagchi said, rubbing his forehead. 'But Ira seems to have something important to say.' He looked annoyed.

'Scheherazade's zine,' Ira said, and looked around, waiting for everyone's response. 'I didn't have time to address this because Solstice had been on my mind for the past few weeks. But I think now, we better talk about it. Do something about it.'

Our Bones in Your Throat had become extremely popular. Zines had never been this widely read in college, but because of Scheher's rising stardom and also the controversial subject of *Our Bones in Your Throat*, it was doing incredibly well. And there was really nothing Ira could do about it. They could ban its circulation, but that could create unrest. Nobody liked censorship. They were bound to start a fight, and she knew it.

The zine was sold cheap, and it sold out fast. I couldn't get my hands on even a single issue, but Ira did. She was not pleased at all.

'Just look at this,' she said, waving the glossy ten-pager in front of us. The cover had weird art and looked like something you'd usually see on a rock 'n' roll drummer's t-shirt.

'Yes,' Bagchi said. 'I have the entire collection.'

Anisha pinched the place between her eyes, looking revolted.

'Well, it's becoming a bit of a problem,' Ira said. I grabbed the zine and read through it. It was beautiful. It had articles on cultural history and socio-political cartoons and comics. Some of the personal essays were really poignant and stirring. The pages in the middle were reserved for bringing grievances to light. Calling out injustice within the gates of St. Margaret's and outside of it. Haikus and contemporary sonnets bridged the gap between the non-fiction pieces. It was so well put together. I now knew why it sold out so early every single time.

'This is...propaganda,' Ira said. 'I mean, she's exaggerated everything.'

'So it's true in some way?' I asked.

'Some of it, yes. But she's made us look really bad. We're not that bad.' She looked nauseous. 'I want this gone. I want this banned. I'm going to talk to Papa.'

'What do we do now?' Anisha asked.

'You can lay low,' I suggested. 'Assignment deadlines are coming. Everyone's going to get busy.'

Ira looked downcast. 'I hope so. But you can't do anything?'

'As in?'

'She's your friend. Talk to her?'

I shook my head. Bagchi intervened. 'You don't need to ambush her. You just need to have a conversation with her.'

'I won't do it, sorry.' So this was why they'd called me in.

'We don't need this drama right now,' Ira groaned, and nobody said a word. 'Papa called her in a few days ago and tried to talk to her. Said we wouldn't tolerate anything anti-college. She was so polite to him, and then she went back and wrote about it in the zine. She's nothing but a hot mess with a messiah complex.'

'Can't she be suspended?' Anisha asked.

'I mean, we could say she's defaming us. But so much of it is true. We can't deny the trees being cut on campus. We can't deny that the warden in one of the hostels yelled at a girl for wearing a sleeveless shirt. And we need a valid reason to send her away. It's not looking good for us. We need a strategy.' She placed her hands on the table and sighed. 'I hate how she's got them wound around her little finger.'

'That's how mobs work,' Anisha said, sullen.

'We need to get them to dislike her.' She looked at me. 'We need to spoil her reputation. She's your friend. Any secrets you know of hers we can spill to the public?'

'No,' I said firmly. I couldn't believe that they thought I would deceive Scheher like that.

Bagchi shook his head, looking disturbed. 'Ira, just listen to yourself. This isn't the way.'

'But...' Ira looked around for support. Nobody caved in.

'None of us like what's going on, but let's not be petty,' Anisha said. I was startled by her remark, because she had always been Ira's yes girl. And then she pointed at me. 'Also, I'm not sure we should be trusting her.'

'She can be trusted,' Bagchi said, cutting her off. 'Also, I think we need a strategy that'll get people to like us, instead of trying to make them hate Scheher.' He looked at me for support.

I nodded. 'I think it'll be good for you if you're on their side and not against. You want to get them to trust you. So stand with them for all their problems, tell them their anger is justified. Make them feel heard. Because often...'

Ira raised her eyebrows. 'Often what?'

I looked at her doubtfully. I hoped I wasn't crossing a line. 'Often you give the impression of being unapproachable. Intimidating. What is appealing about Scheher is that she's not just their idol. She's their friend too. If you've seen her interacting with them, you'd know. She's fierce, but she's also so kind. So be their friend. Stand up for them, put them first. Let them know you can be the first person to run to when things don't go the way they want.'

'I don't know how Papa's going to take that,' she mumbled under her breath.

'The only way they'll honour you as their chairwoman is if you stand up to him once in a while. They'll need to know you're theirs, not the system's.'

'So basically, she's trying to say, don't be the principal's little puppet,' Anisha said snarkily.

Ira shot her a dirty look. 'Is that what you guys think I am?'

Bagchi sensed a small fight brewing, and intervened. 'I think this is a good idea, being on their side. Cabinet members, shall we vote on it?'

Neither Bagchi nor I participated in the poll, because we weren't part of the Cabinet. Nonetheless, we won, and it was decided that the Cabinet would find a way to gratify the students' needs somehow. At least for the time being, until they were back in everyone's favour.

'I'm calling another meeting in five minutes, so be back here. Tea time now, come along,' Ira said, shrugging everyone off. The Cabinet members got up from their seats and left the room, except for Bagchi. He sat there, playing with his watch like he always did when he was nervous. Lines were etched on his face, and he suddenly looked older than he was. It was just the two of us now. 'I think we need to talk,' he said.

'Okay, talk.'

'It can't happen again, Esai.' He wasn't looking at me; he was looking at the door through which Ira had walked out. Everything that was at stake was outside it. 'Last night.'

I felt my throat closing up. I had been dreading this. I'd had this feeling all along that he would get cold feet about us. But what were we, anyway? 'Bagchi...'

He didn't say anything. He continued to trace his watch. He continued to look at everything in the room but me. 'I have a *girlfriend.*'

Why was he making it seem like it was my fault? As if I'd been the only one who'd participated? So what now? Was he going to ignore me?

I turned my back on him and stepped out, inviting the fresh air into my chest as his words hit me like a cannonball. Last night on the tree and all those fireworks spun in my head like a carousel, a ruse of the past. Tears sprung up involuntarily, and I stood there for a while, allowing them. I thought something was going to change. Was I a fool, then?

I took a deep breath. It was going to be all right. I was going to be all right. What was that line from Scheher's closing poem at NCPA? *The tide doesn't lose faith in itself for falling, the glacier doesn't apologise for its hardened heart and messy melting. So how can I ever be hard on myself?*

But boundaries, oh, I was going to build them.

I made up my mind. If he acted like he didn't want me, he was not going to have me. This was foul play, and I wouldn't stand for it. I moved towards the day café, determined not to be shaken by his change of heart. His cowardly behaviour. I ordered myself a cup of chai and devoted myself to it. *Don't think about it. Don't think about it. Don't think about it.*

It's really not such a big deal.

I noticed that Scheher was in the day café as well, and something was amiss. She was patting a forlorn Jewel on the arm, consoling her over something. The same crowd I'd seen earlier in the morning sat around her, as if they were privy to some secret yet to be unleashed into the world. Whatever was going on there certainly didn't look good. Scheher looked up in that moment, and briefly, our gaze locked.

'Why didn't you join us in the morning? I saw you standing there,' she said. Everyone turned to look.

'Oh. Bagchi had called. Ira wanted to talk about something.' I wasn't sure why they were all staring at me, fear in their eyes. As if I was a threat. Jewel tugged at Scheher's sleeve, and then whispered something in her ear.

'Are you with them?' Scheher asked.

I made a face. 'The Cabinet? No.'

Scheher looked hesitant. The others waited for her to say something, but then Jewel got up from her seat and walked away. I didn't know what I'd done, but they continued to look at me cagily. I wanted to ask Scheher what was going on, but she got up too, and went after Jewel. And because the encounter was so uncomfortable, and I wasn't friends with anyone else who sat there, I decided to get back to the meeting. *Weird*, I thought. Whatever that was, Scheher would simply have to tell me later.

Gulping the tea down with complete disregard for my throat's heat threshold, I walked back into the office, delirious and emotional, bandaging myself with pride.

'I've got an idea,' Anisha said, when everyone was seated. 'We should revisit all our manifestos and make sure we're giving them what we promised.'

'That's actually great, Ani,' Ira said. After the tea break, the two women had gone from nasty to extremely courteous with each other. 'I know a lot of us haven't gotten to that yet.'

'I don't think there should be an attendance cut-off for elections. I think anyone who's got the talent should contest for posts,' Bagchi said. Ira scrunched her nose. 'Don't bring your personal agenda here, Bagchi. It's so unethical.'

'I pass out next year, so it's not like I'll be contesting anyway,' he said. 'But I don't think that rule should be there for any of the newer students.'

'Sorry, but attendance is important. Papa's not going to budge on that, believe me.'

'It's not like you've ever brought it up with him,' Bagchi shot back.

'Guys, please,' Ritwik, the Academics convenor said, raising his voice. 'Let's discuss this later, if you're conflicted. What else can we bring to the table?'

Just then, we heard a knock on the door. Ira made a disgruntled noise. 'I hate being interrupted.'

Bagchi rose to open it. 'Joshua!'

Joshua's large, breathless frame entered the room, after which, followed his booming voice. 'Bagchi, there's a situation,' he said, wheezing. Sweat collected on his forehead, and it looked like he'd come running.

'What is it?' Ira asked, alert.

'The VP is out, I'm telling you.' He leaned against the wall, massaging a cramp out of his stomach. 'I came here as fast as I could. Firoza and the others have filed a sexual harassment complaint against Vikas sir.'

'What?' All of us cried in unison.

'You know that girl, Jewel? Apparently Vikas sir has been having an affair with her. There are text messages to prove it, and he's been trying to seduce some of her other friends too, asking her to invite them over.'

'I don't believe it!' Ira said, gaping.

'There are screenshots, Ira. We're going down. Oh God, they're going to think we were part of this.'

'But why?'

'Ira, come on. This man is our vice president. Do the math.'

Ira looked stale. The others turned to one another, a group of petrified children. I could hear the orchestra of their thoughts, a frenzied screaming, seawater in their lungs.

Finally, Bagchi spoke. 'Esai, get out.'

I gawked at him. 'Why?' *Why are you talking to me like that?*

'Get out,' he repeated. 'You can't be seen here. It's going to get really dirty, and you can't be in the middle of this. Your batchmates will brand you a traitor if you're seen with us.' He clasped my wrist and pulled me towards the door. 'Go,' he said. 'Right now.'

'But Bagchi...' I knew he had a point, but it still felt so disrespectful. Just minutes ago, they'd tried to use me to go against Scheher, and now they were discarding me. And the way Bagchi said it, it was as if he hated me.

'I said, *go.*'

I had never heard him use that tone on anyone. I turned and ran, limbs sticky from sweat, until I had no breath in me, until I collapsed in the dirt, caramel dust on my forehead. My head was whirring. I knew where I had landed. I knew it from the celestial orbs that eddied there, I knew it from the triumphant melody spilling into my head like a holy elixir. I stretched my arm to the left, and felt the cool caress of the water, condensing around my fingertips. I remembered Scheher's first show after her heartbreak, and an image of her veiled by all her fans shot through me; her walking home with me, confessing that Jewel had something to tell her. Everything was slowly revealing itself, and it was a lot to take in. Hadn't there been lighter times? Hadn't we been naïve once, hadn't there been more to play

with and less to fear? Infinite nights filled with Sangam poetry
and passionate debates with friends. Evenings spent in banana
markets, carrying wine in water bottles, watching orange light
sifting through pines in Jolly's hometown, Kodaikanal. What I
would give, to go back to that idyllic place again, away from
all this. To wake up to sugarcane juice and peacock sightings.
To sit with Tendral and read Pipi's old letters to lovers he'd
met before Jolly, and then tuck them inside the necks of our
blouses when he came looking for them. To indulge in jasmine
garlands and homemade kohl and not have a care in the world.

My breathing calmed after a few minutes. I became
engrossed in the steady swordplay between the wind and my
flustered hair. I counted till ten, I thought about more good
times. I thought about Scheher and the madness that lay ahead
for Jewel. Enquiries, recounting the same incident to multiple
people, and never being quite sure if she'd ever see the end of
it. I just knew it. Something dreadful was coming.

I'd known it from the time the humming began.

NINETEEN

December was a month of bared fangs and unyielding wariness. Faces, marred by bewilderment, streamed in and out of focus. Even the campus seemed to imitate everyone's collective state of mind. Flies began swarming near the canteen, leaves turned brown and brittle, and there was a breakout of water-borne diseases all over the city. Bombay had always been congested, but lately, it had felt more so. Ever since we'd heard about what had happened to Jewel, we'd all been too disturbed to attend our classes. Wherever I went, I could see students sitting in groups, and everyone was talking about the same thing.

'If I see Vikas sir, I'll throw a slipper at him.'

'Don't call him sir. He doesn't deserve respect. He doesn't deserve anything!'

'If one more reporter uses the word 'allegedly', I swear...'

Time passed, and I was becoming person after person. There was no end to it.

The news had gutted us, bitten into us unforgivingly. I faded in and out of conversations. Shielded myself with a thin wafer of fog through it all, like butter on a knife. Meanwhile, Scheher had created a sort of distance from me. I wasn't sure

if it was because of the strange conversation we'd had earlier
or simply because what had happened to Jewel had taken up
all her time. But we no longer spent time together after class.
She had descended into a state of absolute atheism. I knew this
was yet another version of her that had materialized from her
many moods. All her poems were now tart, acidic, and laden
with stubborn rejection of any sort of institution. They stalked
me ruthlessly, hissing at me, throwing fishing nets at me.

Even the washrooms hadn't been spared. They'd spray
painted the walls in red capital letters, leaving ruins at their
wake.

GIRLS LIKE US GLUE OURSELVES BACK TOGETHER WITH
THE BLOOD OF THOSE WHO BROKE US.

A part of me knew it was for my own good that the
Cabinet had banished me, even though it had felt humiliating.
But while I was no longer associated with them, I also wasn't
sure if I could go back to my own batchmates. I wanted to
be there. I wanted to fight with them. I wanted to stand with
the protestors, but I didn't know how. I tried a few times to
talk to some of them, but they ran off before I could start a
conversation. Word had certainly gotten around that I'd been
seen rubbing shoulders with the enemy, just because of that
one meeting. In the end, rather self-consciously, I made my
way towards the water tower, where they were all coming
together to sign a petition. They didn't throw me out. But
they weren't welcoming either. Scheher nodded at me, and the
others pretended not to notice. Jewel was nowhere around, and
I wondered if they'd taken her in for questioning. I wondered
what kind of action they were going to take against the accused.

Since Jewel had left the group early and had spent entire
days among the professors, her local guardians and the press,
nobody knew exactly what had happened except for Scheher.
But Scheher wouldn't talk, because she said it wasn't her story

to tell. Everyone had to wait for Jewel to tell it herself. And so, when a random girl with fishtail braids told the boy next to her that the police were involved, I wasn't sure how much of it was real. And even if there wasn't a lot of information out there, everyone had something to contribute.

'They've registered a case and taken up investigations.'

'They've got to fire him.'

'And make sure nobody hires him again.'

'*We'll* make sure of that.'

I thought about how brutal the whole year had been. All ignition, all slicing into the flesh. It was hard to believe that Scheher and I used to spend almost every day together, and now I only saw her at the protest. I missed her. Even Ira and Bagchi, who had been my friends in their own silly ways, were now gone. The only person who listened to me was the woman in the lake. And so I went there, evening after evening when class ended, and sat by her tomb, washing off my day.

The protests went on for another week. I began leaving the grounds early because I couldn't take it anymore. My batchmates were all one unit, and I was made to feel like the odd one out. If Scheher tried to talk to me, they all stared with accusation in their eyes, and it was harrowing. All I needed was home and a soft pillow. So I went for it. And skipped a few days of college.

On Friday, the last day of the inquiry, I heard that they'd stayed out for too long. That shops nearby had sponsored the snacks and bottles of water. I heard some of them left before dark. I heard some of them stayed a little past dusk. And then there was Scheher. They said she'd sat there the entire night. Howling. Turning into a creature of the forest. Growing roots into the campus grounds. I imagined the others leaving meat and toddy at her altar. I imagined a black buck staying guard, warding off all evil and protecting her. I imagined her in the exact same way Jolly used to describe Korravai, the mother goddess of war and victory in Tamil tradition.

I slept through the weekend. On Monday morning, I woke up with a splitting headache, and desperately wanted to stay in. But I had bunked too many classes, and my attendance was now critically low. I had no choice but to go to college.

'Where's the paracetamol?' I asked, staggering into the dining room.

'On the top shelf, *chellam*,' Jolly said, folding the newspaper neatly and placing it on the table. I looked at her, one eyebrow raised. She only called me *darling* when she was broaching a difficult topic. 'So.'

'So.' I knew what she was about to bring up, and I hated it.

'They sacked Vikas. Did you know about this?'

I shook my head. Who would I have heard it from? I was the last person these days to know anything at all. Nobody was talking to me. 'I'm not surprised,' I told her.

It was going to be another day of watching Scheher's friends behave like I was a whistleblower. Another day of them telling her not to trust me. Another day of the Cabinet acting highly secretive. You couldn't find them anywhere, and when you did, you found them all together. They were a tight-knit group, always walking together, eating together. I couldn't find out much about the events that had unfolded when I'd been away, but the last thing I had heard was this: the principal had tried to ban Scheher's poems in college. It hadn't worked with the zine, and it didn't work with the poetry.

Scheher was here to stay, like it or not.

She'd simply written another poem in response, and it was called, 'Art Isn't Illegal'. Satire, apparently. She'd performed it at the Fine Arts Cultural Centre, recorded it, and then, of course, put it out for the whole world to see. She'd worn an amber wrap around dress that day, and her eyelids had been painted orange with black stripes. Only Scheher could get away with looking like that. I'd watched it on my phone, when it had been at one lakh views. By the evening, it had hit a million already.

'What does the newspaper say?' I asked Jolly. I had no intention of sitting and mulling over an entire article about how lousy my college was.

'A lot of terrible stuff. I didn't have it in me to read the entire thing.' Jolly looked at me, concerned. She was rubbing her knuckles, tracing the veins on her hands. I knew this wasn't an easy subject for her to broach. The last time she had looked this nervous talking about something was when she'd told me about *Periyappa*, Pipi's brother, dying from a heart attack. 'Do you want to go to class today? There might be a lot of journalists around, looking for students to speak to.'

'What are they saying?' I asked, nudging towards the newspaper article.

She was slouching, crossing her arms. 'There's...' She looked away and shuddered. 'There's a quote from Jewel here about how he started calling her J one day, instead of Jewel. Kept telling her she was so mature for her age, kept saying things like, *you're twenty years younger, but you're twenty years wiser*. And then began the grooming behaviour, and of course, from there, the sexualised behaviour. And it didn't help that he bought her everything she wanted.' Her eyes darted towards me quickly, just to see how I had reacted. I slowly seated myself opposite to her, and rested my palms on the table.

I vaguely remembered Scheher telling me that Jewel lived with her grandmother in a one room kitchen in Borivali. I remembered because I'd seen her raising funds to help her pay off some pending rent. Bombay was known for its socio-economic contrast. It cleaved into extreme poverty and extreme abundance. Alongside all the glamour the metropolis offered was the hopelessness of slums. But it wasn't just the homeless population that salivated over luxury villas. Even the ordinary corporate lab rat and the reasonably successful artist in Juhu and the retiring teacher with her sizable pension eyed every big, beautiful house with wistfulness. That was what the city did to its people. There wasn't a day that went by without a conversation about the rent. There wasn't a day that went by without the hustle. One slip, one lost opportunity, one rip in the pocket, and Bombay immediately went from being a dream city to a city of fiends. This was how the city dwellers lived. Falling, flying.

'What else does it say?' I asked.

'He coerced her into bed,' Jolly went on. She sounded bolder, now that I hadn't reacted as badly as she had expected. 'She was…' She reached for her phone and handed it to me. She placed her index finger on the second paragraph of an online article, and nodded. 'There's a lot more information in here. I think you should read this bit yourself.' I did. I learned that Jewel had been a virgin and Vikas sir had been really rough on her. And because she was in pain, she had asked him to stop. 'H-he didn't listen, and instead said, *slowly, slowly.*' I said, my eyes fixated on the screen. I looked up at Jolly, and scowled. She placed a hand on my shoulder and squeezed it.

'But Jolly.'

'Yes, *chellam.*'

'That's…rape.'

Jolly nodded. 'But a lot of people will say it isn't. Your college, if I'm right, has already exploded with a thousand different opinions. Go and see.'

I shuddered. 'I wonder how long he's been doing this,' I said. 'Jewel's the first to talk about it, but do you think there were others?'

Jolly sighed. 'I hope not, but I don't know. All I know is

that I don't have any peace of mind now, sending you there. Are you sure you're feeling all right? You can stay in for a few days.' She checked my forehead for a temperature and was disappointed to realise I was literally as cold as early January in the hills. 'Fine, go. But if anything or anyone makes you uncomfortable, come back immediately, okay?'

'Okay.'

The classroom wasn't as empty as it had been the previous week. Students filed in every two seconds, and when they got to know the professor wasn't coming in, they began talking among themselves again. To some, Jewel's interest in the professor was consent. 'Read the screenshots, she said she likes him back, right? So what's the deal?'

'If she didn't want to, she shouldn't have gone to his place.'

'She did admit being attracted to him.'

'One minute, she consented, and the next, she didn't. I felt like saying, make up your mind! Stop leading the poor man on. And stop changing the narrative just because it didn't work out.'

And then there were the others. The ones who could look everyone in the eye and explain what was so wrong about all this in excruciating detail. There was this one boy particularly, who sat on the desk all morning, trying to make the other students understand what exactly was wrong about all this.

'He bought her gifts and called her into his office at three a.m. to discuss her assignment. Don't you think that is creepy?'

'She could have rejected the gifts, right? If they made her uncomfortable?'

'She must have definitely thought he was being over the top friendly. But honestly? It was just another manipulative tactic to get her to trust him. None of these predators are explicitly going to say, I want to sleep with you. They pretend to be nice, pretend to care about you. And then they cross boundaries slowly, right? It doesn't immediately escalate to sex, does it? They're touchy-feely with you, patting your back, placing a palm on your thigh, coming too close while discussing that assignment. And look at Jewel, she was definitely his ideal victim.'

'What do you mean?'

'Who'd she run to? She lived with her poor old grandmother, right? Her parents are in the village. And she definitely doesn't look like she's got enough sexual experience, and she's incredibly timid. He must have made her feel special.'

'But she consented.'

'She took back her consent when she was in pain. She said no.'

'Maybe he didn't hear her?'

'Do you hear *yourself*?'

At lunch hour, I looked for Ira and Bagchi. It didn't feel good to admit, but I wanted to know how they were doing. They weren't the nicest bunch, but after the way my batchmates behaved with me, I had a feeling they were my last chance at having friends.

I found Ira in the evening after class ended, standing outside the stationery shop for a Xerox. Bagchi wasn't with her.

'Are you all still mad at me?' I asked, approaching her with caution.

She was baffled. 'Why would I be mad at you?'

'Well, none of you have spoken to me this entire week.'

She pushed her straight, shiny hair behind her shoulders and grinned. 'Work, baby. We're just making sure nobody gets into trouble. But now that things are cooling down a bit, you can sit with us again. If you want to, that is.' I smiled, and she smiled back, patting my head. It was a strange gesture, coming from her. But it felt nice. 'Let's get some chai and head inside,' she said, nodding towards the Cabinet office.

'Were you a part of the inquiry team?' I asked.

'No. It was the principal, Nanda sir, the dean, and some board members. But I still have inside information,' she said with a wink.

Nobody was in the office. We walked in and shut the door tight. 'I'm not okay with how it's all over the news though,' she continued. 'But it's fine. I mean, Vikas sir didn't make a move on me, but then again, men like that, men who are predators usually go for women they can manipulate. Definitely not the chairwoman, the principal's daughter. He wouldn't dare touch the hair on my arm.'

I didn't know what she meant by that. Why was she justifying him not hitting on her? 'So you knew nothing?'

'Nothing. How'd I know who he was screwing behind closed doors? He'd just come in for the meetings with us, then leave. Now I know why he was in such a hurry. That bastard.'

'I was shocked. I actually thought he had a wife.'

'He does!' She shook her head. 'God, and she didn't even believe any of it. Some women, I tell you.' She looked angry at this point. 'And you know what he said when they told him a girl had accused him of sexual misconduct? *I'm sorry she felt that way.* Did you hear that? He was sorry that *she* felt that way. Ha! He did confess at last, though. Papa showed him the screenshot evidence, and he fumbled. And then he didn't know what to say to deny it.' I could tell she condemned his behaviour. It came as a surprise to me, because I had expected her to justify the professor's actions, or at least, deny it to save face.

'I just wish that Jewel girl had told me instead of Scheher,' she went on. 'This doesn't look good on me at all as a chairwoman.'

And she's back, I thought. 'We'll find a way to get them to like you.' I put my palm on her hand, and she smiled.

It was as if I'd summoned it. Because in that very instant, we heard a loud scream. We both jolted upright, and then jumped off our seats and flung the door open. Running towards the commotion, Ira next to me in her high heels, I could tell there was already a big crowd gathering where the sound had come from.

'This place just can't get enough, can it?' Ira muttered, and I couldn't have agreed more.

'He's always doing this to us!' A girl shrieked from the other side of the onlookers. People jeered loudly, and I heard someone next to us say, 'It's Joshua.'

Ira stood on her toes and squinted her eyes. 'And it's Chhangte who's shouting. I know her. She's that Mizo girl from second year who won the hip hop finals during the college auditions.'

The people in front of us shushed us, and we apologised profusely. I stood on my tiptoes as well, but it was a fail. Grabbing Ira by the hand, I squeezed my way through the crowd, and stood at the front.

'You call me Momo or Chinese one more time, Joshua, and I'll make sure you wish you were dead,' Chhangte said, and now I could see her face clearly. Provoked, churning, hungry for blood. Some of the students laughed, some others looked hostile. Joshua, on the other hand, seemed titillated by her reaction.

'They're pet names, babe. I meant it in an affectionate way.'

'I'm not your *babe*.'

'Okay, okay.' He held his hands up high in mock surrender. From the look on his face, I could tell he had no intention of letting this go. I leaned towards Ira and whispered in her ear, 'Do something. You're the chairwoman.'

Just as the girls began walking away furiously, Joshua called out to them, 'Can I at least call you Chowmein, then?'

A lot of people gasped. It was obvious what everyone was thinking. *Oh, God. He just did not.*

I was itching to wipe that arrogant smirk off his face. But before I could say or do anything, Ira darted towards him. Everyone's heads turned. I'd never known time to freeze so fast, but it did. Ira's palm swung back, and then landed square on Joshua's jaw. We all heard it. The loud crack, as if her fingers were leather belts. We all saw the shock on his face, and then the look of betrayal, and then, of course, boiling wrath.

'What the hell, Ira?'

Ira ignored him. Turning to Chhangte, she said, 'I'm sorry he said that. If it ever happens again, you let me know. And I'll make sure it doesn't again.'

Chhangte looked taken aback. And then she nodded right away. 'Y-yes. Of course, chairwoman.'

Mouths were agape. I couldn't read their minds, but it was so clear from their expressions that the scene played itself over and over again until it made sense to them. When it did, the shock subsided and blossomed into enlivened whispers.

'Disperse,' Ira barked at the rest of us, and slowly, everyone began to leave. Joshua still stood there as Ira walked towards me, hand on his cheek, rubbing vigorously.

'That was brilliant,' I told her. I sounded like one of Scheher's gushing fans right after her show. 'I'm so proud of you.'

'Don't be too smug,' she replied disdainfully. 'I only did it so Scheher wouldn't beat me to it.'

'What?'

She tied her hair into a bun and massaged her neck. 'You heard me. This college doesn't need *outsiders* as heroes.'

TWENTY

Ira's slap was only the talk of the town for a few days. Just when students were slowly beginning to trust her again, something awful happened.

I made my way towards the protesting crowd, a feeling of dread shrouding me. It was fourth period now, and I had missed the first half of the day. I had a feeling I was going to skip the rest as well.

Vikas sir had been sacked. So what was this about?

Scheher stood in the centre, wearing an oversized black shirt and denim. There were beads in her hair and paint all over her face. When I got closer, I could see what was written. *We want justice.*

'What's going on?' I asked the girl closest to me.

'The first semester marks are out. Go see.'

I ran to the list on the board a lot of the others were standing next to. There was desolation in the air, and I looked up my name, preparing myself like one would for a medical diagnosis.

Something was terribly wrong. I'd failed most of my subjects.

'No,' I whispered out loud. I turned to the other students, and they were all looking at me sympathetically.

'Join us,' one of them said, bitterness in their voice. 'We've
all failed one subject at least, and how.' The more I spoke to
them, the more I realised everyone who had gathered had an
axe to grind. There were some fifty or sixty students who had
been failed. We all knew what would happen to us if we were
stuck with these scores. It would mean losing one academic
year. It would mean watching all your other batchmates move
ahead, while you sat with the freshers. 'I did well,' I said to
nobody in particular. 'I know I did well.'

I could feel a festival of fury boiling over. The commotion
was too loud, and to make it worse, Scheher was shouting at
the top of her voice, calling out to every student who was
passing by, looking bewildered. 'Today it's us, tomorrow it will
be you,' she warned, pointing at the others who were watching
from a distance.

There were first years, second years, even final years among
the crowd. Two postgraduate students had assembled there as
well, and one thing was clear: everyone was angry. Really angry.

'We tried talking to the Academics convener from the
Cabinet. He said he would speak to the chairwoman, but then
he ghosted me. It's been three hours since he told me he would
see to it,' one of the postgraduate students said. I checked my
watch. It was noon now, and I hadn't realized how far I'd slept
in. Fatigue washed over me, and I could tell my blood pressure
had gone down since joining college. This place was taking a
toll on my health.

Scheher's voice barged in. 'Where is the chairwoman in such
a time of crisis? Where are the secretaries, where are all these
people who promised to help us? They're around when they
need votes, but when we need them, they're gone,' Scheher
said. The other nodded, looking at one another. The crowd was
becoming turbulent, a sea of thunder. Scheher had incited a new
kind of Galvanism. Her words were electrodes making organic

matter come to life, causing dead frogs to twitch upwards, stirring an uprising.

In that moment, I saw the greed in her eyes. She was on a power trip. Everyone was looking up to her, listening to her, making her their *hero*. But was it not too big an ask? Could a mess of a girl really be anyone's antidote?

I loved her, but I wondered if all this was getting to her head. I could understand why the other students had turned to her to rescue them from their problems. Everyone knew how inefficient the Cabinet was. They were slow, and people like Joshua and Anisha were part of it for their own gains, and not because they wanted to help the student community. Ira was capable, but she only existed to make St. Margaret's look posher—even the other day, she'd been writing a proposal to the management, lobbying for a translated books department in the library. They had the power to do enough. They just chose to use it for other things.

And then one angry girl turned the whole system upside down. Scheherazade.

'Jewel,' she said, turning to the girl beside her. 'We've been here for the past three hours. Everyone's seen us. I personally called the chairwoman three or four times, and she didn't pick up. We're going to make it known now that we're mad. Really really mad.'

Jewel looked at her, starry-eyed. 'Yes, Scheherazade.'

'There are some girls making more placards in the canteen. Please go tell them we're going to barge into the Student Union Centre. Right, guys? We're going to stand there and riot till our lungs burst. Are you with me?'

'Yes!'

'ARE YOU WITH ME?'

'YES!'

I quickly pulled Scheher to a side and asked her, 'Scheher,

I think we should just go have a conversation with the Cabinet.
We'll protest against the management if they refuse to help us.'

'They've already refused. So many of us have tried to reach
them, and they keep avoiding us,' she said curtly. I could feel
everyone's eyes on us again. Trying to find out if we were
talking or not.

'Scheher, think,' I said. I knew she was jumping to start a
fight. I knew she had all this unaddressed anger that was begging
to be let out. After what had happened to Jewel, everyone
was on edge. But I didn't want things to snowball. 'Everyone's
been reaching out to individual members. On their own, they
probably don't know what to do. They need to discuss this
together, don't they?'

'Why are you taking their side?' Jewel asked, her lower lip
quivering, and one of her friends rushed to her side. I'd heard
a rumour that she was never returning to St. Margaret's after
what had happened. But certainly I had heard wrong, because
here she was. She did look better, but I couldn't be sure. And
I didn't know what to say without triggering her. So I turned
to Scheher again and said, 'I'm just saying to give them time.
I'm saying, until we know for sure it's a no from their end, we
don't start a fight.'

'No, Esai,' Scheher said. 'You don't know them like I do.
Without a fight, we don't even stand a chance. This is the only
way to get their attention.' She turned back to the crowd, and
they looked at her as if they were waiting for her to lead. I
knew there was no negotiating this. She would carry on with her
agenda no matter what, and I didn't feel too good about that.

Did Bagchi know? And if he didn't, was I supposed to tell
him? Did I owe him that? Questions raced in my head, and
I had no time to answer them. I only knew that a mob was
rising, and that put the Cabinet in a tough spot. They needed
to be informed. I turned around and ran. If I got there before
they did, I could warn them.

They were sitting in the canteen, all the members of the Cabinet. Even Joshua was there, despite the suspension. He glared at me, and I ignored him. None of them were particularly welcoming. Even Bagchi refused to meet my eyes.

He's going to avoid me forever, I realized.

'Ira,' I said, panting. 'I don't know if anyone told you, but there's been some confusion with everyone's marks.'

'I know,' she said, nonchalant. 'It's hard to ignore that gathering over there. They've been scheming since nine in the morning.'

'Oh.'

She stared at me, expectant. 'Well,' I said lamely. 'They're more than a gathering now. They're going to cause a strike.'

From afar, I could hear poems of dissent. Faces began appearing within seconds. Scheher was at the forefront, punching the air with her fist. 'We want justice! We want re-evaluation!'

'Uff! Someone *please* shut her up.' Ira leapt from her seat and turned to Bagchi. 'I told you she was pitting them against us. And you said it would die out.' She rubbed her forehead tersely. 'We need to find a way to disperse them. But how?'

'Why can't you give them what they want?' I asked bluntly.

'How can I promise them a re-evaluation until the management says it's possible?' Ira asked. 'This really isn't in my hands. Papa needs to decide.'

'Then why don't you advocate for it?' I asked her. 'Stand with the other students and fight for them? Because right now, it really feels like none of you care about this.'

Joshua sat in a corner, swiping at a mosquito. He looked uninterested in any of this, and I wondered what was the point in even having him here.

'I can't stand against my own father,' Ira said. I knew the predicament she was in. But I also understood why most students on campus hated her. She was their student leader, and she had done nothing to help them. 'Esai, what should I do?' she asked.

Before I could answer, we were all suddenly distracted by the students' songs reinforcing as they marched towards us. They were getting closer, and something had to be done. Ira gripped my shoulder blades and shook me hard. 'That Scheher, she's your friend, right?'

Wasn't she tired of asking me the same question? 'I mean...'

'Go tell her to stop this nonsense.'

'I can't.' She was being unfair.

'We need you right now for damage control.'

I shook my head. I wasn't going to go against my own friends to save their hide. It was one thing to notify them so they could be prepared. But to throw me under the bus just because I'd delivered the message?

'Esai,' Bagchi said, speaking to me for the first time. 'We're not asking you to take a side here. You just have to stall her while we figure out how this can be fixed. Just go tell her that we're figuring it out, and we need them to be a little patient. We'll talk to the principal.'

I didn't like where this was going. I didn't want to be their dove of peace, their sacrificial lamb. 'Did all of you pass?' I asked.

Bagchi looked at Ira. 'Yes.'

'No wonder you're so chill. And no wonder you don't care.'

'Don't say that, Esai.' He looked defeated. 'I'll try my best to make them look at the papers again.'

'You'll try your best.' It wasn't enough.

Before Bagchi could respond, Ira interrupted. 'That Scheher, she really thinks she's something, doesn't she? Living out some twisted fantasy of being the student leader.'

'I hardly think it's that,' Bagchi said drolly.

Ira's frown was getting more pronounced as the crowd

neared. 'It's obvious she just wants attention. Heard her parents never gave her any,' she said. To me, it seemed as if her vileness was an armour for her fear. I saw her hands close into fists and open again, and I saw that beads of sweat were collecting above her upper lip. She wasn't watching the students. She was watching Scheher.

Joshua grunted in pleasure. 'I love savage Ira.' He clicked his tongue. 'People need to stop listening to Firoza's stupid poetry. It's messing with their brain cells, clearly.'

'Poetry, it seems,' Ira scoffed. 'It's nothing but embarrassing. It sounds like she's a hollering madwoman. What's the big deal? I can also go up on a stage and make a scene.'

'Can you?' Bagchi asked. Suddenly, the tension in the air was sizzling.

Ira promptly recovered from her surprise at his remark. 'I mean…sure. But why would I make a fool of myself like that?'

'Exactly,' Bagchi said. 'Not everyone has the guts to make a fool of themselves in front of so many people. And not everyone has the stomach for it. Women going public about their trauma has always made people uncomfortable, hasn't it?'

I wasn't sure if this was the right time to be having a conversation like this, especially when there was a mob walking towards us. But still, I felt like an old window that had come off its hinges, torn between liking him and not liking him. At times, he failed me so much, and at others, he impressed me significantly. And this was one of those moments when he did.

'Wait. Don't tell me you actually like it?' I could almost see fumes coming out of Ira's head.

'I told you he *likes* Firoza,' Joshua said, inserting his unnecessary wisdom and cackling loudly.

Bagchi didn't give in. 'There's something about it, yes. It's raw and real and gorgeous. I think she writes from the heart, and that's…I appreciate that. Hell, I admire that. I wish I could be like that.'

Oh.

Ira's face hardened. 'She's got no heart. Or else, she wouldn't be coming for us like this.' She had finally met a rival, a nemesis in her political warfare. Someone who actually met the demands of the other students, did the work of a student leader. Now that they'd had a taste of a good leader, would they even want her? Would Scheher overthrow her, take away her power? I knew exactly why Ira felt so threatened by Scheher. But Bagchi was the one to point it out.

'You hate her, Ira, because everyone loves her,' he said quietly.

Nobody said a word. The silence that plunged into everyone stayed for a few good seconds. I knew what they were feeling, because I felt it myself. Disbelief. It was the first time I'd heard him openly stand up for someone. And the first time I'd heard him stand up to her so blatantly. At this point, I was beyond amazed. Maybe I was mistaken about him, after all.

Behind me, Joshua cleared his throat loudly. I followed his gaze towards the main ground. 'There she is!' he said, pointing to the crowd. They were now standing in front of us, prepared for a conflict. 'Star of the show, Scheherazade, the queen. Welcome, welcome.'

'Joshua, shut up,' Ira said, placing her hands across her chest, looking like a statue. Animosity charged in the air like a damaged power cord, now that Scheher and her people had finally arrived.

'I thought you were better than this, Esai,' Scheher said, not looking at me, but glaring back at Ira instead. 'Everyone told me you were working with them. I was the fool for not listening.'

The students who were standing behind her looked at me, censure in their eyes. It dawned upon me that by being here, I had cemented their doubts about me being with the Cabinet. I groaned, knowing that I'd made a very stupid move. I wanted to remind them I'd been upset with my marks as well, that me being here did look disreputable, but I wasn't one of them. Unfortunately, everything was happening too fast for me to explain myself. I turned to Bagchi and Ira, and Bagchi's compelling gaze reminded me of what he had asked me to say. Was this the right time? Would I be subjected to more disapproval? I had no idea. I took the fall.

'I'm not with them,' I said exasperatedly. 'But let's give them a chance to fix things, they said they would.'

'Did they actually say that?' Scheher demanded.

'Yes! They're just asking for a bit more time. An...hour?' I turned to Ira hesitantly. 'Two,' I said quickly. 'Two hours. It'll be done.'

Scheher pointed at Joshua. I could tell that his mere presence had triggered her. And who could blame her? Who wouldn't be upset seeing the way he was sitting, leaning back lazily on the wall and eating a packet of chips as if none of this was his concern? 'And? What's he doing here? Is he the one who's going to fix things?'

Joshua looked offended. 'Stop acting so proud and pretending like you didn't call me four nights ago, all drunk and dying. *Why don't you want me? What did I do?*' he mimicked.

She ignored him, and continued to glower at me. Joshua, not used to being disregarded, decided to change his approach. He flashed her a big smile. 'Firoza.'

She gave him the side-eye. 'What?'

'Come back to me, Firoza. Please. I still love you.' His grin stayed on, bold and unvarying, like that of a wax idol. 'We were good together, weren't we?' he whined. 'I know you miss me. And I know you still want me.' This was no time for such a conversation. He had a habit of inserting himself when it was most unnecessary. I flashed him an annoyed look.

An undistinguishable fog clouded Scheher's face. As if she

was remembering the past. Was she thinking about the good times? Or was she reimagining all those times he'd hurt her? 'Joshua...' she said.

'Yes?'

'Joshua, I want you...' she said tenderly, her lips parting, her breath speeding. '...to shut your mouth. I don't give a damn if you still love me.'

His face turned pale. 'All that fame has turned you into an arrogant cunt,' he spat.

'Oh,' she said loudly, hand on her chest in pretence. 'Are you bothered because you're hearing my name wherever you go? You poor, poor thing. Can't handle how they're all only going to remember you as the idiot who let me go? Well, get used to it. Because that's exactly how you'll be going down in history.'

He took a quick step towards her, and immediately, Ira and I leapt between them. I stood in front of Scheher, and Ira laid her hand on Joshua's chest, stopping him where he was.

Scheher was burning. 'We'll win this,' she said, turning to Jewel and the other students who were standing there.

Scheher looked at me, her eyes glistening. 'Esai, didn't you hear what he just said to me? Why are you even hanging out with him and his friends?'

Him and his friends. That's how she was looking at this. All black and white. I could tell that though she had gotten over him, she hadn't gotten over what he'd done. She was still angry.

I wanted to tell her I wasn't his friend. She was being unreasonably suspicious. I wasn't at all interested in being around him. But I also didn't subscribe to her idea of escalating this to a protest unless it was a last resort. I didn't like the way she was turning this into a boxing ring. I wanted to tell her so much, but she looked so betrayed, and I found myself speechless. There were so many people watching us, and I was getting nervous.

'As your student Cabinet, we will look into this,' Ira pitched in. 'I promise. I'm sorry about what Joshua said. But give us some time.'

'All right. Tell them,' she said, looking at me instead of Ira. I could tell a cold war had begun. 'That if this isn't done by today, I'm bringing in the press.' Had it been anyone else, the press may not have cared. But Scheherazade was calling them, and there was no way they would be able to resist.

One by one, the students sat outside the Student Union Centre, waiting for an answer and singing the songs Scheher had taught them. Nobody was in the right mind to go to class. In the beginning, it had been only fifty or sixty students, but now, more joined in. Even those who had passed sat with them, and it was really something. She had shown them all that she was capable of pulling a crowd. It was stimulating to watch, all these students coming together for a single cause. Joshua began to move towards them scornfully, but Ira stopped him. 'We can't.'

'Why not?'

'Because they're not doing any harm. It's a peaceful protest.' And then Ira looked at me. 'Thank you.'

'I didn't do anything,' I said, looking confused.

'You risked your skin for us. Your friend hates you now.'

I thought about the way Scheher had looked at me when I'd tried to bargain for Ira. 'I suppose she does.'

Ira rested a hand on my shoulder. 'Now tell me. Can she actually bring in the press if we don't get this done on time?'

I nodded. 'She's been interviewed by most of them, so I know she definitely has contacts.'

'Then we'd better get to business.'

But by the time the Cabinet had a meeting with the principal, it was already late evening. Of course, I didn't join them in the principal's office. They didn't think it would make sense for a non-Cabinet member to be there, and thought it would be better for me to try and talk to Scheher again. I did try, but she evaded me. None of the students wanted me around them, so I waited around on my own. The meeting took a while, but by then, everyone had gone back home. Ira had separately filled me in on what had happened over text, and because my own batchmates had withdrawn from me, it somehow felt nice that she was talking to me. That she'd thought to let me know in the middle of such a big crisis made me wonder if she did consider me her friend, after all. It left me conflicted.

I was informed that Nanda sir, Sonali ma'am and all the hostel wardens had come together to discuss the issue. Ira had prepared a mini speech asking them to re-evaluate the papers, and there had been some sort of agreement. I only discovered the entire story when I got to college the following day.

'They only bought more time from us so that they could mint money out of us!'

Scheher's voice was inescapable. The moment I entered the main gate, I saw the crowd seated outside the Student Union. This time, there were more students. I could tell some of them were only here so that they could bunk class. But why? Hadn't the issue been resolved?

Bagchi and Ira had both told me that the management had agreed for a re-evaluation.

I tried to get close to the crowd, but one look at me, and Scheher bristled. They all turned around to see who she was glaring at, and I suddenly felt myself go blank.

'Scheher,' I said cautiously.

'Go away, Esai. You don't belong here.'

This is a misunderstanding, I wanted to scream. But I just stood there for a few seconds, blinking away my tears. And then I turned around and walked away, feeling cheated out of my narrative. They thought I was two-timing. And there was nothing I could do to change their mind.

'Esai!' I looked up. It was Priya, Scheher's old flatmate. I hadn't seen her in a while, and I was glad that my bad reputation hadn't swayed her enough to cut me out.

'I'm sorry they're treating you like that,' she said. 'I don't think you're bad.'

'Thank you for saying that, Priya.'

We exchanged small talk, and then I asked her, 'Any idea why they're still protesting?'

'Oh. The principal said that re-evaluations usually happen with a fee. Five hundred rupees per subject.'

It wasn't much, but for someone like Jewel, it certainly was. 'A lot of us failed. Certainly there's been some mistake, right? Couldn't the management make it free just this instance?' I said.

'That's why they're still protesting. They don't want to pay the fee.'

The silent protest went on for days. When they realised the deadline for re-evaluation was approaching and that there was no escaping the fees levied on them, they panicked. To this date, I believe this was when Scheher made her most timely power move during her entire college life. She promised all the students who had failed that she would pay their fees.

And though she still continued her silent treatment with me, she paid mine as well.

A few days later, when the professors took out their papers from the bank for re-evaluation, they had the shock of their life. The scores on the sheets were different from the scores that had been entered and published.

'There's been an error in entering the marks,' the principal had informed the Cabinet during a one-hour long meeting. I'd heard this from Bagchi, who'd heard it from Ira.

'What?' they'd all said in unison.

'Yes.'

'How?'

'We're still trying to find out how it happened. It's never happened before.'

'Oh God, what do we tell them?' Ira had switched to panic mode.

'This isn't your fault, it's ours. The management will enter the correct marks, and we'll publish them in an hour. So you can go tell them that.'

Now, the entire Cabinet stood outside, dumbfounded. Joshua looked severely distressed with the revelation, and I had a feeling he had been the only one truly happy with the scores he'd received.

The news had somehow been leaked, and the students had started coming together again. I could see Scheher marching towards them. The crowd welcomed her with loud cheering. I stopped walking behind Ira and told her, 'You go ahead.'

'What, you don't want to be seen with us?'

'I want to help you, but I don't want my batchmates to turn against me.'

'Playing it safe?' Bagchi said, from behind me.

I shrugged. 'I've got a great teacher, haven't I?'

From where I stood, I heard everything clearly. Ira told them everything the professors had said about the bug in the computer system, word to word. She said it in a calm voice, and as she was talking, the students began murmuring among themselves. Scheher quietened them down with her hands, and Nanda sir pasted the new scores on the bulletin. A deadly silence hung in the air, and then everyone huddled around it. We had finally received our original marks. I'd done well in everything except the History of English Literature, but I was fine with that. It was still a much better score than what I'd seen earlier. When the commotion died down, Scheher spoke.

'We want a public apology.'

Ira inhaled heavily. 'What did you say?'

'A public apology,' Scheher stressed, grinding her teeth.

'From us?'

'From the principal,' Scheher said. 'And we're going to restart our protest and sit here until we get it.'

'Don't you think you're taking this a little too far?' Joshua taunted. Ira waved at him to be quiet, and then looked at Scheher. 'We will talk to him.' I could see the resentment on her face. I wondered if she took this as an insult to her father.

At first, the principal released an official written statement and pasted it on the bulletin. It was short, generic, absolutely pathetic. It only aggrieved Scheher and the others.

There were now only twenty students clamouring for a better apology from the principal, but they were strong. They showed up every day, and they sat outside the principal's office singing songs and shouting slogans. Every time I crossed them in the corridor, they sang even louder. I didn't know what to think about all this, but I still felt an unshakeable sense of pride when I saw them. Especially when Scheher began performing poetry amongst them, and more students joined in to listen to her. Soon, what started as twenty students, went back to being almost a hundred again.

Finally, the principal interfered. From what I'd heard, he had shown up one morning a little late to his cabin, and they hadn't allowed him to enter at all. 'All right. I guess I do owe you an apology.' He'd looked sincere. 'I'm deeply sorry about what happened. And you have my word that it will never happen again. You are safe with us.' He'd nodded at Scheher, and then everyone had parted and made way for him to get into his office. Once he'd gotten inside, they'd looked at each other in stunned silence.

The reaction since then was deafening. They took to the streets of the campus in jubilation, and there was an outbreak of cheering and clapping. Some of them picked Scheher up and danced, as a ripple of euphoria spread through the throng. Ira and the rest of the Cabinet stood there, watching helplessly.

Until the day ended, the students continued to move around in big, animated groups, with Scheher's poem in their mouths as if it were the gospel. They shouted new incantations as they made their way out the main gate in the evening. I strained my ears to catch hold of the words as I walked past them.

Serves you right, now you've got stuck
our bones in your throat.
Swallow all you want—
we refuse to go down.

All night, I heard the same words in my dreams. *Serves you right, serves you right.* Vocals merging into one, harmonic and passionate. *Now you've got stuck, now you've got stuck.* It came in waves.

Our bones in your throat.

TWENTY-ONE

After that incident, Scheher and I stopped being friends. I'd stopped attending her shows as well. I wasn't used to being shunned, especially because I had always been her biggest supporter. It wasn't easy adjusting to the fact that I was no longer invited to sit in the front rows of her performances anymore. It wasn't easy accepting that all everyone could ever talk about these days was the breakup of our friendship. I'd been there when she'd forgotten her lines on stage, I'd been the first to snap and encourage her to keep on. But now the verdict on me was apparent: my batchmates thought I was on the Cabinet's side. And I didn't know how to prove them wrong.

To make matters worse, the Cabinet also had begun to assume I was with them. Ever since that very public clash with Scheher, they had started inviting me to their meetings. It had begun innocently, when I'd been sitting alone in the canteen with a new book from the library. Bagchi and Ira had seen me all by myself and joined my table, and one thing led to another, and we'd begun discussing internal politics again. Everywhere I went, I could feel people stare, and it unnerved me. Sometimes my only comfort was the lake, a trapdoor into a different world.

Sometimes all I did was climb the rope ladder the waves threw at me, accept the invitation to be a tenant of her dreams. And when I returned to the balmy grass, a bedspread of its own kind, I felt rejuvenated. And she was always there to see me back to my world, a guardian spirit, standing near the trees. Sometimes in a flimsy white gown, all drenched. And sometimes decked in silver amulets and headdresses, gem stones and flower crowns.

Because I couldn't go for Scheher's shows, I watched her performance videos in private. Nothing could stop me from being a part of Scheher's new memories, and nothing could take my love away. I mouthed the words to her poems because I'd been there when she'd written them. She'd practised them in front of me, time and again, and they'd become a part of me.

'Men before you have tried to wear their crowns in my lands, only to find out that I am freedom. Freedom?' She'd waited for me to approve. 'How about democracy?' I'd suggested. 'Oh! That's even better, thanks.' She'd started over. 'Men before you have tried to wear their crowns in my lands, only to find out...I taste like democracy. You showed up at my show sceptical, but you fall for me. Bury me in the sky, the ground is for the ordinary, I growl into my mic. Bring stars to my grave, not flowers, I say, and the audience screams into a maelstrom. Someday when a stranger folds my obituary into a plate for roadside vada pav, the entire town will hunger for poetry...'

St. Margaret's thrived on our dispute. Everyone could feel the animosity between us, and they found it exhilarating. Even Ira constantly quizzed me on the status of our friendship, and I could only shake my head. A part of me understood that she needed reassurance I wouldn't go back. That this was beyond mending. It gave her more agency to badmouth Scheher in front of me.

Meanwhile, the zine became a cult phenomenon. Everyone was reading it now, even the professors and their children.

And everyone was up to date with what was happening in St. Margaret's, because not knowing meant not having read the zine. And that was simply too embarrassing to admit. There were columns Scheher had written jointly with other students who were let down by the management, and conversations that turned into discussions about how things could get better. I wanted to tell her I was so proud of her. I wanted to know how she was dealing with this new rollercoaster life, and I wanted to know if she was all right. She'd been so busy with her work lately. And she'd been so busy avoiding me. But I wondered if she was still going for therapy, still on medication for her anger issues. I wondered if she still went to consult her reiki grandmaster, still went for Mass with Jewel every Sunday morning, still read her tarot cards, still turned to every other thing except herself to rescue her heart.

Because sometimes, she still looked sad. All these people in her life, and yet not one of them could bulldoze the hollowness in her chest or keep her from blasting her heartbreak manifesto wherever she went. Or convince her every morning not to down a bottle of Hennessy and stare out the window like she wanted to jump.

No, nobody could steal Scheher away from the loneliness of herself.

I knew she didn't want to be associated with that incident anymore, but at times, it was still the first thing that came to my mind when I looked at her. I couldn't help it. It was as if I was always searching for tactile evidence, something that said, *yes. I am clean. I am whole again.* I needed to be sure she had finally cut the cord. That she had left that version of her in the past. I needed to know how she had lived so many lives and survived each and every one of them, despite being so young.

The only thing that rescued me from all the havoc on campus was the arrival of the Christmas holidays. This meant

I could hide inside my house for a whole week and wait for things to settle down. This also meant I had more time to spend with Jolly, Pipi and Tendral, the only people who truly cared if I was okay. I'd felt like a pawn in everyone else's game, and it hadn't been a good feeling.

The first few days of staying home were blissful. I read books, cleaned my room, even learned a few new recipes. And then on the nineteenth of December, Jolly and I took a train to join the anti-CAA gathering in August Kranti Maidan, the place where Mahatma Gandhi had given the Quit India speech. The protest was against the Citizenship Amendment Act, which granted Indian citizenship only to non-Muslim persecuted minorities. It was a direct attack on the Constitution and secularism because it was discriminatory.

We'd been warned about a counter group rallying at Churchgate station, so we'd chosen to get down a stop before. When we finally reached the maidan, it was full of disciplined citizens who shared the same horrified reaction towards the new anti-Muslim law. I met a girl who was sharing copies of bail in case anyone got detained. Three days later, I found out she'd been taken to the station.

And then Christmas arrived in Bombay, and to my consternation, I was unprepared. The world had been spinning so fast, I'd had no time to catch up with the beautiful things it had to provide. All at once, I was fraught with the urgency of being elsewhere. So on its eve, when I saw Tendral getting dressed up, I quickly jumped in. 'Wherever you're going, I'm coming.'

'Raza and I are going to see the lights outside Mount Mary Basilica. It's the most happening place in Bombay during this time. Did you go there yet?'

'No.'

'No? I'd assumed you'd gone with Scheher. I have a

classmate who goes to that church, and she sees her and her
group always hanging around there.' I shrugged. There was
no point explaining that Scheher had been giving me the cold
shoulder.

'No, I've never been,' I said. I opened my wardrobe and
pulled out an embroidered tunic. 'Will this do?'

'Of course! It's going to be very crowded, though. Not
inside. Inside, they'll be having prayers. We're going to go to
that candle place opposite it. We'll light a candle, and then
come back. Works?'

I nodded. 'Works.'

That night, the Mother Mary idol standing two floors above
the ground, looked exquisite. Street vendors were selling burfi
on the side. Bombay was a big city, but it was tradition for
everyone in college to show up at Mount Mary. I did run into
a couple of students, and they all looked so different in the
colourful lights. Joshua entered the church with his family, and
wondered if he was here because he'd been dragged to come,
or because he really was a devout person. It was disconcerting
that there were so many things I didn't know about my peers,
even though I met them almost every day. But then again,
there were so many things they didn't know about me either.
Somehow, that was a comforting thought.

'Look! Scheherazade!' Tendral said, pointing at a familiar
face in the crowd. Scheher had a shawl over her head, and she
was holding an orange candle. She had some friends with her,
and they were all standing near the entrance, singing carols.

'And do you recognize that man?' Tendral said, tapping
Raza's arm eagerly. 'He's in that toothpaste advertisement! The
one they play in between cricket matches!'

'There are a lot of stars here today,' Raza said. 'I come
here every Christmas eve, and it's become a sort of tradition
for everyone in Bombay. Besides, it's such a lovely sight.' He

leaned against one of the stone walls and stared at the church. It was lit in blue and purple, with yellow fairy lights streaming down from the top like waterfalls. There were pink and orange candles everywhere, as well as paper stars. Amidst all this, the street lights continued to glow.

'It truly is,' Tendral said, seconding what Raza had just said.

We stood there for a while, lost in reverie. It felt like a renewal, where I was being guided into a new beginning. At the close of the night, I told myself, I would make myself strong enough to face anything again. I'd borrow from Scheher's valour.

When class began again after a few days, everyone had something new to obsess over: Scheher had just released her debut album, *Our Bones in Your Throat*, with one of the biggest distributors in the country. She was selling her own merchandise now, doing twice as many shows, giving more interviews and signing autographs. Her attendance had dropped badly, and she only came to campus when there was drama involved. At times, I wondered if she even remembered a life outside of all that, when she'd just been Firoza, the girl her parents had never understood, the girl who had been insecure about her tallness and overshared when she had too much sangria and didn't always have to be performing in front of an audience or the camera. I thought about how all this overnight glamour had extinguished something so priceless in her: her simplicity, her joy, her authenticity.

I wondered if Scheher was happy in her new world.

But Scheher was the least of my problems. Bagchi, for one, had taken my avoidance of him to heart, and rightfully so. He hadn't expected me to cut him out so easily. He'd texted me during the holidays, trying to make amends, but I hadn't responded to his mixed signals. When college reopened again after the New Year, he was the first person to seek me out during break. He waved at me when he saw me cross the street, and tried to get to me by being in the library all the time. I saw him lounging near the bookshelves, making his presence known. I ignored him all the time, but it never once discouraged him. Finally, one day, he came up to me and asked me what I was reading. 'You really want to know?' I said.

'Yes.'

He was going to be sorry that he asked. 'It's about two lovers who don't end up together because one of them didn't have the guts to admit there was something going on between them.'

'Ouch.'

I closed the book and got up. He had a good view of the front cover. 'It says Amrita Pritam's poems. You liar.'

'My bad.'

'Is it any good?'

'What?'

'The book.'

'I don't want to really talk to you. So if you could just move aside...'

'I was in my school's Rabindra Nritya team once.'

'What?'

He took a deep breath. 'I was in my school's Rabindra Nritya team. The evening we performed our dance drama, my parents were the only ones who didn't show. I waited so much. And then I cried. And then I felt guilty.'

'Why?'

'Because my brother was in the hospital. Of course that was more important than my stupid play.' I could tell it was hard for him to talk about this. He'd never had a dignified childhood. And now it haunted him. 'What I'm saying is, I stopped crying at one point and trained myself to not really ask for anything in life. Nothing mattered enough to fight for.' He looked tired. 'I get it, I'm not passionate and full of fire like you. I'm passive. I don't take sides, I just mind my business and I keep going. But this passiveness helped me get by. It's not that I don't want you. It's just that I've made peace with never having a single damn good thing in my life.'

While a part of me wanted to cry *bullshit* and stalk off, a part of me also wanted to hug him and tell him I really cared for him. I wanted to hide him, I wanted to keep him safe. From himself and the rest of the world. And maybe even from me.

I bit my lip and contemplated. This wasn't easy at all. All along I'd hated that he'd been so apolitical. All along, it had gnawed at me, left me in two minds about him. How could someone not care, and yet be so sweet? How could I be friends with someone like that?

How could I be so damn attracted to someone like that?

I decided to take the middle ground for the first time, and extended my hand. 'Fine. Friends?'

He took my hand, but he didn't let go. He held on for a few seconds, and my breath hitched. His fingers lingered on my knuckles, and then gently retreated, and the library no longer looked distorted. Every book fell back into place, every table and chair, every person in the periphery of my vision.

'I'm tired of this place,' he said. 'It brings out the worst in everyone. Let's get out of here, just for today?'

To celebrate our rekindled friendship, we went to town. And on our way, I asked myself what it was about him that I liked so much. Did I like him because he was always so soft-spoken, so shy? He'd never hijacked any conversation, and had always made space for others. For the first time, someone didn't just desire me, they liked me for my spunk and my heart. For the first time, I felt like I was finally wearing my own skin. I liked talking to him. I liked standing near him. I liked the wordplay and the tension. I liked the ghost of that kiss between us.

After lunch, we stopped by Haji Ali for Rose faluda. In the evening, we got drunk on cheap alcohol, headed to Chowpatty beach and sat there for a bit. I watched him as he watched the Arabian sea in all its dreamy grandeur. Did the sunset make everything look more beautiful? The sky, the sea, the man in front of me? Why was the beating in my chest fluctuating every time he looked at me and smiled? Why did I feel like pressing my body onto his every time I locked my gaze with his intense eyes? And why did my hand move towards his, like a trick of gravity, when he spoke about something that still cut him in half every time he thought about it?

'Back home, when my brother hadn't been sick to the point of being bedridden,' Bagchi said, still enraptured by the crashing of the waves over the rocks. 'We used to go to the beach a lot. He loved going on the fisher people's boats, and they always took him along because they had such a soft spot for him. We'd go surfing on a thermocol board because we couldn't afford the real ones.'

'It actually sounds fun. I'd like to try it one day,' I said. He looked at me, a little discomposed, trying to understand if I meant what I said.

'Do you think I was selfish? Asking for attention from my parents when he was dying?' he asked me, and then looked away, as if he couldn't bear to wait for my answer.

It occurred to me that Bagchi's childhood was ridden with guilt. Guilt for wanting more from his family, guilt for taking up their time as the healthy child, survivor's guilt. Every time he mentioned his brother, he winced as if the loss had wedged itself somewhere within his body and was now causing physical anguish. I imagined Bagchi's little brother as a younger, lankier version of him. The same mischievous, roguish grin. The same serious eyes. I imagined him at sea, learning new things outdoors until his illness caught up with him.

I rested my head on Bagchi's shoulder and stared at his point of focus. He rested his head above mine. Another wave came by. Another wave dived back in. 'You were just a child.' I looked up at him. He turned towards me too. 'Don't be too harsh on yourself, Bagchi,' I said. He nodded, suddenly aware of how close we were sitting. His gaze skidded to my lips. They parted. Our arms were touching. Our thighs were touching. He curled his fingers through the gaps of mine, and time slowed. Stopped, even. And then someone threw a rock into the waters, and we realised where we were. He fell back, and I did too.

We sat there until the sun disappeared, and then I got up from where I was sitting and dragged him into another liquor shop. He protested at first, and then finally relented. 'What're you afraid of?' I asked, teasing him.

'You, Esai. You.'

I put my hands over my head. 'Me? What're you saying! I'm harmless.'

We got a few more bottles and spent the evening talking about our wildest drunk escapades. I told him about that one time Scheher and I had gone to a restaurant and ordered wine, only to realise it had been a dry day. Furious, we'd whined and begged them to make drinks for us, but they'd told us they didn't have the license to sell for the day. We'd finally coaxed a phone number out of them to buy in black, driven all the way to Andheri metro station, and met a few shady men underneath it. And then we'd gotten drunk senseless in my room until we'd passed out. He told me about being kissed by an older woman on an inebriated night, and then later realising she had a husband. We'd laughed all the way to dinner at Leopold Café, holding hands, falling onto each other, walking around upmarket old Bombay like lovers.

From there, we got a taxi, and all the way to the Bandra Worli Sea-link, we speculated about Kiran Desai and Orhan Pamuk's romance.

'I thought they were still together,' Bagchi said, faltering. 'I thought they were married and living in Istanbul.'

'No! But I do wish they were still together.'

'Look at us, gossiping! We're no different than everyone else in college.'

'But we're gossiping about literary figures. Don't you think that's cooler?'

'Elitist gossip is still gossip.'

'Are you calling me an elitist?'

'I'm calling you a gossiper.'

We were on the bridge now, and I rolled the windows down and put my head outside. 'Esai! What in the world?'

'Shh.' I dived back in and turned to him. 'Quickly! Put your head outside. On your side, *kid*. And look up. Do you see it? All the golden-yellow?'

'Damn. It's…stunning.'

The wind bolted through our hair, causing it to spread all across our faces, but we didn't care. As we faced the sky, taking in the lights above us as the taxi drove on, I had a feeling this night would never happen again. Not like this, not as captivating. I wouldn't want it again with anyone else, even if it was just as beautiful. I felt like I was watching two constellations merging and illuminating each other, like if I made a wish right now, right here, it would come true.

I closed my eyes and asked for nothing.

When I finally sat back on my seat, I realised I'd been crying all this while. Bagchi put his thumbs under my eyes and gently massaged me. I closed my eyes, drowsy from the sensation. 'Every time people cry, they usually look away, or look down, or even try to wipe their tears away. I saw you that day, outside the Cabinet office. Crying because of what I had said. Most people cry and feel ashamed about it. Or pretend they aren't crying. You cry with pride, Esai.'

Looking back, I know now that the night couldn't have ended any other way. I had been drawn to him since the very first day.

I moved towards him, staring into his eyes, willing him to make a move. He did.

His kiss was slow, and then searing. We devoured each other with our hungry mouths. I could feel my heartbeat escalating. My hands acting on their own accord, looping through his hair. I climbed onto his lap, and whispered his name. He stroked the side of my neck.

And then he put his hands under my shirt. The chemistry that exploded between us in that moment was astrophysics. I had a distinct vision of black holes dancing to electropop when he did that. Every kiss that followed after left me feeling like a test animal sent to space. Left my heart pounding like a drum festival. He did not ask the taxi driver to drop me at my place.

Instead, we went to his apartment.

One minute we were in the cab, a ritual of hands, and the next, we were cutting into sheets, collapsing into touch. Screaming, gasping, grasping. A low purring at the base of my throat, a sigh escaping him and crucifying me to his body.

His flatmates were asleep, it was two. It was the night of the blood moon, and we made out in panic and glory, in all the colours of the electromagnetic spectrum. Twin Houdinis, bodies moving magically. Tonight was different, tonight we were hounds in the dark. I wanted him, and he wanted me. He gripped my jaw, and then my mouth. Two fingers clasped around the jutting lower lip, and then he closed in on me. The sky changed hues. It was marvellous to see his face in different lights. Psychedelic purple. Coral. Homemade marmalade. Arousal in a kaleidoscope of sorts, and it was here that he fucked me.

He fucked me raw and hard. He pounded me till my ears

rang. Tongued the wetness till I was shaking. Made me come faster than a trapeze artist swinging.

And then we fucked some more.

When he finished at last, I slumped against him. I replayed the old dream of legs entangling and unknotting, as he outlined the quiver in my thighs. I could still taste the throbbing. I could still feel the dripping. I could see it in his eyes, nothing would ever be the same again.

In the morning, after his flatmates left for work, he made us breakfast. Joked about the size of my hair and how it kept getting between us. Held my hand while I spoke. Cupped my hips, stroked my back. Oscillated between silence and conversation. Didn't let go until I refused to undress for the fourth time. Pouted, made a sad face, told me he would call me. Told me that he loved me. But I couldn't love him. I could only show him there were consequences to being touched by temporary people.

And so, I didn't make any promises when I left. And I hoped to God that he didn't notice.

TWENTY-TWO

❖

The days that followed, I found myself in a liminal dream sequence. I stared at the hickeys on my neck. I traced the roadmap of his touch. I made nameless shapes and drew continents on my skin until guilt tickled me. Guilt was a thief. It didn't let me stay in the warm memory of last night for too long. Guilt admonished me for slaying the innocent. For turning Bagchi into collateral damage.

I'm sorry, I said, staring at the ceiling. How would I ever face Bagchi again?

He was in love with me. I cared about him. It was not the same.

He had called in the morning. I had pretended to still be asleep. He would call again. He would look for me on campus. What would I do then? Skip class? Avoid the library? Hide in the lake? And then to make matters worse, Ira had left a message on my phone. It had been vague, confusing and distressing. And no matter how many times I read it, I couldn't read between the lines.

Meet me, she'd said.

And so, during break, I found myself standing in front of

the principal's house. I had waited for the principal to leave, because I had no intention of running into him. He didn't know me and it was better that way. But what was I supposed to do now that I was here? And had Bagchi told Ira anything at all? What was I in for?

It was her mother who opened the door for me, and let me in. She looked like an older version of Ira, except for her eyes. Her eyes were pleasant, humble. They didn't have the regal, arrogant glint that her daughter and the rest of the family had been born with. 'She's in her room, upstairs,' she said, as if she had been expecting me, and then traipsed back to the big television set in front of her.

'Ira?' *Are we good?*

She was leaning against a computer chair, feet on her desk. She still had her satin loungewear on. A bottle of brandy was on the table, emptied out. Hiccupping loudly, she offered me some, and I didn't know how to tell her there wasn't any left in it. Apart from that, it was too early to be drinking.

I looked around at the clutter. 'Come on, Ira, don't do this to yourself.'

'Stop judging me. Everyone judges me. I thought you were my friend. That's why I called you here. I suppose that was a bad idea, after all.'

Shame ate at me. I thought about muscles rising, muscles falling. The in and out, it happened in heartbeat timeline. I looked at my hands, because there was nowhere else to look. 'I can help you, but only if you tell me what's wrong.'

'Ah. Saint Esai. Always ready to help the weak. Oh, wait. That's Scheherazade. I'm getting confused.'

I sucked in my breath and willed myself to tolerate her. It appeared to me that Ira wasn't the best of company when she was hurting. 'Are you all right?'

She closed her eyes for a good five minutes. I thought she'd even fallen asleep. And then, suddenly, she straightened, and kept her feet back down. 'You know, Esai. I've been thinking about how stupid everything is.'

'What do you mean?'

'Everything is so futile! Life is so damn expensive. Like there's literally a price to pay for everything. A broken heart for love. Death for a pet you adore. War and ruin for the homelands that made you. The impermanence of youth. When old age comes knocking, your mind forgets your favourite memories. There's no escaping it. So why do we name the things that don't last? Why give ourselves identities, experiences...why bother, why bother falling in love? Such a fucking waste of time. All of it, I tell you.'

Oh.

'In case you're wondering,' she said, slurring. 'Bagchi broke up with me.' And then she burst out laughing. 'You probably think I've gone insane.'

'No,' I said quietly.

'I'm laughing because we both thought I'd be the one who'd leave first. When it started out, I really wasn't thinking. It wasn't supposed to go on for this long. I knew Papa wanted me to marry some business tycoon, or you know, someone well-established. Not *this boy*, as he would so often say. Bagchi knew it too, he knew Papa didn't think highly of him, and he knew I'd never once fought with Papa for anything. I was my father's daughter, I'd been like that since the day I was born. We had zero expectations from the relationship. But then,' she said, her voice quivering. 'I fell in love with him.' A single tear dripped down her cheek. 'That idiot boy, I fell in love with him. My fault, right?'

I stood there, hands in my pockets, trying to make sense of the entire situation. So she didn't know I was involved. Bagchi had only told her he wanted out, and he had left it at that.

I was free to walk away clean, if I wanted to. But then she'd called me, not anybody else, when she was deteriorating. Why?

Because she thinks I'm her friend, I realized. Something punched my gut. I wanted to run and hide my face. *I'm not your friend*, I wanted to say. *I was never your friend*.

A framed photograph of Ira with her father sat on her desk. It had been shot the day they'd gone to the National Gallery of Modern Art. She looked so tiny and frail in that, and he looked so young, like how he'd looked in Minaxi's memories. He did not look like a man who had lost a loved one to a lake. He did not look like anything terrible had ever happened to him. *Like father, like daughter*, I thought. Laxman Dalvi. *What did you do? And where were you when she drowned?*

Ira caught me staring, and turned to look at the photo as well. She didn't say anything, but instead, disappeared into her own thoughts. Was she wondering when they'd gone from looking so happy to the countless arguments they had now? They hadn't always been at war. For example, in that photograph. He'd been funny, loving. But time had moved on from this childhood memory, and like age-worn wrinkles on the flesh, it had drawn between them boundaries of mistrust. The closer she looked, the more she could see the loose stitches and the wide holes that had made the relationship irreparable.

Slowly and deliberately, she turned the frame around. I diverted my gaze away from it, almost apologetically. 'You always have the best advice,' she told me. It pinched me that she trusted me like that, but I didn't counter her. 'Tell me, what should I do?'

'I think you should stop drinking,' I said feebly. What else could I say? 'We can go for a walk in the evening, get some fresh air,' I offered. 'How about that?'

She looked jaded. 'Don't tell me to stop drinking. I don't know how I'm going to get through the next few days without drinking. Or months. Or years.'

'We'll just take it one minute at a time, actually.'

'That's a good idea.' She pondered over it for a moment, and then looked at me. 'I think a walk would be nice. But not inside the campus.'

I nodded. We could have some tapri chai on the way to the park. Stop by the nursery and look at some flowers. Maybe I could buy her a pet plant, and maybe it would distract her for a while. 'Be ready at five?' I said. 'I'll come pick you up and we'll roam around. I was thinking of tea.'

'Tea would be perfect.'

But at five, when I knocked on her door again, she wasn't at home. Her mother had no idea when she'd left the house, had no idea where she'd gone. I called her a few times and then headed back home, dejected, feeling sorely responsible for her situation.

At eight, she finally returned my call.

I couldn't hear her voice over the loud music. *She's at a bar*, I thought. 'Ira?'

'Esai, I've texted you the address. Wear your best dress and come!'

She was partying in that newly opened club Joshua's father had a stake in. I didn't want to go there, but what if she was in trouble? She did sound sloshed. I ransacked my wardrobe hurriedly and pulled out a bell-sleeved dress I had borrowed from Tendral and never returned.

It was a shisha bar. I walked into the sequin-walled terrace, searching for Ira, assuming she was sitting in some corner, crying her eyes out. But then I heard her call me from one of the group tables, and I had no idea whose lap she was on, but he looked like he didn't know her either.

'This is Lohit.' Ira said to me, patting her new friend on the back, completely oblivious that her burgundy lipstick was smudged. And then she coiled her arms around the man's neck

like a gold chain. She kissed him hard, and then took a drag
from the hookah.

'Ira, let's go,' I pleaded, soft enough for only her to hear.

She met me with obstinacy. 'No, I'm going home with
Lohit.'

It annoyed me that she was behaving like this. Looking
around for the counter, I said, 'Fine. Do what you want. I'm
going to get something to drink.' I walked towards the bartender
and ordered a Bloody Mary and some fries to go with it. It had
been hours since I had eaten, and I was now angry and starving.

My drink was the first to arrive. As I sat on the bar stool,
blowing a fuse all by myself, I heard someone call me.

'Esai?'

I could recognize that voice anywhere. I turned around
swiftly, and there she was, standing in front of me in a
marvellous baby pink slip dress. 'Scheher,' I said.

'Wait, why are you drinking alone?' she asked.

I looked over at Ira, and then back at Scheher. Scheher
followed my gaze, and she understood.

'You're not with friends?' I asked Scheher.

'I was, but they've all left, and cabs kept cancelling on me.'

I smiled. 'I'm telling you, it's divine intervention. Can I get
you a drink?'

She seemed a little unsure. 'Okay. I'll have what you're
having.'

'But you're a wine person.'

She chortled. 'You know me too well, Esai.' I did. It was
no secret. Despite our very public blood feud, we were still
sisters. I could never hate her.

'So...you didn't tell me you and Ira went clubbing together.'
She looked let down. 'New best friends.'

'Hardly,' I said. 'I'm here only because someone had to
check on her.'

She looked at Ira closely from where we stood, and then nodded. 'She's binge drinking.'

She was the last person I wanted to talk about. 'When is your next show? I want to come watch.'

'Delhi. Piano Man. You'll fly with me?'

'I'll fly anywhere with you.'

She laughed. 'I know that.'

She looked around, letting the place creep in on her. 'We've never been here together, have we?' she asked. 'Although the two of us did cover most of Bombay. Remember?'

Yes, I remembered. We'd gone around the city as if we were tourists visiting for the first time. But there was something special about experiencing your own home with someone new, someone you could talk to for hours. Suddenly, the pollution and the dead rats during monsoon and the ugly houses built so close to one another that they put cursive letters to shame, became bearable. Suddenly, the museums and bookshops and highways became noticeable. Suddenly, everything was rose-tinted because of the conversations that were had there. We'd snuck into the Taj during lunch hour and while everyone else was eating from the buffet, we'd ordered the cheapest thing on the menu. Cold coffee. The waiter had judged us when we'd asked for two straws. We'd left as soon as possible, only to run into an old, weary man who'd been feeding the pigeons outside the hotel. We'd shared a glass of tea with him and his cab driver friend, and he'd told us, 'Years ago, I'd heard fireworks at an event around the corner and cleared out, because when I was a young boy, someone had yelled at me for blocking the wedding baraat.' Later, he'd learned the ghastly truth: there hadn't been any fireworks. It had been the sound of men gunning down guests at the Taj during the 26/11 assault.

And then hadn't there been that time we'd met a man with free VIP passes for a music festival? He'd been so enraptured by

Scheher's glitter eyes that he'd taken us along. But then we'd disappeared on him the minute we'd gotten in. And then, of course, how could I ever forget shopping at Colaba causeway? When I had picked up a bracelet for fifty rupees and asked the shopkeeper, 'Kiti zhaale?' Scheher had been swayed. She'd blurted out, 'Wait, you know Marathi?' And then the walk to the next café had been all about how there were more Hindi speakers in Bombay than the Marathi ones because a lot of people from different parts of the country were coming into the city for education and work. 'Even though Marathi is the official language around here,' Scheher had said. 'Some of my friends are from here, and they tell me they hate that it's being sidelined.' 'It's the same where I come from,' I'd replied. 'As a Tamilian, I feel very protective of my culture and nativity.'

We'd gone to plays together. We'd done karaoke at some extremely disreputable bars. We'd done the first day, first show for a movie nobody had ever heard of. We'd solved puzzles together in escape rooms. We'd walked past old movie sets in Film City. We'd played tic-tac-toe on a small board in an indie patisserie we'd discovered between two industrial buildings in Ghatkopar. We'd organized a story slam together to honour Mohamed Mattar, who'd been shot while trying to protect two women in Sudan. The whole world had turned blue for him because it had been his favourite colour. This had been back in June, when it had been hard to get anywhere because of the rain. We'd even binge-watched old serials together, learned from belly dancing tutorials on YouTube and ended up bumping into each other so many times we'd given it up. Nothing compared to the joy, love and wisdom we'd shared, nothing ever would. Because as far as college life was concerned, my best moments had always been with her.

At eleven-thirty, Ira puked over her expensive dress, and we knew it was time to go. She drunk-called Bagchi, and when he sounded afraid for her, she assured him that she was with me. He asked her to give the phone to me, but I shook my head, and made her cut the call.

'Wasn't that sweet? He was checking on me,' she said.

'You called him, not the other way round,' Scheher said bluntly.

'Yes, but he asked me if I was safe.'

'Bare minimum, Ira.'

'What's she saying?' Ira turned to me.

I laughed. 'You know, never mind.'

We got her into the cab, and sat on either side of her. She passed out, and we were thankful that she'd stopped talking. But then there was silence, and the silence was even more daunting. For the first time, I was glad to see St. Margaret's. I didn't think I could stand the awkwardness, and Ira's inebriated chatter every time she stirred awake. We walked from the campus gate, because they didn't allow vehicles in at this hour. The guards wouldn't have let us in either, but then, they saw Ira, and they didn't deny entry. 'Bigshot,' Scheher mumbled. 'Anyway, here we are.'

'You hold her,' I said to Scheher. 'And go ring the doorbell.'

'What? Why?'

'Because you're already in so much trouble. If the principal sees you being there for his daughter during a time of crisis, he'll warm up to you.'

She nodded, and hauled Ira towards the door. I walked away, and as I did, I watched them exchange small talk. He didn't notice me. It was odd to see the principal in normal clothes, in just an old t-shirt and capris. He folded his hands over his chest and looked at Ira sternly. She stood up straight at last, and then she wept. He took her in, and from where I stood, I imagined he was thanking Scheher for bringing her home.

And then Ira threw up again, this time, on the front of his

t-shirt. She burst into big, slurred apologies, and he immediately sent her to her room.

I watched Scheher take a step back, as Ira waved at her from inside. The principal then smiled curtly at Scheher, and shut the door on her. Cold war, I thought. He definitely wasn't going to warm up to her any time soon.

'Such a shallow man, I tell you,' Scheher said later, as she caught up with me. 'Anyway, see you?'

I nodded, looking back to see if the principal was watching through the window. The lights were off, and the curtains drawn. Had we woken him up? No, it seemed like he had been waiting for Ira to get back safe. I had seen him, even though he had not seen me. He was still the same petrified young boy in the dream. Underneath all that power and authority, he was still *Lax*. I could see it now.

I dropped Scheher to the back gate, and watched her leave. Once she had completely vanished from my sight, I turned on my heels and ran.

I wanted the forest to myself. I wanted to swim in the lake. I wanted to know the truth.

Somewhere, a light gleamed. I was thirsty for water, and I was in too deep.

The truth was, I had seen her again while Scheher had been talking with the principal. She had stood in between two big Banyan trees, and she had been staring at us. I had a feeling she had come out of the lake to say something, and I couldn't leave without hearing it.

As I got closer, I heard the singing all over again. I sang along, and then I danced. A mirror appeared before me, made of mist. The dancing girl in the reflection wasn't me, it was her. I swayed to the rhythm of the lake, and in the mirror, she did the same. Her piercing stare consumed me.

The lake looked beautiful tonight. It was decorated with

lamps and coloured lights. The whole place basked in a pink hue, and there were butterflies everywhere. Somewhere ahead, there was an apparition of a swing, its ropes loose and long like the stems of magic mushrooms. Its seat was the yellow-brown of old books, and when I sat on it, it disappeared. Yet another deceptive illusion. She giggled, and so did I. She picked a flower from one of the bushes and dropped it behind my ear. When I touched it, it dissolved into petals. I plucked more flowers. Ixoras. Tulips. Daffodils. Violets. But in my palms, they all turned to dust.

She was laughing now. 'You're playing with me,' I said to the mirror.

The clouds took on shapes and blew close to me. The head of a lion. A sitar. A battleship. I swiped at them and continued dancing to the private view of stars.

'Terrible, isn't it?' Her voice carved its way into my head. 'To be young and doomed.' I looked into the iridescent water, and saw her face, serene and smiling. I dipped my feet into it and let myself fall into the depths, as the orbs bobbed up and down. In harmony with the cosmic dance of the waves. I loaned my body to the water, and my muddy feet awakened into dark turquoise scales.

The Lake Woman's outstretched arms rose from below, morphing into a cradle. Drugged by her perfume, I slept like a foetus. Her dreams were my dreams now.

TWENTY-THREE

Nanda sir once told me how Joan of Arc had screamed prayers so loud that she'd drowned out the roar of flames. I wanted to be just as loud when it all ended.

Sometimes, I dreamed about the life I had before spending an entire half year with shaky legs and a weakened heart. The girl who'd entered St. Margaret's, so full of questions about science and existence, was now a sleepwalking sisterhood of bones. Maybe I could just run away from all of this and start again someplace else. After all, hadn't Galileo been a college dropout?

But dropping out was the least of my concerns. I knew it had to happen at some point. With what I knew now, how could I not?

I'd been so depressed that I hadn't even noticed how long it had been since I'd had my last cycle. I'd lost my appetite a very long time ago, and it hadn't made a difference in the world or to me.

At first, I comforted myself with lies. *It's the stress.* But I couldn't bring myself to stay with it for too long. Now that I had my doubts, I also began to notice how my body had changed.

Hadn't I been running to the bathroom a little too often the past few months? Hadn't I had such ugly mood swings despite the medication I was taking?

And then another month passed, and I couldn't live in denial anymore. I had a sick feeling in the pit of my stomach, and I saw a doctor to confirm what I already knew. He'd said *congratulations* at first, and then when he saw my shattered face, he'd quickly registered the situation. It was too late for an abortion, he'd said, but adoption and every other option was laid out before me in hopes of making me feel better. In hopes of fixing this accident.

Now what? I kept thinking, throughout the auto ride back home. I thought I was dying, but clearly, I was two lives now.

I spent the whole night crying after coming back to my apartment. I stared at the ceiling for hours, wondering how to tell Lax about the baby.

There's going to be a baby.

I decided to break the news to him the next evening, when his class got over. I hadn't gone to college in a very long time, and my attendance was so abysmal that I probably wouldn't have been allowed to write my exams either. Why was I concerned about ruining my future if I already didn't have one?

I could do this, I told myself. Rose, crescent moon, starlight and the sweetness of my mother's milk—that's what I was made of. I wouldn't be afraid. I waited till dawn, and then I washed my face and got ready. I had to get my life together, just for today. I waited until the last bell rang, and then I saw him. He was standing at the entrance of the Physics lab, talking to a classmate.

He strode towards me in his usual diffident style, wearing an exorbitant black shirt. It was the first time I took notice of how different we both looked. He was neat, always civil, and from an affluent family. It showed. And I? I was poor and shabby and cut open. I wasn't the least bit lovable. So what was he doing here, holding my hand?

'I can't stay for long,' he said. His father needed him home to help out with some official work. After a few minutes of grumbling and cursing his father, he told me he loved me, hugged me momentarily, and took his leave. He apologized countless times and told me he would make it up to me. *I've to say something important,* I screamed inwardly. *There's a baby. Do you hear me? There's a baby!*

I could feel myself growing agitated. I almost made my way to Nanda sir's office, the one place I could cry in peace, but then I'd felt the shame. I'd bunked classes to a point of no return. And I was in no state to drop by for chai.

So I stayed away. I stayed away from everyone except Lax. I completely disappeared from college, and nobody even noticed I was away, except for Nanda sir. Lax told me he often stopped him on the campus streets, asking why I wasn't coming to class. The last time I'd seen him was in class, when I'd been sitting in a corner and staring out the window, crying. I'd turned my face away from him so he wouldn't notice. But he'd seen me the minute he'd entered the room, and when it had ended and everyone had begun streaming out for break, he turned to me and said, 'Are you okay, child?' He hadn't once been offended that I hadn't paid attention to his lecture. And he'd mindfully waited until the bell rang so he didn't have to draw attention to me when everyone was watching. I couldn't stand how beautiful he was.

I missed Nanda sir's goodness. But he couldn't know, nobody could.

When I finally mustered the courage to tell Lax, I'd already made up my mind. I was not going to see this as a mishap. Maybe this was a good thing. Maybe I needed a child in my life to love me.

Maybe Lax needed it too.

But I was wrong. Lax had gone weak at the knees when I told him. And when he finally opened his mouth to say something at all, he said, rather brusquely, 'Minaxi, I'm not ready for this. I'm so young! *You're* so young.' Tears collected in his eyes. 'My father will hate me forever if I ruin my future like this. He has all these plans for me, Minaxi, and I just can't...'

But I'd had plans too. I'd dreamed of a future too. For a moment, I felt really bitter and cheated in life. Here he was, being groomed to run an entire college. Where did I fit into that picture? 'You just can't what?' I asked.

'If...if you're going ahead with this, we can't be together,' he blurted out.

'What?'

'We can't be together.' He suddenly looked and sounded like his own father. What had I been missing all this while?

'Lax...'

I couldn't stand to see him let me down. It hadn't been the first time. He'd never fought for me when the seniors maligned me. He'd never once publicly acknowledged me. He'd never done anything but look after himself. He'd swung from wanting everyone's approval to wanting me. And now he'd lost me.

I called up my little sister. She immediately quit boarding school and came over. We held each other the whole night and cried. The last time we'd cried like this was when our parents had died.

It had been the summer of our chicken pox and the festival season in our local temple. My sister and I had locked ourselves up in our room, covered in the medicinal variety of red sandalwood known as *raktachandanam*. We'd tormented ourselves by scratching our skin to perdition.

But then our grandmother had told us a story, and the pox hadn't felt so bad after all. It was about a demon who'd

been murdering children by inflicting them with a deadly fever.
And to protect them from this demon, a goddess called Shitala
appeared with her silver broom and holy water and entered
their bodies in the form of rashes.

According to our grandmother, the pox was a good sign. It
meant that the goddess had visited us. And because the goddess
was already in our house, she'd declared that there was no
reason to go to the temple.

But our parents wanted to see the ritualistic mime dance
being performed in front of the shrine, so they went anyway.
And as fate would have it, one of the elephants there went
berserk, trampled its keeper, and ran amok. People escaped
with their lives, but in this stampede, we lost two people who
meant everything to us. We lost our parents.

Ever since, it was our grandmother who had cared for us.
She used to work in a garment factory. She could sit in front
of a sewing machine for hours and still not feel too tired to tell
us stories about kings and demigods and boons and curses. She
died quickly in the early hours of the morning, crying for her
deceased son. It was only after her death that my sister and I
were allowed to turn to our inheritance. We'd been lucky in
the sense that it had been enough to fund our education, but
it still always felt like we were scraping by. We turned into
misers, and we overcompensated by working part-time and
committing to our books, and in turn, we were rewarded for
our hard work with scholarships. Making it to St. Margaret's,
with all that had happened, was not easy. But I'd seen the city
and fallen in love with it, and then I'd seen the campus and
couldn't be convinced to leave.

Now I was here, at these crossroads, unable to decide where
to go. I felt lonely and unhappy.

And then one day, Lax knocked on my door. I'd been too
startled to consider whether I was still upset with him or not.

He barged in, confessing he couldn't lose me. 'Ever since we met, I've never lived without you. Don't ask me to do it now.'

I made him some tea and together we discussed what we would do next. 'An abortion isn't possible, is it?' he asked me dejectedly, and I shook my head.

'If you don't want to be around, I will try and understand that, Lax,' I said.

He flinched. 'Of course, I want to, Minaxi. How poorly do you think of me?'

I ran my fingers through his hair and smiled. 'I'm just in a very bad place right now. I don't know what to think of anyone.'

'We can make this work,' he said, a little wobbly. I could tell it took a lot from him to say something so audacious, and I wasn't sure if he could ever live up to his word. But I took it anyhow, because I was so needy for hope. He left an hour later, dispelling most of my fears. I rinsed the tea cup and kept it back on the shelf. I ignored the crack on its side.

In the evening, my sister and I sat on the balcony of our makeshift apartment. I caught her staring at me raptly, and raised my eyebrows. 'What?'

'Have you spoken about money to raise the child? Marriage? You know, all the important things,' she asked, and then looked away. My insides writhed. But I couldn't show her that it bothered me as well. So I said, 'Lax is looking for a job in another city. We'll be out of here soon. You, me, Lax and the baby. We won't be living on our inheritance or our savings; I'll find a job immediately after the delivery. You won't have to work anymore.'

'I don't mind it.' She had stopped her studies indefinitely and taken up an accounting job in Bombay. At first, I had raised objections, but she'd been determined, and both of us knew we needed it. Lax hadn't offered any financial aid or spoken to his father about it, and I was too proud to ask.

'I want you to go to school,' I told her. 'I already hate myself for taking that away from you.'

The way she handled it was so elegant, and I was grateful she was my sister. 'You took nothing away from me. I wanted to do this. One year off is nothing. I'll catch up,' she said, and I believed her.

It was not an easy pregnancy. My body didn't feel like my body anymore, and my mind played tricks on me. A part of me was frantic about dropping out of college, and a part of me couldn't see what lay ahead for me. This hadn't been my plan, and on most days, I felt disappointed in myself. I even felt rattled when Lax talked about his semester exams, and reminded myself the jealousy was natural. I would go to college again someday. I would have my own laboratory and in-house telescope someday, just like Nanda sir.

In my third trimester, I could barely get up. My sister took me to the obstetrician once a week, and the scans and tests left me unbelievably fatigued. She was with me all this time, and she stayed up with me whenever I couldn't fall asleep from the pain.

Towards the end, my blood pressure went up, and Lax had not come to see me at the hospital. I lay there, staring at the ceiling, while my sister slept on a metal chair in the same room. We did breathing exercises together, and though it had just been a few hours since the labour pain began, it felt like an eternity had passed. And then I saw the healthcare provider, and she smiled at me. I suddenly felt very safe.

Minaxi, push.

Push harder.

Gentler.

When it was all over, my stretch marks looked like claw marks. But there was a baby. God, yes. A healthy, tender baby watching me with fresh eyes. Making me feel so brand new.

It shocked me how quickly I could love something I'd sworn I wanted nothing to do with. All it took was one pair of big, wet eyes, and my heart defrosted. Her softness thawed the ice away, and I relented. I couldn't help but adore her. I was crying now, and laughing too. My sister stood next to me, staring into her face, looking besotted. 'She's beautiful,' she said, her voice shaking. I could feel a knot in my throat. My whole body ached, but nothing mattered. I had just witnessed a miracle. For months, I had felt like dying. But not today. Today had changed everything. One baby had changed everything.

'You should name her,' I told her.

She looked scandalized. 'Me? Name a baby?'

Initially, she wasn't sure she could take up the task. But as the days progressed, she began writing down names in her notebook and then scratching them out. I had never seen anyone take anything so seriously in their life. It had amused me and been my source of entertainment for a while.

Eventually she made a decision. She came up to me one day as I was lying on my cot, and said, 'Esai. Her name is Esai.'

It meant music. I loved it.

When I wasn't too fatigued, I watched Esai sleep. I woke up every two hours, because that was how often she did too. My little sister was a fast learner as well and picked up every trick in the book when it came to caring for the baby. I couldn't have done it without her.

The only time I didn't feel that way was when she nagged me about Lax. She had never been one to hold back from expressing herself. And so, as more days passed, her questions about why he wasn't involved augmented. It even led to arguments in our house, and a mental breakdown.

I said things like, *exams.*

His father would get suspicious.

He was busy finding a job.

But my own excuses distressed me. And she further fuelled my worry by asking, 'If he wanted to, he would, right? He's not avoiding you, right?'

I thought about the number of times we'd met up over the past year. I'd been so caught up myself, with the pregnancy and then the childbirth. And of course, through it all, the depression. But this happened to new parents, didn't it? They get so busy with the child that they don't have time for each other.

But I'd been the one busy with the child. So what had he been doing all along?

I started showing up outside his class every day. And then twice a day. I was getting restless, uncertain, and above all, panicky. He assured me he would find work somewhere, and then we could elope.

But what about your father? I wanted to ask. *Won't he have a problem with you leaving college behind and running away with me?*

I never asked. I was terrified of him getting cold feet again if I brought up his family. So instead, I waited for him. I waited for him to apply for work and I waited for him to tell me he'd heard back from one of them, at least.

But nothing changed except for me. I was on my medication again. I increased my Buspirone dosage, I paced the ground more often. On the side, I was looking for work too, in case he failed at it. Maybe he could stay home and take care of the baby, I told myself angrily.

The day I got signed on to work at a call centre, I told Lax that we could pack up and leave.

'No, we're going to Ahmedabad,' he told me, elated. It was a Sunday evening, and the campus was empty. We stood near the Botany tank, and as if touched by serendipity, we both had the same news to share.

'What?'

'I got a job in Ahmedabad! Get your things, meet me outside my place, and let's run away.'

I didn't ask what it was. I didn't think twice about anything, because I was leaving. I ran back to my room, packed my trunk, and lifted the baby from the cotton cradle. I pulled a shawl over us, and left a note for my sister, who was fast asleep.

The guards at the main gate didn't notice the baby, because they were talking with each other, and she was sleeping. A couple from second year, who hadn't been there earlier when I'd met Lax, gave me strange looks as I walked in, but I didn't care. I kept going. When I reached Lax's house, I rang the doorbell. I was in for a surprise.

It was his father who opened the door. 'Come in, Minaxi.'

Perplexed, I walked in. The same old familiar house, and yet, so many unfamiliar faces. Lax sat there, in one of the armchairs, palms on his knees. There was no suitcase. And he was in his pyjamas.

My intuition turned into a bowling alley. All pins dropped in unison when I saw the look on his face.

There were others in the room. I recognized Dr. Raja Dalvi, the founder of St. Margaret's, and Lax's grandfather. 'These are the members of the founding council,' Dr. Dalvi explained, studying my expression. 'But not all of them,' he added, turning to two men with shaved heads, and masks on their faces. 'Old friends,' he said. 'I've a lot of connections, you see.'

There was a gun in their hands. My brain froze.

Dr. Dalvi saw what I had seen, and threw me an insidious smile. 'What to do, Minaxi. Times have changed. We've moved on from trading in illegal drugs and smuggling gold and human trafficking...to real estate and film production and sometimes even universities.'

I looked at Lax, but he was staring into his lap. Why had

he never told me about this side to his family? Was this why he had always been so afraid of them?

'See, I'm not going to let some *randi* ruin my grandson's future.' The baby began crying. That was when Lax looked up. Our eyes met. His were moist, painfully apologetic. 'And I'm not going to let some *randi* destroy St. Margaret's legacy.'

His words jabbed at my throat and left me speechless. I could see it now. Lax had never wanted the baby. That day, when I'd broken the news to him, I should have known how he'd felt from the way he reacted. I'd been stupid to trust his change of heart when he came back that day. He'd probably run to his father and told him everything when he realised I couldn't abort. And then, of course, the rest of the family got involved.

How did a love that had first felt like hugging a tree, like crying into soft fur, like a childhood friend, now turn into something so vicious? Our entire illicit relationship blazed before me like a pipe dream. I saw myself standing outside Richardson Hall after Lax had confessed he loved me for the first time. I saw myself walking beside him one rainy evening, and then closing the distance between us when nobody had been around to watch. Our friendship had eased into love. Once we had even dreamed of a beautiful future together.

And now? Now it had all gone up in smoke. Now there was nothing left of it but regret.

I hate you, I wanted to scream at him. *Your love is nothing more than backstabbing.*

'I built this college from the dust on my spine. From my very veins. And you dare soil it,' Dr. Dalvi said angrily. Esai cried harder, and he glared. 'That thing is not ours.'

'I agree,' I said, nodding. 'I'll take her somewhere far from here, raise her on my own. You have my word.'

He shook his head. 'But what good is a word? Can't it be

changed tomorrow? You say you will stay away, but what if your little love child grows up and comes back to claim this land? What then?'

'I'm not like your grandson,' I said coldly. 'I don't make false promises.'

He shook his head sadly. 'It's too late, girl.'

The hitmen moved towards me, their eyes on the baby. I swiftly turned towards the door, flung it open, and skyrocketed out of there. I didn't even realize where my feet were taking me, until I found myself in the residential compound of my apartment. I lost them for a while, or so I thought. They were professionals, it wouldn't be long before they found me. I ran up the stairs, and I banged on the door. I should've woken up my sister the minute I'd decided to leave. Why hadn't I consulted her? Why had I been so impulsive? 'Jolly! Jolly, please. Jolly, open the door!'

'Minaxi?' My little sister stood there in her night gown, looking confounded.

'Take her,' I said, panting, handing the baby over to her. From where I was standing, I could hear their approaching footsteps on the staircase. I hurriedly filled her in.

'Wait, where are you going?' she asked, mortified.

'I...don't know, Jolly.'

'When will you come back?' Her voice was a whimper.

We were both crying now, and my heart went out to her. The footsteps got louder, and I pushed her in and closed the door on her. We had run out of time. And I truly was sorry.

By the time the men arrived, I was hiding behind the neighbour's gigantic shoe rack. I let them scurry towards the opposite end, and then I quickly got up from where I was crouching and ran down the stairs. They could have been well-trained at gymnastics for all I cared, but I was running for my life.

We were going in circles. I led them out of my place, grateful that Esai had stopped crying by the time we'd been at the door. Maybe the comfort of the house had caused her to calm down, or maybe she'd been too shocked by all the running.

My ribs hurt, and my lungs felt like they were stitched together with cold air. I didn't stop, even though I didn't know where I was going.

At one point, I realised I had reached the back gate of the college again. The men signalled at the guard to grab me, and I had no choice but to run inside before he could.

I was on campus again. I was in their territory.

They were getting closer, and I could feel my stamina begin to die out. I still kept running through the woods, my hands slapping against the branches, and only ever stopped when I reached a dead end. Beyond this point, nobody knew what stood, because I was staring at the forbidden lake.

This is it. I could feel them behind me.

I realised Esai's blanket was still in my hands. I hurriedly gathered some rocks and dropped them inside it.

I lowered the bundle into the lake, hoping for a reaction. They just stood there, staring at me, with nothing much to say. 'There, she's dead. Isn't that what you wanted?'

One of them moved forward. He had a gun in his hand, and he placed its mouth on my forehead. I could smell the paan on his breath, the apathy on his face.

They said that when you died, you had seven minutes of brain activity left in which you watched a dream-like sequence of your memories. I thought it was beautiful, the idea of being cast in your own private short film. Of starring in your own story and then becoming the audience in the final throes of existence. What was it like, to watch the art you created flit before you like the supercut of an unfinished masterpiece? Wouldn't it be like the universe saying, take a bow? Go, but with thunderous applause.

'Turn,' the man ordered. I took a deep breath, and turned. *It was a good life. And if it wasn't, then at least, it was mine.*
'Now jump,' he said.
I prayed for gills.

TWENTY-FOUR

When Laxman Dalvi and his father came looking for Minaxi in the depths of the forest, they already knew she was dead. Their men had said she'd jumped into the lake the same time they'd fired the bullet. They'd waited for her to resurface, but when she did, it had been as a lifeless body, floating in the water. There had been no baby. They'd searched everywhere, and I'd stayed missing.

Jolly had taken me to Kodaikanal, where she'd spent most of her school years, and raised me there. It was here that she'd met Pipi, and five years later, they'd married. Jolly and Pipi had loved me like their own child. Even when they had Tendral, they loved me like their own child. Nothing changed.

I grew up hearing stories about Minaxi. About her kindness. About the difficult pregnancy and the uncertainty. Jolly had kept her photos and everything she'd owned, but nothing had given us closure. We had both lost someone so dear to us—a mother, an older sister—and we clung onto each other throughout our grief. 'That place,' she'd said to me, more often than once. 'That horrid place built by those murderers is still there. And there's no way I can prove what they did to her.'

And she'd been right. I'd arrived at St. Margaret's just to see how prosperous the Dalvi clan had become, how unfazed they were by the incident that had happened twenty-five years ago. Laxman Dalvi had married, and his daughter, Ira, was now running her own government on campus. The only proof of my mother's existence was the ugly rumour that there was a spirit in the lake. She'd been reduced to a witch, and he had been elevated to the principal. They had bought more land, and they'd built more wings and opened more departments. It had been agonizing to watch. And then I'd met Scheherazade, first a wannabe poet, and then, a glamorous teen icon who could not be stopped. She was ambitious. And she'd hated the college as much as I did.

I still remember the day everyone had laughed at her poetry and she'd told us about the Lake Woman. The day I'd taken her to dinner and told her I was going to help her write better. 'It just needs a bit of tweaking,' I'd said. 'Let's make your dream happen, Scheherezade.' She'd looked at me like I was some talent manager who'd dropped from the sky. She'd asked me why I was doing this for her, and I'd simply said, 'I want you on my side.' I hadn't told her anything else. There had been nobody I could trust.

And during dinner, she'd told me again, 'You're always the one taking care of me. I want to take care of you too someday. I want to be there for you.' And I'd taken a deep breath and told her about everything that had happened to my mother. I'd told her that it had been exactly twenty-five years since Minaxi had been killed, and that baby had survived because Jolly had taken care of her. That I wasn't eighteen like the other students, but twenty-five years old. That because I'd spent all my life around Tendral, it had been easier to masquerade as a younger student. She'd even cut my curtain bangs for me, and curated my entire college wardrobe. She'd done everything to make sure I would fit in with the crowd, without raising any suspicions.

Scheher had listened without interruption. She'd kept
oscillating between shock and awe. And then I'd revealed
to her my plan of bringing the college down to its knees. I
couldn't prove that they'd killed my mother, but I could still
destroy them.

'They killed someone, and covered it up,' Scheher had said,
clenching and unclenching her fists. 'Do you think they started
that rumour about her too?'

'It doesn't matter. What matters is, we pull out every bad
thing they ever did, be a sort of loud speaker to their corruption.
Amplify it.'

Back then, Scheher had fit into the agenda so perfectly.
Sometimes I did ask myself if it was opportunistic of me to
have enlisted someone so fragile, someone so easily influenced.
Sometimes I felt a stab of remorse too, especially because I'd
grown to care about her. I wondered what she'd think of me
if she knew.

And now here we were, almost winding down. When I
returned home, completely drenched, she was sitting on my
chair, notebook in her hand. She was waiting for me, and
when she saw me, she shook her head. 'You went for a swim
at this hour?'

Almost every day after class had ended, we'd met at my
place or hers. We had faked a fallout to avoid suspicion that
we were working together, and to ensure Ira's trust. Scheher
had become her enemy, and it had opened up the door for me
to become her advisor.

It hadn't felt good to ignore Scheher on campus. It had felt
worse when we'd had to stage that fight in front of everyone
and sell them the idea that we weren't friends anymore. But
it had all been worth it. Ira had taken me in completely, and
she had listened to everything I'd told her to do. She had been
provoked enough to slap Joshua. And Bagchi had been gullible

enough to open up about Cabinet secrets. Scheher, being the Journalism student that she was, managed to unearth a lot of gold too. Everything she had written in the zine had been true. Exaggerated, but still true.

'Every time you return from the lake,' Esai said, interrupting my thoughts. 'You have this weird, lost look in your eyes. You know that, right?'

I thought about how the lake had been looking so clear lately. How the hints had felt like breadcrumbs leading me towards a destination. I looked around for my towel as I rubbed my feet on the carpet. 'It was cold,' I said.

'Of course it was cold!' Scheher cried. She'd been staying over almost every weekend this month. 'It's the middle of the night, and you were inside a lake.'

'I have a feeling this was the last time,' I said.

I'd awakened to the sound of running anklets. Surrounded by ruins of an age-old temple. I'd emerged out of the vortex, a Trojan horse. I'd lain plastered to the earth for a while, as if heavy paperweights were on me, holding me down. And then suddenly feeling inadequate, like I could never be sacred enough to be there, I'd gotten up, and made my way back.

'Anyone else would think you're mad, swimming in the middle of the forest at this godforsaken hour.'

I smiled. 'I made sure nobody saw me.'

She leaned forward and pulled at my wrist. 'So listen. I need help. I've been waiting for an hour.' She made me sit on the bed, completely unbothered by the puddle I was creating from my wet clothes. 'What do you think of this?'

'One look at me, and death becomes a flower.'

I mulled it over. 'I think it's great,' I said, wiping my hair with the towel. 'But go with something more specific. Like, one look at my beautiful face and the noose bursts into a garland of flowers.'

Her eyes lit up. 'Oh, that's brilliant! I'm using that.'

'New poem?'

'Yes. I guess.' She sighed. 'I wish I could write like you. I've said that a million times, I know.'

'Don't mention it,' I said. As she continued to brainstorm, I began changing into dry clothes. She suddenly looked up from her book. 'Esai, did you tell your new boyfriend about what we've been up to?' she asked me.

'What new boyfriend?' I asked tepidly. 'And what *have* we been up to?'

'Come on!' She threw the pen at me, and I swerved. 'I know Bagchi broke up with Ira for you. I'm not stupid, I see how you look at each other. And before long, I'm sure everyone's going to find out anyway.'

'Some secrets can be kept well,' I said, laughing. And then I grew solemn. It hurt my conscience to be joking about Bagchi, even though I knew I could do nothing about it. 'But really, I can't be with him. Because he doesn't know me.'

'He doesn't know anything?'

I shook my head. 'You know, that day in Nanda sir's house, when Raza came in as the electrician, Bagchi almost caught me smiling at him. I think he knew I knew him. I don't know. He even asked me about it. Close call.'

There was a forced cough near the door. Both of us turned. 'Did someone say my name?'

Raza, Tendral's boyfriend, was standing there, smiling widely. 'What're you scheming about now?'

'Raza!' Scheher said, moving in for a hug. *Humara ladka*, she always called him. *Our boy.*

Tendral appeared by his side too, a bowl of bhel in her hands. 'You were eavesdropping,' I said, scolding her. It had been dangerous to tell her everything, and I'd only been looking out for her by not involving her in the entire plan.

'So what if I was?' she said, grinning. Turning to Scheher, she said, 'To date, Esai has no idea how the hacking worked. Ask her to explain?'

'I will, I will. But tell me, were you ever scared?' Scheher asked Raza. I got up and bolted the door so that nobody else would overhear us.

'I was,' Raza admitted. 'I literally had to walk into some nutty professor's house and secretly install a small camera facing his computer. And he wouldn't stop watching me and talking to me.'

I laughed. I would never forget that evening. Nanda sir had been so engrossed in Raza's work that he had refused to take his eyes off of him. 'But I got him off your back for you, didn't I?'

'By then, I was melting in my own sweat.'

'So you installed a camera in Nanda sir's house, masquerading as the electrician. Then what? Did you even fix his light?' Scheher asked.

'I did, of course I did,' Raza said. 'Didn't Esai tell you anything?'

'I'm not into tech,' I said, taking offense. 'I couldn't imagine where to begin while telling her any of this.'

Tendral stepped in. 'Okay. Let me try to explain it in layman's terms. We put the camera there, so we could see the professor's keyboard when he logged in. This way, we could track his finger movements. And this way, we got the password to the staff Wi-Fi.'

'Very smart.'

'Once we had access to this password, we could easily get into the server. All the marks that were entered into the system, we altered them. I mean, it's a crime. We're definitely criminals.'

'But not bigger criminals than St. Margaret's fabulous management,' I added.

'And the Cabinet,' Scheher said. 'Don't forget them.'

'Going back to Nanda sir's house to remove the camera was close to impossible. I had to pretend like I'd given him a faulty tube light, and that was why I was coming back.'

'Raza, Nanda sir is not scary,' Scheher said. 'He's just a bit loony. A mad scientist of sorts.'

'He talks too much, I'm telling you.'

We didn't have a lot of time, and because I had to speak to Scheher privately now, I said to them, 'Anyway, both of you, out. You've heard enough.' I motioned for them to leave.

'I'm honestly glad I don't have a bigger sister,' Raza said. After a bit of mewling and grumbling, I was able to send them away.

I closed the door and looked towards Scheher excitedly. 'So, what do you know?'

She beamed. 'I've been speaking with Joshua, you know this.'

Yes, I did. We both knew, after Ira had slapped him, that he'd become their weak link.

'How is he?'

'Angry, upset. He gave me a lot of content for the zine. He's a raging bull with no brains.'

I shrugged. 'No surprises there.'

'So easy to manipulate, and God, I'm enjoying it.'

'That's why I thought you should do it.' I sat on the bed again, this time, a little on the edge. The pool of water had dried up under the fan. 'So how has it been going?'

'Remember you and Ira ran into me at the new hookah bar in Versova? I was actually with him there. I was buying him drinks to get him talking, and acting all sympathetic to how Ira had humiliated him in public. I had to lie and say I still loved him,' she said, pursing her lips. 'He called her a bitch, said he knew things about her to bring her down. The more I agreed with him, the more validated he felt, and the more provoked he became as well.'

I imagined Scheher doing to Joshua exactly what she'd done to her. I imagined her alienating him and turning him against his own friend after he'd been deceived. Scheher, a crusader for the enemy's rights as well. 'Good,' I said, and nodded at her to go on.

She frowned. 'He told me he was still angry about her choosing Bagchi over him.'

I did a double take. I'd always had a feeling there was something between them, but it still caught me by surprise. 'What?'

'Yes, listen to this. I can't believe he never told me when we were together. Apparently he liked her. And they'd gotten really close in their first year, so he thought they would date. So all that rejection came back again, and he was like a leaking tap. He just had to talk about it, and I was his free therapist. Of course, it was the same thing on loop: I've always been there for her, doing her dirty shit. Who does she think she is, anyway? We even bunked classes on the same days, she bunked more than me, in fact. But when the attendance sheet was put up, she had her seventy-five per cent. I caught her on it, told her I knew. She said, fine, I'll talk to Papa and get yours to normal too. So they rigged it. She did it for me, not for that shit show, Bagchi. I covered up for her, and she thinks she can slap me in front of everyone? Who does she think she is?'

'Oh my God.'

She told me Joshua had descended into a bottomless pit of self-pity. 'I should've slapped her back,' he'd kept saying. 'I should've never covered up for her with the attendance.' And then Scheher had wondered out loud, 'You know, the best way to destroy someone like Ira would be to take away what she loved the most.'

'Bagchi?' he'd asked.

'No,' she'd replied, irked by his stupidity. 'St. Margaret's. *St. Margaret's.*'

He'd gone home inebriated and simmering from the idea she'd put in his head. Scheher had been successful in reducing him to nothing but a pit of hot coal. But I was too busy thinking about what she had said earlier to feel moved by Joshua's reaction.

'Scheher,' I said, as I let all the information set in. 'If Ira didn't have enough attendance...'

Scheher's smile was loud and blinding, a chandelier. We both looked at each other as if we'd stumbled upon a gold mine.

'That's right, my dear Esai,' she said, her eyes shining. 'Our chairwoman had no right contesting for the post of chairwoman. She didn't have enough *attendance.*'

TWENTY-FIVE

Once, in a summer reserved only for the magnificence of mango trees, I had sprawled across a lover's bed, listening to him talk about chaos theory and the butterfly effect. How small changes could lead to large-scale repercussions. One momentary slip of the wheel. One tiny hole in the tire. One baby pigeon flying into a plane during take-off. One lovely smile. One kiss. But of course, the greatest butterfly effect was whittled into history, as they say, on that fated June 28, 1914, when the driver of Archduke Franz Ferdinand, heir to the Austro-Hungarian empire, made a wrong turn into Franz Josef Street in Sarajevo after a narrow assassination escape. Ravaged by the failed plan to execute Ferdinand and stopping for a sandwich on his way home, on the very same street, was Gavrilo Princip, the Bosnian Serb student and cohort of the earlier bomb thrower.

To say the least, a wrong turn and a sandwich started the First World War.

Words, in that sense, were a lot like butterflies. Everything that was said, had its own monumental outcome. Words could be opinions. Ideas. Ideologies. Weapons. All winged, all equally gorgeous. All destined to align someone's stars or tear them apart. Designed to be little wars.

All it took was a woman's reckless laughter to begin a war.

Something as fragile as an anklet could lead to the burning of a capital city.

In the end, it was brazen, enticing gossip that caused a college to dismantle like a standard chair.

To this day, it left me wholly and unreservedly mesmerized, like a child watching the miracle of a wind chime unfold. Mellow light raining on the stained glass. Melodies tinkling through the hanging bells. Colours flaring up and then easing. And eventually, a silence overlapping it all like a snug blanket.

How easy it was to start a fight.

We marched in through the gates, colour in our cheeks, slogans in our throats. First years, second years, third years, postgraduates, even students from other colleges that Scheher and her friends had managed to get into the campus. It was out of control. The minute the news broke out, Ira had called me in hysterics, asking me what to do.

'I can't help you here,' I'd told her. 'If I stood by you right now after what you've done, my conscience would destroy me. My batchmates would hate me.' And then I'd hung up.

We had painted our faces. We had instigated and sensationalized their con. We had demanded justice; we had insisted on vengeance.

'We will not be silenced,' Scheher bellowed, and everyone around her echoed along, 'No, no, no, we will not!'

Some of us blocked the main gate. Some of us sat hungry in front of the Student Union. Some of us hollered outside the Cabinet office, shouting slogans louder when the professors passed by, taunting them. I was worried for Nanda sir, praying the students wouldn't harass him like they did the others, but before they could, he joined us. He stood there, nodding at every word being yelled, clapping when Scheher ended her speech. I saw Sonali ma'am sitting on the steps of one of the Science block buildings, talking on the phone. I realised she was informing the other faculty members living on campus, because soon, they all started coming out. I saw them with their families, some in their night suits, some in half formals, looking overwrought. All of them, victims of circumstance. Or had they been a part of it? How many of them had studied with her? How many of them even knew that she'd been killed on these very grounds?

'This is so discriminatory,' one of the seniors said, as the crowd grew in numbers. 'They didn't let me sit for my end of semester exams because I didn't have enough attendance.'

'They didn't let Bagchi contest for the post of Literary and Debating Secretary while your Highness had everything fed to her with a silver spoon,' someone called out from behind me. I turned around to see some of Bagchi's friends standing with us, the ones he'd sat with to watch our initiation. And among them was Bagchi too, looking sad, tormented, and double-crossed.

I wondered what he was going through. I wondered what had pushed him to finally show up at a protest.

'If they aren't coming to meet us, we're going to meet them,' Scheher said. 'Who's with me?'

The crowd roared.

'WHO'S WITH ME?' she repeated, eyes blazing.

They screamed louder. They screamed and they screamed until they snowballed into mutiny.

And so, all of us began moving towards the principal's house, chanting Scheherazade's renowned chorus: *Serves you right, serves you right. Now you've got stuck, our bones in your throat. Swallow all you want, swallow all you want. We refuse to go down. WE REFUSE TO GO DOWN.*

We stood outside the big house, shouting, crying out for

them to come out. They were only making it worse with their silence, their indifference. If they didn't respond soon, the mob's insurgence would get out of hand.

And I was the first to show signs of it. Without a blink, I picked up a stone and threw it at the window. 'Esai!' I heard Bagchi say reproachfully. But the damage was done. The others picked up stones as well, and began pelting them at the house. It worked, and the principal came out. Behind him was an old man in a wheelchair, and I recognized him instantly. It was his father, the founder's son. My blood stewed and simmered. As far as I was concerned, they were all turncoats. And they were about to watch this place go down.

'You deliberately fail us and think we won't notice,' Scheher began. 'You groom our girls and you allow your boys to be racist. You save your own child's ass; you destroy everyone else's future. How could you?' Her voice wavered, her hands shook, and before she could say anything more, the principal moved towards her.

'First thing tomorrow, expect a legal notice for defamation,' he said, pointing at her.

He was met with boos from the others. 'Then you'll have to send us all a legal notice,' a junior shouted.

'I want my lost year back,' another student said. 'You want us to win competitions against other colleges, but you don't give us time to practise. You want Solstice to be amazing, but when we give our time to put in the work, you take away our attendance, you cut us down. Your management is fucking corrupt! Your chairwoman is a privileged bitch! You can all go to hell!'

'Go to hell!'

'Go to hell!'

'Go to hell!'

Amidst the commotion, nobody had noticed the college

buses being set on fire. Suddenly, flames erupted from behind us, and we all jumped.

'Fire!' Jewel shrieked, covering her head. 'Ente daivame!'

Pandemonium broke out. Everyone began running in different directions. I was being pushed from everywhere. Scheher held out her hand to me, but I couldn't reach her. The tips of her fingers grazed against mine, and then I fell back, gasping and sputtering. It was Bagchi who pulled me to a side, and asked, 'You okay?'

'Yes,' I said breathlessly.

'Look!' Jewel said. 'Joshua!'

From a distance, I watched as Joshua moved from one building to the next with a torch in his hand, the ancient Roman kind with the rag wrapped around one end. With him was his army of goons, masks on their faces as they followed suit, setting aflame everything they could get their hands on.

'Has he gone mad?' Ira screamed. Her hair was no longer in its neat bun, but standing upright, as if she'd been electrified. Her eyes were bulging, and she kept biting at her nails while calling out to Joshua. Her derangement distracted me for a moment. I did not notice the tall figure running towards the burning towers, until I saw his hands flailing manically.

'No! No, no, no, no, no! Stop it! Stop it, boy! Stop!'

It was the principal.

Scheher and I stood transfixed. The whole scene was surreal. The trees, once a sublime caramel and green, now roared into maroon.

And there it was again, that primitive song. It got closer and my knees buckled. Scheher gripped my arm tight as I kneeled, the music nailing my mouth shut.

'Can you hear it?' I whispered to her.

'Esai, not now.'

'She's calling us,' I muttered feebly. 'We have to go.'

A tree collapsed. Everyone screamed. Somewhere in the deep, the man in the coat fainted from the smoke.

'Papa!' Ira sobbed wretchedly and started running towards him. 'Ira, no,' Bagchi said, grabbing hold of her. 'There's too much smoke.' She struggled against him, put up a big fight, but he was stronger, and he held her close.

'I'll go, child, don't worry,' Nanda sir said, and quickly turned to Sonali ma'am. 'Call the ambulance, the fire department and the police. In that order. And gather the professors and get every student out of here. Their safety is our priority.' With that, he disappeared into the fumes.

I gripped Scheher's cold wrist. 'Let's go,' I said, coughing. The smoke was everywhere now.

I turned around to take one last look. Sonali ma'am didn't have to call the police. Someone had already tipped them off, and they'd arrived. Ira was limping, and leaning on Bagchi for support. As they moved towards safety, he turned to look at me. I knew he was still shaken from watching me stone the window. I knew he had so many questions. I could not answer them. And so, I would never face him again.

Briefly, I felt a sharp pain in my gut. He'd done no wrong, and yet he'd suffered. All over again, I saw myself bent over his kitchen table with his fingers inside my mouth. Us sharing a cigarette in a bathtub. Kissing under the fireworks. All that intimacy, both innocent and erotic. He'd soaped my back and I'd cried. There had been laughter too—the kind that turned our stomachs into fists. So what if he had not been the one?

Did that mean it was any less beautiful?

'Esai,' Scheher called. 'Come now.'

There were barricades near the main gate. Everywhere we turned, we saw students running for their lives, and they were blocking our way out. Every exit was packed, and there was too much panic. The sky was now the colour of raspberries. We found ourselves escaping into the woods, in search of a place to hide, in that exact place a woman I loved very much had vanished years ago. And as Scheher and I drew close, the orbs began to light up in ecstasy. There was music whistling through the skeletons of the leaves like a cradle song. Through the grass, growing taller by the second, we ran, feet hitting thorns and eyes tearing up—and somewhere far away, the sirens blared.

The sudden burst of lightning startled me, and I tripped.

'Esai!' Scheher cried. We could hear footsteps behind us. 'Get up! Hurry!'

'In here,' I said, pointing to the lake, and she halted. 'Oh no,' she said.

'Do you trust me?'

'With my whole life.'

We jumped into the water, and at the same time, the ground beneath it opened up. Hands rose from it like weeds, and pulled us down. And as the men came close, we shut our eyes, ready for the harbinger of our sentence, our impending capture—but the dragonflies began levitating, neon blue reflecting in their huge eyes, and the moonlight sprinkled itself on us in a show of solidarity—there was diamond dust everywhere, and as they settled as fresh frost over the lake, the water rose over and around us. The trees surrounding it grew taller and taller as if they were ancient towers shooting up into the early hours of the night, as if they were a savage uprising, an army of protective deities blocking the others from reaching us—and it went on and on, until we were engulfed completely, inside her womb.

It was the last time I saw her.

EPILOGUE

The aftermath had been a swarm of journalists. Glass had exploded, buses had been turned to soot, a man had been hospitalised. We'd learned that Nanda sir had made it out alive, half carrying and half dragging an unconscious Laxman Dalvi with him. Everyone had managed to get out, including the guards, and they all had a different story as to what turned to ash first.

According to me, it had been the Student Union centre. I'd never liked that place anyway. But Scheher swore she saw the Botany tank go down earlier than anything else, and that had left me muddled all over again.

But one thing was clear: they had decided to close down the college. Jolly had been the first to tell me when I'd come down for breakfast. 'So it's done.' Her eyes had been brimming with tears. We'd hugged each other and cried.

I had grown up on my mother's stories. I had grown up detesting St. Margaret's, cursing its very existence; and yet knowing it had finally paid its price only left me feeling more displaced. Like a grand finale without the applause. I thought it would restore something in me, but I felt no different.

Still, I felt empty.

Scheher and I stayed locked up in her apartment, watching the news. For three days now, the media had only shown videos of Ira Saanvi walking out of the hospital with her weeping mother, her head held high. They'd lapped up her stoic demeanour, her lack of chest-beating and display of grief. They'd found in her a new tragic hero, a new star. She was pale and tight-lipped, answering all their questions courteously, speaking like a public figure, or perhaps, a politician.

'My father is a good man. He didn't deserve this,' she told them on repeat. In one of the news channels, I also saw Bagchi standing on the side, waiting for Ira to finish her interviews with the press. It looked like they'd gotten back together, but I could never be sure.

A part of me wondered what Ira was going through. I still couldn't make up my mind about her. She'd surprised me with her solidarity towards Jewel and her love for Bagchi. But she'd also been cold and heartless and selfish so many times. All I knew was I neither wanted to be her friend nor her enemy. I wanted to possess the gift of being forgotten by someone like that.

'The boy who caused the arson is now behind bars. Weren't you friends?' I heard a reporter ask her, and I tuned back in.

'Clearly not, if he was thinking of murdering my father.'

'You mean to say it was not an accident? That your father didn't walk into the fire?'

Her head went up an inch higher. 'He lured him into it by burning down the very thing that meant the world to him. St. Margaret's.'

The reporter had nothing to say to that. 'Who do you think started this riot?'

'Scheherazade,' she said, looking into the camera. The conviction in her gaze gave me chills. 'This girl has been trying to ruin our college since day one. She's a troublemaker, a manipulator. She turned our people against us. Why? Because she's desperate for fame. That's right. She'll do anything to see her name everywhere.'

'Are you talking about the poet, Scheherazade?'

'Yes. Her.' And then she went on a rant about how Scheher had provoked everyone, all because of a personal agenda against her father. 'She was obsessed with him. I think she wanted to pursue something with him, because she was always around him, flattering him, trying to get to meet him outside the premises. Between you and me, I think the whole Jewel incident with Vikas sir was also staged by this woman. She got her fan to lie for her, and she framed him. The accusation definitely made a dent on St. Margaret's otherwise flawless reputation.'

'That's outrageous!' Scheher said, staring at the screen. 'It took Jewel so much strength to talk about what happened! And I've never even spoken to Laxman Dalvi one-on-one. Never. Except for that time I dropped her at her door.' Ira had been so fragile that night, and now she was back to being a chameleon.

'She's hated you since the day you overthrew her in popularity and power. You had the people on your side. She just had her stupid chairwoman post and privilege.'

But while we knew that, the media held a different trial. They displayed Ira's interviews everywhere, and edited Scheher's performance videos to make her appear the villain.

In no time, the reputation Scheher had built for herself came tumbling down. She earned the city's spite, she became the public's new fallen starlet. People drew moustaches on her old posters, they boycotted her shows, they sent her death and rape threats. They celebrated her fall from grace, they welcomed the reversal of fortune.

Scheher retaliated by retreating into her bedroom for days. I wondered if I had to show up at her door every day to wake her up and cook for her again. I wondered if this time, the process of recovery would take longer.

But then one day, I found her packing.

'No,' I said, putting my hand on the suitcase and forcing it close.

'This city, it isn't for me right now,' she said, a half smile on her face. 'Come on, Esai.' She pushed my hand away.

'Where would you go?' I asked her. I had grown accustomed to her taking my hand in hers, saying with unbending conviction, 'I'm with you in this and everything.' To her making this city and my life tolerable, sometimes even lovable. To the nights we'd spent wide awake, being each other's shelter when the world had crashed on us. To the days that fluctuated between glamorous parties and introverted getaways to cabins with sunset views and meadows. I had grown to love our unconventional friendship. It had started in darkness and ended in darkness, but there had been light between.

'Will you be all right?' I asked her, my voice a little rocky.

'Yes,' she said, giving in to her uncontrollable, full-fledged smile. For the first time since I'd met her, she looked peaceful.

'And you?' she asked. I nodded, unable to speak.

Pipe in her hand and headphones on, she hugged me. 'This is it, then.'

'Really, Scheher?'

'Really. Good bye, Esai.'

And then it was finally over. I had to do the most heart-breaking thing I'd ever done. I had to watch her walk into the warm, humid outdoors, only for her to disappear from my life forever. I'd hoped she'd write to me. I'd hoped I'd run into her someplace. I'd hoped for a sign somewhere, and I'd received none.

For years, I looked for her everywhere. I left letters addressed to her in all our favourite places, I hunted the news for any word of her. I searched in Bandra's Mount Mary church and what remained of St. Margaret's and every theatre she'd performed in. New poets came and went. Eventually, the city forgot her name.

But once in a while, a rumour resurfaced, and as time passed, it turned into a new myth: Scheherazade was still out there, telling her stories. Telling it to fascinated kids in libraries, for they had seen her. Telling it while sharing drinks with strangers in bars, for they had seen her too. They'd all seen her. A hooded figure in a bookstore. A masked woman bent over her notebook in some quaint little café. A phantom moving through auditoriums, poems in her mouth. Beyond censure or erasure.

Another rumour went like this: anyone who spoke of her poorly lost their appetite. They couldn't speak for days. A cold case of bones stuck in their throat. Which was also probably why most writers invoked her name before they began new manuscripts. It was a good luck charm, a blessing. Absurd as it was, it was a children's fable. One they loved passing on.

And last, but not least, was my all-time favourite: all writers who wrote under pseudonyms were Scheherazade. And I was willing to fight just about anyone on that, because I'd started this one off.

I'd lit it like a lantern and then pushed it into the sky.

I'd seen it with my own eyes.

I'd seen it fly.